WOLF CODE
A Sheltering Wilderness

For April —

With appreciation,
Chandler

DIRE WOLF BOOKS PRESENTS
IMAGINATIVE FICTION BY
CHANDLER BRETT

WOLF CODE
A SHELTERING WILDERNESS (Book 1)
WILDERNESS WAR (Book 2)*
WILDERNESS END (Book 3)*

WOLF CODE
A Sheltering Wilderness

CHANDLER
BRETT

DIRE WOLF
BOOKS

This is a work of fiction. All characters, organizations, and events portrayed in it either are products of the author's imagination or are used fictitiously.

WOLF CODE
A SHELTERING WILDERNESS

Copyright © 2015 by Chandler Brett

Dire Wolf Books
3300 North Main Street
Suite D 153
Anderson, South Carolina 29621

www.direwolfbooks.com

Library of Congress Control Number
2015954220

ISBN-13: 978-1-943934-01-0
ISBN-10: 1-943934-01-0

First Edition: January 2016

Printed in the United States of America

0 9 8 7 6 5 4 3 2 1

To my white wolf
and to our pups
with much love

Wolves are neither demon nor deity. They are smart, social, family-oriented creatures that work together for survival. Indeed, they are quite a bit like us.

—Jim and Jamie Dutcher

THERE is a wolf in me… fangs pointed for tearing gashes… a red tongue for raw meat… and the hot lapping of blood—I keep this wolf because the wilderness gave it to me and the wilderness will not let it go.

. . .

O, I got a zoo, I got a menagerie, inside my ribs, under my bony head, under my red-valve heart—and I got something else: it is a man-child heart, a woman-child heart: it is a father and mother and lover: it came from God-Knows-Where: it is going to God-Knows-Where—For I am the keeper of the zoo: I say yes and no: I sing and kill and work: I am a pal of the world: I came from the wilderness.

—Carl Sandburg

CONTENTS

1
WHITE WOLF

KAN AWOKE WITH ONE THOUGHT—HE HAD TO FIND HER. Pushing off cold rock, he stood and focused on the valley ahead. A labyrinth of snow-dusted trees stretched in all directions. Towering pines, spruces, and firs dominated skeletal oaks, birches, and maples, the multitude surrendering ground only to a great river snaking into a lavender horizon. Monstrous gray mountains, tipped in winter white, guarded the valley's boundaries on the far left and right. As thick clouds invaded the sky and ushered in an early twilight, a biting wind drove him back. Was there any hope he could find her in that wilderness?

Breathing in deeply, the black wolf approached the edge of the overlook, checked the distance to the ground below, circled in place, and finally jumped. The rush of the fall ended when he broke through icy crust into softer, engulfing snow below. He kicked his legs, twisted, and pulled himself up out of the hole.

Once he regained his footing, he shook himself and settled into a steady trot, following the slope of the hill down to the forest line. The movement felt good; it helped to shake loose the stiffness in his legs. In little time he came to the edge of the trees, a place where several branches jutted up out of the snow like misshapen claws.

When he spotted a familiar spruce, Kan ran to it, pushed past the low-lying branches, and began to smell the base of the trunk. The scent was too weak. Whining, he clawed to clear away the snow and ice, and after he had burrowed several inches, he thrust his snout deeper. Yes, this was the marker, the border of their territory; he had not been mistaken. The smells sparked memories of running with his mate under the evergreens, past streams, sharing in the hunt, enjoying the freedom of the mountain woods.

Yet something was wrong; the scents were thinner than he had expected. Members of the pack had not passed this way in many days, perhaps weeks. What did this mean? What had disrupted the pack's patrol? What kept them away? He whined again, scratched at his trench in the snow, and then marked the spruce trunk with his own scent. Though there were advantages in leaving no signs of his passage—avoiding unwanted trackers who might cause him trouble—he placed his marker in the slim chance she might circle past him in the woods, so that she could follow his scent if necessary.

Jumping away from the spruce, he paused to examine the woods before him. Branches above creaked under the weight of accumulating snow, and shadows obscured the path ahead. A heavy stillness rested beneath the trees. Why had the pack retreated? Were they in danger? Was she okay? With growing concern he dashed forward.

Tracking while it was snowing was difficult; the wind, moisture, and white blanket would cover, dampen, and disperse scents. With his snout low to the ground, breathing in the frosty air, Kan followed as best he could, relying as much on familiarity of place and routine as on the smells he could differentiate. After several minutes he spotted the pack's next marker at the base of a Korean pine, sniffed it, and discovered that it was just as neglected as the first. Lifting his head, he listened closely. There was little sound in the woods, most of the animals apparently having migrated or gone into hibernation. Kan continued onward, studying the terrain for any signs that could help him understand the neglected markers or give him a clue to her present location.

His mind flashed with possibilities; he wondered what it would be like if another wolf from the pack found him first. It would be a gamble whether he would find a friendly greeting or a fight, for pack politics could have changed while he was away. Even if she were there to soften the tension by being the first to approach him, the first to nuzzle in close, to sniff him, to bite playfully, there still might be a male who decided to take advantage of the moment to make a move to exert dominance over him. Leaving the pack for any extended time created an uncertain return, and if she were not there—he did not want to think of that—but if she were not there, then there would be an even greater chance he would find conflict.

He made good time as darkness descended, but an unexpected scent suddenly brought him to a stop. Lifting his snout, he breathed in the odor and studied it; there was now another reason to be cautious. He quickly scanned the forest around him, snow dominating the landscape even under the trees, only the tips of some leafless twigs peeking out. Taking a few cautious steps forward, he focused on the trees nearby and found what he was expecting—long, deep gouges a few feet up one nearby pine, the scratch marks of a tiger. First, the size of them troubled him—he had never seen gouges that large—yet as he studied them, he began to find their location equally disturbing.

The last few times Kan ran with the pack, they had come on signs of a tiger possibly encroaching on the farthest edges of their land. The scents were strange since tigers and leopards normally kept to themselves, offering no real threat to the wolf pack, but this marker, deep in wolf territory, now gave testimony that a large tiger was hunting on land the pack patrolled. Certainly the pack would have sighted this competing predator in the middle of their woods—that had to explain the neglected markers Kan had found earlier. What drove this tiger, though, into open competition with the wolves? Scarcity of prey, no doubt. A starving tiger, particularly one of this apparent size, became a significant problem for the wolves. The pack would be in danger not only in the loss of food, but wolves traveling alone through the forest, as he now was, could become this predator's next meal.

A crunching sound from behind startled him. Quickly he turned and scanned; there was something large moving a distance away behind several trees. Kan felt the presence of another. Reacting, he growled, bared his teeth, and crouched, ready to defend himself. At first all became still, save for one of the creaking branches above, but then he caught sight of movement between the branches several leaps away, a dark form raising its antlered head. For a moment its eyes locked, frozen in panic, with Kan's, the uneasy communion between predator and prey. When instinct took over, the elk finally kicked and dashed away in the other direction, leaving behind a mist of snow and the scent of fear drifting in the wind.

Resisting the temptation to give chase, holding firmly to his purpose, Kan relaxed a little. As he straightened, he found himself out of habit throwing his head back into a howl, announcing to his pack the sighting of prey. When only silence followed, he regretted not controlling the impulse. Was his pack anywhere near enough to hear the signal? The tiger certainly heard it and now knew a wolf walked in the woods. Would the call bring the beast down upon him? The lone howl would reveal he traveled alone. No hungry tiger would pass such an advantage in a hunt.

Kan had to pick up his pace. Resuming his search for the next marker, hoping he was moving away from, not toward, the tiger, he jogged faster, his paws shifting rhythmically through the snow. The ground sloped up for several yards and then finally gave way to a large icy rock overlooking a lower bed cut out by a river, the one Kan had seen earlier from a distance. At the river's edge, the view opened up to the left and the right. Though the pack smell was stronger, it was not as powerful as he had expected, and now the snow was falling harder, frosting his muzzle.

Strangely there was the faint scent of something else on the air. What was that? He pushed forward, his desire to catch up with his packmates running strong. As he had done many times before, Kan dropped from the rock down to the bed several feet below with the intention of following the river along to where he expected to find his pack. This time, though, as his paws broke the fresh snow, he caught movement in the corner of his right eye and heard a peculiar growling increasing in pitch and volume as he turned.

At the edge of the thick darkness of the river-worn alcove, directly under the rock ledge from which he had leaped, lay some sort of carcass, well-scavenged, ribcage exposed, and behind it, just visible, a squat form squirmed in the shadows. Kan had barely identified it when a mass of black fur, led by a tight ball of a head, jaw open and teeth forward, shot out at him, charging through the snow. Before Kan could flee in the other direction, the wolverine had knocked him back, coming up under him, clamping sharp teeth on his left side.

Kan shifted his weight, just barely holding his balance against the wolverine. He struggled to push the attacker off, but it would not let go; instead, it wrapped its arms around his body, scraping and digging with its claws. Kan jumped and turned, trying to shake himself free, but the wolverine was closer to the ground, had better footing, and reaped the benefits of first sighting. Unable to escape the wolverine's hold, Kan felt one of the attacker's teeth finally break into his side; he yelped in spite of himself.

The pain brought new effort, and Kan reached and bit toward the wolverine's snout. The first time he missed, filling his mouth with snow, but the second time he hit the mark. The wolverine finally lost his grip, and Kan was able to spring free. At the moment when he thought he would escape, though, Kan felt a sharp pain clamp down on his back left leg. He whipped his head back to see the wolverine's teeth deep in his leg, blood clumping around its mouth and running down into the snow.

That's enough!

Now fueled by anger and pain, Kan twisted to bite down on the back of the wolverine's neck. It took several tries to get a good grip on the wriggling form beneath, but he eventually found it. Even though he had gained a commanding hold on the wolverine and was biting down with some force, his stubborn opponent refused to let go of his leg, so Kan shook his head and bit harder, finally feeling his teeth tearing into some flesh beyond the ball of fur in his mouth. The wolverine finally let go of his leg, but then rolled and dug its claws into Kan's chest. With the release of his leg, trying to minimize the wounds from this new attack, Kan pushed off, first slipping, then getting just enough purchase from the rocks beneath the snow to clear the reach of the wolverine. Without looking back, he ran, splashing across the river.

Only on the other side did Kan confirm that the incensed animal was not following. Obviously hurt, the wolverine stood dazed, yet still growling, teeth bared in a horrible grimace, daring him to come back. They stood a moment glaring at each other until the wolverine was finally satisfied and turned to retreat into the darkness. Only the broken ribs of the stripped carcass remained in view.

Kan did not like the thought of being bested by this wolverine—what would his packmates think? He was not interested in the carcass and would have preferred avoiding the fight altogether. What had it accomplished? It was so stupid. He was soaking and chilled now, cuts on his chest and side, and a long torn stretch on his leg, which he sniffed and licked despite the pain. It was going to be a problem, but he did not have time to rest. If he was going to find her, he had to press on.

After taking a drink from the cold water, still wary of the wolverine, Kan resumed his quest, following the bed alongside the river, stepping around the icy rocks, now limping to take as much pressure off the bad leg as possible. He began to worry. The smell of blood from his wound would announce his presence sooner than he would have liked, and it made him an even easier target for the Amur tiger roaming this forest. It also would complicate the politics of his return to the pack. If another wolf saw a weakness, then there was certain to be a challenge. Trying to counter these anxieties, he focused on finding the gait that was the least painful, yet could cover the most ground.

The flow of the river was strangely comforting in the darkness; it spawned memories of a happier time. In the summer he would come here with her to play, to cool down, splashing in the water at the river's edge. On the first run, he would chase her up the bank, nip at her tail, twist, and then she would chase him back down. In the winter they were more cautious about getting wet. With this thought he noted the irony of the chill on his chest and legs, wet from his run from the wolverine. She would laugh at him for his sloppiness.

He finally sensed he was nearing his destination—that gave him strength—yet he did not hear the howls and the barks he associated with this space. Surely the pack would have sensed his presence by now, two or three of them at least, bounding down, scouting ahead to be first to greet him. No one came, however. What was wrong? He climbed out of the riverbed, hobbled his way up over the icy rocks, past several more trees, and finally entered a familiar clearing. The pack's scent was strong around him, but a quick scan revealed that no wolves currently found shelter there. Kan stood alone in the snow, tired, confused, his leg throbbing.

Sniffing about, he discovered the pack scents were indeed weaker, days old now. Differentiating the scents, Kan identified the alpha male and female, as well as several mid-ranked males and females, and the omegas at the bottom; he did not linger over any of these. He was searching for hers. When he eventually did find it, he breathed it in deeply, some of his anxiety fading. For a moment he was comforted with a vision of Lana, milling among the others in the pack; the peacemaker, the soul of the tribe, she moved with grace, wisdom, and beauty. In the next moment, though, the scent drifted, and Kan shook off the dream, for it could not satisfy. He wanted to see her in front of him now, her amber eyes glowing, her fur thickened for the winter. He wanted to feel the captivating mystery of her presence. Above all he wanted to know she was safe.

Why was she not there? Why had the pack abandoned this spot? What would have caused them to leave? He should have picked up on the signs, the neglected territory markers, the scratch marks of the tiger, the scavenging wolverine—the pack would have allowed none of these when it was running strong. Where did they go? Frustrated, looking for some answer, Kan threw back his head and howled, his voice sounding loud and long in the night sky. When he needed a breath, he stopped to listen, but again there was no reply. Releasing the pain in his leg, the desperation of his search, and the concern over the absent pack, he howled again and again.

When no answering call echoed back, he felt the urge to

drop into the snow, to give up. His quest had failed. All he had found so far this evening was a spooked elk, an inhospitable wolverine, and the ghost of a tiger. All he could show for his effort was a mangled leg and several scratch marks on his chest. He needed to rest.

But he had not come this far to stop now. She needed him, so fighting against the impulse to give in, he breathed her scent again and set to work inspecting all corners of the site, carefully distinguishing the directions of the most recent markers. He eventually determined the pack had moved, apparently as a group, toward the south. He left his own scent markers in the abandoned camp, next to hers, and took off after the southern trail, relying more on his nose than his eyes in the dark night.

At least, he thought, the snow had dropped off. Only an occasional flake now drifted in front of him. While tracking was a little easier, he still had to contend with his leg, which was burning now despite the cold. He would have to take a break, after hobbling for some distance, and try to lick his wound. Fortunately the forest seemed rather quiet. Quick shadows occasionally did appear and disappear, but he did not have time or the desire to identify them.

Coming on a short spruce, he inspected its trunk and found a marker with a scent more acrid—at last, one that was fresher. He had found his pack's trail. After lifting his head and howling, he listened as his call faded into the night. Was he correct? Were they nearby? He searched the silence for a hint of a response, the night air icy on his muzzle. A returning howl immediately surprised him. For a moment he doubted, but then another voice followed and then another. Although the pack was still miles away, Kan yipped in excitement.

Listening closely, he sought to identify the voices. The first howl had to belong to Danuwa. Of course he would be in the scouting party. How strong had Danuwa become in his absence? How would Danuwa receive him? Much would depend on who else traveled in the party. Who were the others? Those voices belonged to Noya and Sasa, the twins, from the same litter as Danuwa, but of radically different temperament. Kan was glad to hear them, for they in the past had been close to his beloved, running with her on many hunts. And then there were two other howls mixed in. Even though Kan could recognize both of them as young males, he could not identify them specifically; they were not familiar enough—they had to be the pups from the litter born last spring. That made only five total, a small group from the pack. Where were the others?

Kan continued to search for Lana's howl among the others, but when he still could not locate it, fear crept in. Why was she not calling? Where was she? Was she hurt? Abandoned? Or was she truly gone as he feared? And how was he going to face these others, wounded, if she were no longer running with them? For one uncertain moment, he did not know what to do—and then he committed. For good or ill, he was going to find them. If she is gone, he thought, then let them turn on me.

Though in pain and anxious about how his former packmates would receive him, Kan limped on, occasionally stumbling. This part of his journey was punctuated by occasional calls that with time grew closer. As the five wolves approached, he learned from their howling that Danuwa was in the lead, and that the two other male voices were close to him. Noya and Sasa also were running nearby. Kan began to hope they would be able to temper their brother as they had sometimes done before. The tenor of Danuwa's voice troubled him, and when it sounded obviously near, Kan paused to lick his leg again to lessen the smell of blood with saliva. There could be trouble, and he must not appear weak before the patrol.

As the scent in the air confirmed Danuwa was near, Kan remembered an earlier time when Etsi, the mother of the pack, had given birth to a large litter of seven pups. Even when she had lost two of them, the five remaining had become a challenge to the seven adult wolves. Each adult, including Kan and Lana, had been required to help. From the beginning Danuwa had stood apart from his brothers and sisters. He was a troublemaker even then, Kan thought.

One day stood out in Kan's memory. Several in the pack were chasing the pups back and forth through a field of tall, golden grass. While he was still trying to decide whether to join, Danuwa broke off from the others to chase and nip at him. It was all part of the game, but when he thought Danuwa's bites were getting too intense, Kan rolled the presumptuous pup onto his side. Instead of turning his belly up as the other pups in the litter were doing, Danuwa growled and bit up at Kan's neck. Not wanting to be a part of this challenge, Kan opened his mouth wide and clamped down on Danuwa's muzzle. He held the pup in place, but the growls continued. Finally Kan gave up, released him, and ran over to the others, hoping someone else would distract him. The ploy worked, for the alpha male, the leader of the pack, had jumped on Danuwa and put him in his place.

Now in the chill of night, Kan looked for a place to greet the wolves who approached; he wanted as much an advantage as he could get. As soon as he found a tree that had fallen partially to the ground, another tree holding it up at an angle, he stepped carefully along its trunk toward a high perch where he could see who was coming first. It was not long after he was in place that he spotted a swift shadow bounding through the distant snow. Stealth is not on his mind, Kan thought. He intends to intimidate.

Several trees away, the shadow slowed, and Kan knew the other wolf had spotted him. A low, guttural rumble, not yet a growl, sounded as the shadow continued moving toward him. In the dim light, the darker fur of Danuwa's undercoat, snout, and eyes blended into the darkness, leaving visible only the lighter fur of Danuwa's exterior coat in a mask eerily resembling a skull.

Two other shadows, smaller than Danuwa's, came trotting up behind him, stopping before they got within two lengths of him. While keeping his eye on Danuwa's approach, Kan breathed in the scents of these two males and was finally able to identify them as the pups from Etsi's last litter. They had gotten bigger since Kan had seen them last, and he wondered how loyal they were to Danuwa. This was not the welcome he had wanted.

Danuwa chose not to approach Kan face on, but to head toward the base of the tree. Following Danuwa step for step, Kan twisted slowly to the point where he was looking down the length of the tree at Danuwa. Kan could see his eyes now, could see the nervous energy and the cold ambition.

At this moment the two females, Noya and Sasa, emerged from the forest shadows. Although they warily kept their distance, they whimpered restrained greetings and wagged their tails. Danuwa did stop a moment to look them over before he placed a paw on the tree. If the encounter went badly, maybe the sisters would be able to keep the three males from killing him.

Kan had to put up a good front. Despite the pain that wagging his tail brought to his leg, he tried to stand tall for this inspection, demanding to be greeted as an equal. Danuwa confidently walked over Kan's paw marks in the snow along the trunk and came to stand in front of him. Kan bowed in greeting, lowering his head to his front paws, yet keeping his eyes looking forward. Danuwa brushed up against him, mouth open, sniffing him—here was the situation that Kan had dreaded. Danuwa had approached tail wagging, but when he located Kan's leg wound, he started to growl. Kan immediately tensed, and in a heartbeat, felt the masked wolf's paw strike his flank. He tried to keep his balance, but his bad leg gave way, and he stumbled sideways, hit the trunk below him at the wrong angle, and rolled off, falling to the ground below.

As he tried to catch his breath and stand at the same time,

Kan panicked and was not able to get out of the way quickly enough before Danuwa jumped down on him, pinning him to the ground. As he breathed in snow, Kan heard the growls of the other males nearby.

Here was the test; he had only a moment. Even with Danuwa's weight pressing on his shoulders, Kan managed to push off with his front legs and twist out of the hold, leaping in the direction away from the other two approaching wolves. He had to use his wounded leg in the process and did not get as much distance as he wanted. He knew the others would be on him soon. Cutting sharply, he managed to get himself mostly turned around in time to face the charging Danuwa, who hit him and sent them both rolling, thrashing legs entangled, teeth gnashing wildly. Kan found himself on the defensive, trying his best to keep his opponent's jaws away from his throat.

One lucky turn, and he was able to grab Danuwa's ear, producing a yipe that kept the other two males at bay. Only temporarily, he knew. Danuwa pulled free and stood, head lowered, hackles raised, growling low. Just able to get to his feet, Kan crouched in answer, meeting his opponent's stare. He had to end this quickly, or he would fall to the order of the pack.

Danuwa, though, with something to prove, charged again, hitting him hard. Kan managed to stay standing this time, but his opponent knew to press his attack, causing him to pivot onto his bad leg. He fell again, Danuwa biting down on his shoulder and then the back of his neck. When he tried to force himself up, Danuwa held him. Kan tried to twist free and failed again. He was losing his will; he felt darkness closing in. He did not want to surrender, but the snow was frigid on his chest.

Suddenly a heavy jolt from above pushed the pressing weight off him. Despite the burn where his opponent's teeth raked the back of his neck, he felt some strength return. A familiar scent in the air filled him with hope, and he stood to see another wolf standing over his enemy, her mouth closed over Danuwa's muzzle, the moonlight glimmering on her fur, her growl demanding attention. Here she finally was, Lana, his white wolf. He wanted to rush to her side, but instead found himself transfixed by her display of authority.

Danuwa struggled beneath her and was finally able to jerk free and stand. He glared back at the white wolf, and the other two females, who had joined her, before he cut short a growl, shook himself, and shoved the smallest male to the ground as he finally trotted away.

Lana turned around and walked toward Kan. When her muzzle touched his, the tightness in his shoulders eased. Dropping back into the snow, he felt her nuzzling in, licking his face and ears. Was she really there?

The other two females finally approached too, playfully nipping at him, joyfully barking. They offered a quick greeting and then retreated. He was back with the pack.

But he was too tired to care, and his leg hurt. Although he wanted to run with his mate, he closed his eyes and felt his breath heavy. He was aware someone licked his wounds.

Her voice fell softly into his ear. *I'm glad you're back, Kanati. I'm glad you found me.*

2
FEATHER

"I PREDICT YOU WILL NEVER MARRY, TOVARISHCH," MICK goaded me while we climbed the steps to our second-floor apartment.

Tovarishch, the Russian word for "comrade," had become an inside joke for us. One of those times that first year we were flung together by fate, or by the Admissions Office at least, when our suite of fellow graduate students had gathered for dinner in an attempt to get to know each other better, Mick had asked me and the other four guys gathered around the table what we knew of Russia, and I flippantly joked everyone there called each other "comrade." When he frowned, his eyes dark in the low-lit restaurant, I doubted my attempt at humor—until his eyebrows lifted a second later and he said sarcastically that he had much work to do to educate us culturally-challenged Americans. By this point Mick had lived in the States several years and taken enough university courses to know the language of political correctness. Despite his corresponding jab, I did apologize later just to be certain, and he promised all was well. As he walked away, though, he said, "Do svidaniya, Tovarishch Williams." See you later, Comrade Williams. There always seemed to be an edge to the way he said it, but the deep, warm timbre of his voice dispelled any thoughts he had somehow insulted you.

Again sensing that challenge, as we neared the top of the stairs, and not wanting to be outdone, I said in a tone of mock indignation, "And what would you know?" Jumping past him to open the apartment door, I continued, "I suppose you'd tell me I need to move to Russia to improve my prospects."

Stepping inside, Mick said, "If you were so lucky, you would learn Russian women keep their men fat during day and warm at night."

"You better not say that too loudly here in America. Our women will jump you for such chauvinism."

"Ah… but I have accent, and I know how to dance," he boasted.

"Yes, you're a regular Don Juan, aren't you?"

Mick tossed my suitcase and backpack on the floor in my room. Since he lifted weights, my luggage caused him no problems. I looked around at all the stuff I'd been able to cram into my sedan and lamented the task of unpacking even as I was also excited about the possibilities of setting up the apartment again.

"The place looks good," I said, walking back into the hall and catching a glimpse of Mick's room behind the half-closed door. There was a pallet bed on the floor, and on the far wall, a large poster of a tiger jumping, claws extended, mouth open. No luggage was out, so he'd already had time to unpack and settle in.

"I was looking to improve over last year, and anything beats the closets we lived in first year," he agreed.

The first year we had lived in university housing in a suite with a small common area that never evoked a sense of comfort, a shared bathroom which none of us liked, and six even smaller bedrooms, each just large enough for a bed, a desk, and a closet. While living there, feeling confined and claustrophobic, I frequently cursed the moment of weakness that led me to think on-campus housing would be a better option for financial as well as social reasons. Ultimately the decision would pay off, for the shared plight, the feeling we were ascetic monks committed to our cells, did pull us together despite our different degrees and varied departments. All brand new students to Duke University, we six shared a similar goal, the slow process of building a network of friends from the ground up. It was here I met Mikhail Lossky—"Mick" to his friends—a Russian pursuing a doctorate in biology. Later I would wonder if we would have met any other way.

"So how are things in Vladivostok?" I asked. We had only talked once over the summer, a time he called me from his native homeland to brag about sailing in the Golden Horn Bay since he knew I loved the coast. He had also announced he'd been tracking an Amur tiger in the Zov Tigra National Park— who wouldn't think that was cool?

"I enjoyed the time at home. And you? How is Atlanta?"

"No real changes," I said. "My parents are still as busy as ever."

"Did you get to visit the Outer Banks?"

"No, we're not all so lucky as you. My parents were tied up, and I wasn't happy about it. I told my uncle, though, I'll be going next summer without them. You may have to watch out this semester. Since I didn't get my coastal fix, I may be a bit stir-crazy."

"That's too bad," Mick said with mock sympathy, dropping on the couch in our living room, propping his feet up on the coffee table. I saw he'd been true to his word and put up a new poster print of the Golden Horn Bay on one wall to go along with the decorative anchor on another. We'd decided the year before in setting up our bachelors' pad a nautical theme would be best.

I sat on the sofa chair we'd picked up secondhand and could feel the wooden slats under the thin cushion. "No, the real highlight of the summer came a couple weeks ago with the release of *Transylvania Nights VII*. I can't wait to show it to you. The game is immersive!"

"I look forward to hunting werewolves with you," Mick grunted as if we were Vikings going out on the battlefield.

Smiling, I said, "I also got a new pair of Reality glasses for my birthday."

"I was wondering. You look less like a geek."

"Thanks, man." I took the glasses off, held them out in front of me, and watched Mick's reaction in the blue-tinted reflection of the lenses. "They're pretty wicked. You get Augmented Reality and Virtual Reality with the flip of a switch. It's amazing how sharp the pictures are you can take with them too, and it's difficult to distinguish them from regular sunglasses anymore."

"I got the surround sound set up already," Mick said, changing the subject, wanting to show off his own new toy. He reached for the remote control and within seconds had a European rock ballad blaring from the phalanx of speakers around the room. The sound was sweet.

"I brought the wall screen and projector," I added. The screen would cover an entire wall in our apartment and would be our gateway, with our Reality glasses and an Internet connection, to some intense adventure gaming. Back in Atlanta my parents would frequently upbraid me for how many hours I'd be online, so I was looking forward to gaming without a conscience standing in my doorway.

"Shall we set it up?" he said, a sly grin on his face. It didn't take much to tempt me.

Within the hour we had the screen set up and were testing

the connection speeds, graphics capacity, and sound quality. At first the display did not measure up to what I was expecting, so we spent more time than we intended troubleshooting the problem, eventually locating the source of interference. When the graphics were crystal sharp, I made the mistake of logging into my gaming account just to see how it looked, and of course, I then logged Mick in. We were soon sucked into the massive online gaming world of *Transylvania Nights VII*.

Only taking a break to order pizza for supper around 9 p.m., we chased monsters through Romanian castles late into the night, quitting when headaches and sore eyes told us we'd pushed ourselves too far. We logged out finally and headed to our separate rooms. I pushed past my luggage, found my mattress, and pulled a blanket over me since my Russian roommate loved to keep the apartment so cold.

❧

I forgot to set my alarm for the next day and slept through the first session of a class I was supposed to attend. Since my parents pressured me to work my way through graduate school, and my finances were tight, I had signed up to be a teaching assistant. My hope, though, was that I could instead find part-time work at some gaming company in Raleigh, but the executives out there did not come through on my timeline. They kept promising something would open up for me, but my second year was close to ending, and I had to make a plan for the next. When I finally committed to being a teaching assistant, it didn't take a week before I got the job offer I'd been waiting for. Although I wanted to drop the TA assignment, I knew I had to keep my word—particularly when my parents didn't give me a choice.

By sleeping late I had missed the first session of Dr. Stanley's Special Topics in Technology. Thinking I should at least head off any trouble, I did write a short email apology to Dr. Stanley, who also happened to be my dissertation director. To my relief, later in the day I found a laid-back response, asking me just to look over the included syllabus and informing me I'd have to make my own introduction to my discussion group since it would meet before the large class would gather again.

So the next day as I worked my way to the assigned room in the engineering building, I found my mind still was not on the class, but pulled in other directions—setting up the apartment again, looking forward to starting my new programming job, and anticipating exploring new ground in Transylvania Nights. I'd like to think I'm not entirely anti-social, but I wasn't looking forward to the prospect of standing up in front of a group of students, all their eyes on me.

After climbing a couple flights of stairs on the way, I was surprisingly winded when I reached the classroom. I wasn't going to enter in that condition, so I took several more steps down the hallway to a corner where I pulled out my phone to provide just enough cover from the attention of the students rushing past. After momentarily closing my eyes and breathing deeply, I finally turned back and walked deliberately into the room. As soon as I entered, several students already in their seats looked up at me, nervously, expectantly. At that moment something happened; some spirit of mischief possessed me, and I didn't walk to the front of the room as everyone expected, but instead impulsively ducked my head, turned, and climbed the steps up to the back row to take the seat in the far corner. It wasn't difficult to blend in; my clean-shaven face was youthful enough, and I was wearing jeans.

From the highest point in the room, I quietly observed the undergraduates who were milling about, obviously a little agitated themselves. I cannot remember their conversations exactly, but I'm sure the students were expressing their typical first-of-the-semester anxiety about course assignments and swapping stories about what had happened over summer break, movies watched, jobs taken to raise a little spending money, trips squeezed into their busy schedules. I noticed a few international students and, as the room filled, discovered the gender breakdown actually favored the women, unlike several computer-engineering courses I had taken which much more often went the other way.

The clock on the wall was about a minute away from the class start time, and the twenty or so students who were there started to look around at each other.

One, a male student with frizzy blond hair and large shoulders, broke the ice, "Has anyone seen our TA?"

Several students looked away, too embarrassed to answer his indiscrete directness.

But a dark-haired young man who hadn't shaved in a while and was dressed in a skull-and-crossbones t-shirt took up the cause. "No, he wasn't there when Dr. Stanley introduced the others. He may not be here."

Another student asked, "Has anyone heard anything about this Williams guy?"

Still another inquired, "How hard is he?"

Others said they had asked around, but could not uncover anything.

One declared, "He must be a computer geek to be a TA for this class." I cringed at the stereotyping.

Frizzy Blond saw his opportunity. "Well, let's give him ten minutes. If he doesn't show, then we'll pass around a sheet of paper, write our names down, and leave."

On the front row, a walnut-haired young woman with dark glasses forced herself to speak, "What happens to the list?"

Skull-and-crossbones batted the question down. "Leave it on the desk."

Dark Glasses continued, "What if the next class throws it away?"

Skull-and-crossbones, evidently irritated at being challenged, shot back. "Why don't you take it to Dr. Stanley then if you're so worried about it?" His eyes ran over her. "The walk would do you some good anyway."

Several noted his harsh tone and looked away, not wanting to get involved. Some of the women in the class flushed with anger at the implication of the last statement, but remained silent. I was about to stand up and end the foolishness when another female voice entered the fray, a slightly deeper voice, melodious, clear, commanding, "You shouldn't talk to her that way."

A good part of the class turned to look at her. She was on the other side of the room on the second row, and I had to stretch a little in my seat to see her. Her long, straight, dark hair, gathered loosely behind her, was adorned by a single white feather, several inches long, with a black tip. Before I knew it, I felt my hand tapping the button on the side of my glasses, taking a 3D scan of her profile; some part of me wanted to remember the moment.

Skull-and-crossbones stood, a bit confused. "Really?"

Feather looked back at him, her gaze unwavering. "No, you shouldn't. Your comment was insulting, and all she was doing was thinking ahead, unlike some of us."

Skull-and-crossbones growled, "Who do you think you are to tell me what to do?"

Frizzy Blond reached out and put a hand on Skull-and-crossbones' shoulder. "Man...."

Addressing Dark Glasses, Feather said, "Don't worry. I'll take the list."

Having observed we were several minutes past time, I finally stood, saying, "That won't be necessary." As I walked down the steps toward the front of the room, I felt the class inspecting me. How did I measure up? Tossing my satchel on the table, which I then pushed against the wall, its legs screeching on the floor, I finally turned to face the class. All were seated again, and most of them were frowning, some in confusion, one or two mouths open in surprise; others, a little quicker, were bitter at apparently being tricked.

My tongue tripped. "M-my n-n-name is Donovan Williams." I recovered, "I will be your TA for Dr. Stanley's Topics in Tech— or that's what I call it."

A general, indecipherable muttering passed through the class, revealing I was not scoring highly on student satisfaction. I looked down at the information on my tablet. In the search for normalcy, I started to call roll and discovered the fringe benefit of identifying those who had starred in the pre-class drama: Skull-and-crossbones was Dave Littleston, Frizzy Blond was Larry Trask, and Dark Glasses was Katie Menken. I found myself stumbling over an unfamiliar name, Tsula Watie.

"T-t-t-sool-ay What-i."

The melodious voice spoke again with controlled patience. It was the woman with the feather, the name I most wanted to learn. "The *ts* is one sound, almost like a *j*. Tsoo-lah Wah-tee. I'm part Cherokee. Most people have trouble with my name."

I immediately made a phonetic note on my roll. I wasn't going to repeat the mistake; I didn't want to be counted among "most people."

Reaching the end of the roll, I moved on to reviewing the syllabus and requirements for the course, then asked the class how their assignments were going, and finally began to relax myself as I realized most of the class seemed relieved to get on with our work. I do not remember much more from the actual session. I stumbled through as best I could.

When I finally dismissed the class, two or three anxious ones, including Katie from the front row, came up to me to clarify their understandings of the class projects. While they were asking these questions, I noticed Tsula remained seated, waiting. The others finally left, walking out into the hallway pushing past the line of students eagerly awaiting the sign they could enter the room and claim their seats for the next class. I turned to gather my books, but her voice stopped me.

"Why didn't you say anything?"

She was standing, watching me closely. I had to acknowledge her. Since butchering her name, I had largely avoided glancing at her side of the room.

Her hair was dark brown down her shoulders, accentuating a face of golden complexion. She wore blue jeans and a brown blouse with an intricate blue-bead pattern, suggesting a bird with wings, outstretched over her chest. She was slim, but there was nothing fragile about her appearance. Her amber eyes, deep and sincere, measured me.

I was not prepared. "Excuse me?"

She rephrased her question. "Why didn't you interrupt Dave when he was insulting Katie?"

I didn't know what to say.

She broke the awkward silence. "You could have made a difference."

Before I could decide how to respond, she walked out of the room without another word. Her exit evidently was sign enough for the students waiting at the doorway to start pouring in, and I was forced to move too even though I felt I was leaving something unfinished. Out in the hallway, I looked for Tsula, but she had already vanished in the crowd. I tossed my satchel on a wooden bench to collect my thoughts.

That didn't go as planned. What a wonderful mix of students for my first class! And who did this Tsula think she was? It really wasn't any business of hers how I conducted my class. And was Dave really that out of line? I didn't like what he said either, but did Tsula need to make a scene? Wasn't Katie being just a bit annoying? This was college after all. Time to grow up.

The more I thought about it the more irritated I got. This TA assignment was going to be more of a headache than I had imagined. Not a good sign. I decided the best policy, though, was to ignore Tsula's challenge for the moment. I had plenty of first-of-the-semester errands to run, anyway, enough to occupy the rest of the day, so I went straight to work and was mostly successful in keeping the headache at bay.

That night, though, was a different story. Lying alone in my room, I was unable to keep my mind from rehearsing that class session. When I remembered the picture I'd taken, I pulled it up on my Reality glasses. It wasn't as clear as it would have been on the new wall-screen Mick and I had installed in the other room, but I didn't want to risk his coming in on me, and the image was sharp enough for my late-night eyes. I studied that dark hair, the turn of her nose and lips, the line from her ear down her neck to the suggestive curve of her blouse, but I paused longest on the white-and-black feather and the serene intensity of her eyes. Cherokee. I was intrigued.

Her words returned to me. *You could have made a difference.* A difference? What did that mean? What did she expect? There was something in the way she said it. What was it? She said it like she was wounded, like someone had hurt her. I was suddenly disappointed in myself. Had I blown my first day? But then anger resurfaced. Who was she to judge me? I shut the glasses off and tossed them onto my bedside table.

Although I tried, I found I couldn't sleep. I played out different scenarios in my head. What if I had walked to the front of the class from the start, what if I had intervened earlier, what if I had held Dave in check? But I didn't do any of those things, and Tsula had challenged me. Her criticism could have been worse, though; she could have asked her questions as soon as I walked to the front of the room. She could have tried to embarrass me in front of the whole class. But she still chose to confront me. She still presumed she knew the best thing for me to do. The thought kept bruising me like a pebble would inside my running shoe.

❧

Rather than getting to the classroom early, I showed up precisely on time for the next session and started calling roll, thereby declaring I meant business; I would not be caught unprepared again. Only two or three students hadn't returned. Dave, Larry, Katie, and Tsula were all there. Since I had practiced Tsula's name beforehand, I managed to pull off a decent approximation, and when she smiled at the attempt, I found myself curiously satisfied and irritated at the same time.

After the roll I returned to class policies. "Although this is an engineering course and most of the assignments will be clear-cut, I do like to promote group problem solving. Look around you at the others in this class. Treat this group as a think tank. Learn their names. We will be given certain tasks throughout the semester, and we are going to work on them together. We will value each person's voice." Here I looked specifically at Dave, who glared back, Katie, who looked down, and Tsula, who nodded.

I continued, "We will, of course, reward excellence. Creative ideas will always help your grade, but think tanks always work best when we allow each person to contribute his or her strengths. If you cannot agree to these terms, if you cannot treat your fellow classmates with at least a measure of respect, then I would suggest you leave now, go find a drop form, and bring it to me to sign before the end of the day."

The class stared back at me blankly, no one venturing to respond. Once I'd gotten that out of the way, I turned to reviewing the material for the week. The rest of the session ran fairly well, and over the next several meetings, to everyone's relief, we settled into a dependable routine.

I only slowly warmed up to the prospect of teaching, never entirely losing the feeling the sessions were an obligation. Tsula's presence in the course continued to be a complication; I could never relax. I had to give much more to the class than

I wanted, knowing she would ask the tough questions the other students did not care to ask.

"I think Dr. Stanley was dodging the real issues here," Tsula said during one memorable session, breaking the general silence after my recap of one of his recent lectures in ethics and technology. I noticed Dave roll his eyes.

"How so?" I had to admit I was curious.

"I didn't feel he ever addressed how we should be using technology."

"Wasn't that the point? We each have to make the decision for ourselves?"

"Sure. There is individual responsibility, but we each should think also about our social responsibilities."

"What do you mean?" I asked. "Give me an example."

"Why should we use all this fancy technology to create spellbinding games or jaw-dropping special effects in movies? What is the purpose of all that work and money? How much time will we give to finding new ways to separate us from the real world around us where animals are going extinct, and pollution and war are raging, and children are dying of malnutrition and hunger? Are we going to get more excited about blowing someone up in a video game than we are about tracking a wolf through a living forest?"

Larry jumped in, looking over at Tsula, "You need to relax and have some fun." I saw some of the other students quietly nodding.

I continued, a little defensively, looking around at the class, "Is entertainment inherently wrong? Don't we need some downtime?"

Katie said, "I probably could spend a little less time with the games on my phone." She often would back Tsula up in an indirect way. She hadn't forgotten what Tsula had done on the first day.

Tsula wasn't finished. "The problem is people have too much

'downtime' now. They define themselves by their 'downtime' and wake up in the morning organizing their lives around it."

"What if these moments are more real to them than their regular lives?" I asked.

"Good one," someone whispered. I got a momentary charge out of the affirmation.

"That's the problem, isn't it?" Tsula continued.

"Why?"

"Because it's escapist," she said, leaning forward. "We have too many problems in the real world, for people to be playing games with no ultimate point. Technology has become the opiate of the people."

Her revision of Marx was provocative, but before I could respond, Dave spoke, "So you're hoping some solar flare will come along and fry all our tech?"

Tsula frowned back. "It might force our society to remember what is important."

I realized many in the class were not paying any attention to our argument, and those who were were just watching, curious spectators with no desire to enter the fray. I tried to divert the back-and-forth by calling on some other classmates to voice their opinions, hoping to pull them into the discussion. Tsula must have realized what I was doing and backed off a little. After class, as she was getting ready to walk out, I called her by name—the only time I initiated a private conversation during the semester—and she walked over.

She had a questioning look on her face.

I asked, "What do you think we should do with technology?"

"It should be a tool, and we should use it to make the world a better place."

"Isn't that a bit simplistic?"

"Life isn't as complicated as we make it."

I said sarcastically, "So our tombstones will read, 'We could have made a difference.'"

She grinned. "Maybe."

Her smile disarmed me.

She spoke again, "I'm afraid I dominated the discussion today."

"The others have just as much of an opportunity to speak. Don't worry about it. I doubt they have given these topics as much thought as you have."

"My parents taught me to speak up for what I think is right."

"I'm curious," I started. "Have you ever played a virtual-reality game?"

"I'll have to confess I've never really played any video games. In high school I had friends who tried to get me to play, and I tried some games that responded to body motions. The dance game was a little fun."

"You admit to having fun?"

She ignored me. "I never really saw much of a point."

I defended, "Role-playing games are like an interactive story. If you get some creative people behind them, they can be just as immersive as a good book."

"You get to be a part of the story?"

"Yes. My favorite games have always been a mix of role-playing and strategy, those that tell a good story. They create a world you can live in and enjoy. If you want to stop following the story and just explore a place in the game, you have that opportunity too."

"Again, isn't that escapist?"

"It depends on what you want. If you want to ignore the world around you, you can turn anything you do in that direction."

"I've gotta run," she said, moving toward the door. "I don't have much time for lunch before my next class."

"Would you like…" I started to ask her to lunch, but caught myself.

"What?" She looked back over her shoulder.

"Nothing. See you next time."

She smiled, and I watched her walk out, admiring the hug of her jeans. In the quiet following, I couldn't decide whether I was more relieved or sad to see her go.

§➤

The semester progressed, and despite how Tsula vexed me, I remained keenly aware of how we both shared the same campus. On those days when Dr. Stanley lectured, I was required to sit toward the front with the other TAs, for he would sometimes call on us to demonstrate a principle. It was also an understood honor that we were separated from the undergraduates who populated the rest of the lecture hall. Before class, though, I often would stand looking up at the seats, and I could spot Tsula when she came in. I recognized her dark hair, lithe form, deer-like steps, and the earthen colors of her wardrobe. Occasionally she would spot me and wave—what I felt was a polite, distant wave.

Despite what you might think, a university campus can be large enough so you don't see someone even if you are looking for them. I only bumped into Tsula once outside the classroom. I was headed into the engineering computer lab, and she was rushing out, a stack of books in her hands, and we almost collided.

"Sorry," she said, and when she recognized me, she seemed embarrassed.

"In a hurry?" I asked.

"I've got a deadline." I noticed the topmost book in her arms was titled *The Return of the Wolf.*

"What're you reading?"

"I'm tracking the wolf population in the United States over the last century."

"Wolves?"

"It's a project for one of my classes. I'm a biology major, with a zoology emphasis," she offered as explanation.

I nodded.

"Have you ever seen a wolf?" she interjected.

"I've seen a fox or two run across the road, and I've seen all sorts of animals in the zoo, but I don't think I've ever seen a wolf."

"You really should. They're beautiful creatures," she said, her amber eyes fixed on me.

"I take it you've seen one."

"I've had a chance to follow a pack and watch the alphas interact with the other wolves."

"Alphas?" I asked.

"Every pack has its leaders. There is an alpha female and male guiding each pack. Different alphas have different styles of leadership, different personalities. Wolves are social animals, and each has a way of contributing to the survival of the pack at one time or another."

"Sounds fascinating." I couldn't come up with a better reply at the moment.

"But I need to go turn my paper in," she said, a bit apologetically.

I stepped to the side to let her pass. "Then I'll see you in class." After watching her disappear around the corner at the end of the hallway, I finally entered the lab.

୧ଈ

Semester's end eventually came, and my class gathered for their final exams. If you've never seen a group of people take a difficult test, it can be quite entertaining, with the frowns of concentration, the furious writing, and the poor soul who is constantly blowing his nose. I went into the class looking forward to finishing up this responsibility, and as each student turned in his or her last assignment, I grinned. We were playing "and then there were none." I admit I breathed a sigh a relief when Dave walked out the door.

After an hour only three remained, Tsula among them. I

suddenly felt a tinge of regret, looking at the mostly empty classroom. I didn't understand it. Despite my resistance our little group had formed a bond over those months together. I put down my work and watched the final three. When Tsula gathered her things together and walked forward, I stood, whispering, "Thank you," as she handed me her paper. She smiled, paused a moment, then turned and passed through the doorway.

Returning to my seat, I held her paper in my hand, admiring her handwriting, a lingering sign of her presence. I flipped through the exam and was thrilled to discover a quick note at the bottom. "Thanks for a great semester. I trust one day you will make a difference!"

She spared a thought for me—was it a note of admiration? Certainly hope. Again I was confused. My dominant feeling was that I had lost something I didn't want to lose. Would I see Tsula again? I knew already she hadn't signed up for the course I was TAing in the spring. Would I see her on campus? But then I doubted. Did I really want more complications? Shouldn't I just quit while I seemed to be ahead? The semester had been exhausting.

The end of the semester was "crunch time" as I struggled to get my studies completed, to get those exams graded on time, and to keep up with my new programming job off campus. It is a fog now, but one image stands out clearly. My subconscious evidently understood my commitments better than I did, for in that last week, it brought me one of the most vivid dreams I've ever had.

Tsula and I were out walking in the woods, autumn leaves drifting around us. As animated as ever, she was arguing wolf habitat was again in danger, despite recent successful efforts to bring their numbers back from the brink of extinction. An eerie howl suddenly sounded above and beyond us, distracting my attention. As I looked in the distance for the creature who claimed dominion over the woods, I realized night had come upon us and I no longer heard Tsula's voice in my ear. Turning back toward her, I discovered she was no longer with me; I was alone in the woods in the dark. The howl sounded again much closer, and I started to run. A presence was gaining on me; I felt the hot breath on the back of my neck. Though I tried to run faster, my legs seemed caught in honey. Darkness overtook me, and I struggled, swimming with no destination, nothing to hold onto. But then the darkness gave way to an approaching light until all that was left was one shining feather, white at the base, black at the tip.

3
BITTEN

"DO YOU THINK IT IS WISE TO ENTER THE DARKNESS, Ms. Washington?" he asked, pulling aside the last wooden beam to expose the hidden weakness in the stone wall—a gaping hole and black emptiness beyond.

"I don't think we have much choice. Process of elimination. This has to be the spot we're looking for," she answered, catching only a glimpse of Ahmed's face in her lantern's flickering light before he passed through the hole and disappeared into the tunnel.

"The dangers of working with a partner," she whispered to herself, "but I don't have much choice." Taking a deep breath, Brie ducked her head and jumped after him, landing softly on the other side. Though the tunnel had looked expansive at the opening, Brie found she had to stoop slightly now she was inside.

Ahmed, who had walked forward several yards, turned back, his own lantern momentarily blinding her. When her eyes focused again, she saw he was standing, without having to crouch, right next to her, his khaki-colored shirt and pants hanging loosely about him, framing the golden skin of his bald head and arms. Behind circular spectacles, his restless eyes kept moving from the path ahead back to her.

"I wonder if this is how it'd smell if you were buried alive?" he asked.

"A pleasant thought," Brie responded sarcastically.

Ahmed grinned, his dark goatee accentuating a twisted smile.

"Are you sure you can handle this, Professor?" Brie continued.

"I have to find my wife." His voice was devoid of emotion. "It's been three days now. The more time, the less chance I'm going to find her alive."

"This is not going to be pretty."

"We will find what we will find," he said, then turned and started to follow the tunnel downward, no longer waiting on her.

"Yes, we will," she whispered, her hand checking the placement of the long-barrel shotgun in her shoulder harness before she followed.

Brie watched closely as Ahmed descended, his stride tight, but quick, his lantern bouncing, releasing his shadow to dance on the wall and ceiling. All was quiet except for Ahmed's raspy wheeze and the thumps of their feet on the rocky path. The incline ran steadily down for several minutes before easing and finally leveling off. Glancing over her shoulder, Brie noted the long climb back to where they had started; they were committed now. When she turned forward again, she noticed Ahmed had paused his advance and was twisting his head one way and then the other, lifting his ears. She resumed her pace, but before she caught up to him, he stepped forward again, and this time she lost his shadow. In a few steps, she confirmed he had passed out of the tight tunnel into some larger chamber, immeasurably large *since their light failed to reach the ceiling or the far walls.*

"I have a bad feeling about this," Ahmed whispered.

Brie was looking up, wondering how large a space they were in, when she heard a rush, a thud, a man's yell, and the crash of glass. As she turned, she lifted her lantern with one hand and reached for her shotgun with the other. A hairy shadow had Ahmed pinned to the ground, and the thin man was frantically trying to hold the shadow back as it continued to lunge at him. The snapping sound told Brie she only had seconds. Quickly and quietly, she placed her own lantern on the ground and reached up to steady the shotgun. Just before she had pulled it into position, she heard Ahmed howl in pain.

With the gun lifted, she shouted, trying to keep her voice from breaking, "Here!"

The shadow did not respond, so Brie fired one barrel in its direction, keeping her aim high so that she did not accidentally hit Ahmed. The edge of the blast evidently did find its mark, for the creature lurched to the side with a guttural grunt, leaving Ahmed to scramble back, blood soaking his shirt and arms. The creature turned, and Brie finally made out its face, the long lupine snout, the fiery eyes, the pointed ears, which twisted low and outward when it spotted her.

Brie held firmly onto her shotgun.

The werewolf growled, tensed, and then sprang toward her, high into the air, arms extended and mouth open. She fired the second barrel at point-blank range into the creature's head and chest. It collapsed into a bloody heap just before her.

"Professor," she called while rushing to Ahmed's side.

His head low, breathing hard, his right hand gripping his left forearm, Ahmed did not open his eyes for her. She quickly noted, beyond the bloodied shirt, the deep gashes in his chest, but it was his arm that concerned her—the wrist and hand were twisted at a wrong angle, and blood flowed past his fingers. Though she reached to examine Ahmed's arm, she could not move his hand.

"Did it bite you?" she asked.

Ahmed did not answer.

"Did it bite you?" she repeated, pulling stronger on his good hand. When she finally broke his grip, he groaned and fell on his side. There were deep holes in his arm, and white bone could be seen. His mangled arm was definitely broken.

She cursed as she unbuttoned her long-sleeved blouse. When she finished pulling it free, she used it to wrap Ahmed's arm, and he moaned at each touch. His breathing had slowed, and he was going limp in her arms.

"Don't pass out on me!" Brie shouted.

Ahmed's eyes flicked open for a second and then rolled back.

Hearing movement nearby, she tensed and looked back. Her lantern still sat where she had left it, only feet away, and its yellow light flashed over a massive ball of thick, brown fur hunched over the werewolf she had just shot. This second creature nudged and sniffed the bloody carcass and whined when it received no greeting. Carefully Brie laid Ahmed down and reached for her pistol, but at that moment Ahmed groaned, and the ball of fur lifted its head, bringing its face into the light. This werewolf was much larger than the first. As it focused on Brie, its lips pulled back to expose fangs and gums, thick grayish saliva dripping down. Over the barrel of her pistol, Brie watched it closely from her crouching position near Ahmed. The creature did not move, did not make a sound, but remained coiled, ready to strike.

Keeping her hands tightly around the gun, Brie stood.

The werewolf jumped, and Brie pulled the trigger, but as the light went out with a crash, Brie discovered the creature had not leaped at her, but her lantern. In the darkness that followed, Brie fired again and again.

§♠

"You've got a sweet setup here, mate," Uncle Jack observed, as he leaned back on the cheap sofa and kicked off his sandals. My uncle knew how to make himself "at home" just about anywhere. This was his first visit to my apartment, not long after the semester began, just weeks after I'd first met Tsula. Mick was out, and I was showing my uncle around.

He frequently called me "mate." Once when I asked him why he did, he said it was a sailor thing. He had spent several years in the Navy, but I had a suspicion it was also a result of his two-year station in Australia. He always said the word with just a hint of an accent.

"I don't know how you're going to get a Ph. D. with this wall-screen greeting you every time you enter your place."

"Thanks for the encouragement," I said.

"So you're going to tell me you haven't played *Transylvania Nights VII* any time when you should have been studying? You haven't played it late into the night and fallen asleep in class the next day?" His voice was searching and teasing.

"I did miss the first session of the class I'm TAing," I confessed. Uncle Jack always could draw me out.

"I knew it!" he declared like a lawyer who'd just gotten a witness to reveal the crucial piece of evidence. "I'll give you six months and then you'll abandon this foolhardy plan and go work full time."

"No," I defended. "I'm committed to this degree."

"And how does it fit into your plan of being a great video game designer?"

"I want to be the expert in my field."

"Is that you or your dad talking, mate?" he asked, his eyes narrowing.

"You know Dad doesn't want me working for a video game company."

"You don't need this degree to work at Tsunami Games."

"But if I'm going to design the ground-breaking tech necessary to pull Immersive Reality off the ground, I need to know my field better than anyone else."

"You are your father's son," he said finally and then pursued another idea. "Immersive Reality? Is that what you're calling it now?" He seemed genuinely intrigued.

"I think my idea is a game changer, one that will put Virtual Reality to shame."

"Wow! Someone thinks highly of himself," he said, a large grin spreading across his face.

A scraping sound at the door told me Mick was back unexpectedly. A second later the door opened to confirm his return. He had a startled look on his face.

"Sorry, Mick, I didn't get a chance to tell you my uncle was popping in for a visit."

Mick was silent.

"I brought Don a copy of *Cobalt Blue*. We were just going to get it cranked up. Would you care to join us?" My gregarious uncle was always pulling people in. He and Mick did share that in common.

"Yes, I would love to see the new game." Mick had recovered. He had met my uncle a few times the year before, but they had never had much time to talk.

After Mick threw his backpack in his room and rejoined us, we started.

Mick asked, "So you continue to keep Don in the latest games?" Mick had met my parents and heard me defend my plans to them several times on the phone.

"I may have taught him to sail, but he is the captain of his own ship these days," I heard him say as we were thrust into the game's opening scene—some tropical jungle, perhaps in Central America, our avatars dressed in soldier jungle gear.

My uncle was being modest. He and I would meet online a couple weekends a month, and had done so for years; we didn't spend much time talking before we would jump into our latest game. We had explored all sorts of worlds together; we had been pirates, car thieves, superheroes, and soldiers of various stripes. Those were memories I treasured. He had been my mentor of sorts, and without his help I don't know how I would have survived my childhood.

&

I was five years old when the massive, tiger-like dog came bounding around the azalea toward me, and I did not run, for I thought it had come to play. My mother was visiting with someone who was sick, one of her "charity cases," as my father called them, and I was in the yard kicking around my soccer ball with the daughter of the woman my mother was treating, a girl who was taller than I was, smudges on her face, her hair in pigtails. Though my mother had asked me to stay close by, I don't think she realized how strong my little legs were. After a game-winning kick, my ball rolled well down the hill into a yard where sand dominated grass.

"Be careful!" the girl yelled as I started to run after the ball.

"I'll be al'right," I shot back at her. What did she know anyway?

The ball had slowed, but it was still rolling, and I wandered far. I did look back once to see the girl, shaking her head, her pigtails swinging, her hands on her hips.

My ball came to rest finally next to a car, in the space where a wheel should have been, and I was curious (all of our cars had wheels) and ran my finger along the ridges in the rusty studs that jutted out. I heard the thunderous bark first, and I did not know what it was until the dog cleared the azalea, its heavy paws throwing dust up behind it. The next events could not have taken much time at all, but whenever I rehearse them today, the images always creep; the dog is ever closing in on me—its brindle coat, black stripes on orange, one incongruous white patch on its chest, the chain collar, and that drooping face with hanging jowls, as if it had been made of melting cheese.

As it neared, I held up my ball, inviting it to play, but its dark mouth opened wide, clamped down on the ball, and shook it with a ferocity that startled me. I heard the girl with pigtails scream behind me, and then I knew pain. The slobbery mouth and wicked teeth were around my arm, and I could not pull away. I stood transfixed, looking into its eyes, observing something I'd never seen, a wild predatory spirit, and I was its prey. Although I did not fight, the dog did not let up, and under the pressure, I felt my arm snap. Darkness closed in, and I struggled to breathe.

I heard voices around me and recognized my mother's. Someone was on top of the dog in front of me, hammering at the back of its neck, yelling at it. "Let go! Let go!"

When the jaws finally released, I fell to the ground. I do not remember what happened next, only the warm firmness of someone's—my mother's?—arms around me, carrying me to safety.

I opened my eyes next when I was in the car. We were speeding down the road, and she was on the phone with my father. I hazarded a look at my arm, which I couldn't feel, and discovered my mother had already wrapped it. My hand was blue, though, with a streak of dried blood my mother had missed, and the angle of my arm wasn't right.

Before I knew it, we were at the hospital, pulling past the sign reading "emergency" and up to the curb where a man dressed in white was waiting. He opened the car door, reached in, and lifted me into a wheelchair. Within seconds he pushed me through the automatic door and into the hospital as my mother came running up behind us. There were others in the emergency room waiting, but my parents had the quick track, and the man in white immediately wheeled me back beyond another door he opened by hitting a large metallic button on the wall. Cold air surrounded me, and I was shivering by the time I reached a room.

My father intercepted us at the doorway, his voice the only thing I could hold onto in this strange world. "Donovan, everything is going to be okay. Dad is here, and I'm going to make everything right. Don't worry. I'll take care of you." I felt his hand grip my shoulder for a second.

Then I heard my mother's voice. "Richard, I'm sorry...."

"We'll talk about it later," my father cut her off as we entered the room, a small one with pale florescent light and no windows.

My father's hand was again on my shoulder. "I'm going to fix your arm, Buddy, but in order for me to do that, you're going to have to take a nap. One of my friends is going to come in here and help me get you ready. Do you think you're ready?"

"Yes," I croaked, still shivering a little under the blanket he'd given me.

"You hang in there, Donovan, and everything will be okay."

My mother grabbed my father, and they argued to the side for a little, but then he winked at her in a strange way and walked out. A nurse soon appeared, her abdomen round as a beach ball, and she talked to my mother about babies as she stuck a needle in my arm. When my father returned, another doctor was with him. While this other doctor worked in the background with the clear tubes hanging above me, my father checked on me again. My mother kissed me on the forehead, and I drifted away.

I went under thinking my father would be the one working on my arm, but years later I found out hospital and insurance policies forbade surgeons from operating on their own family members. I was shocked as a teenager to learn my father had given in to the policy. If there were a way around regulations, he was the type to find the loophole or to make one. Of course, I was also shocked to learn my father had lied to me. He said it was a "benevolent lie" to make me feel better in a difficult situation, but when I found the truth, I began to wonder how many other such lies might have shaped my childhood.

At the time I wasn't thinking about such things. The surgery went well—my father's friend knew what he was doing— but in the succeeding hours a staph infection set in, resisting the antibiotics the surgeon had prescribed. It was my father who identified it first, but even he had difficulty getting the rest of the hospital staff to acknowledge the need for more aggressive treatment.

The next couple days were fuzzy since I was wrestling with a fever. When my eyes were closed, the nightmare of the dog attack haunted me, and when my eyes were open, my vision was soft as if I needed glasses. There was enough of me present to record impressions of my father's animated discussions with others in white coats and to feel my mother's gentle caresses across my forehead. After over a week in the hospital, I emerged mostly myself again, but my arm was scarred, the infection having undermined the surgeon's work. My mother kept telling me it would fade with time and the application of creams, and my father would nod, but I could tell he was not pleased. Today, when remembering this scene, with the knowledge of what really happened, I imagine him whispering, "I would have done a better job."

When we got home, I discovered, sort of accidentally since my parents tried to hide it from me, they had also been arguing about something else—what to do about the dog. It was the day after I came home from the hospital, and I overheard part of a phone conversation my mother had with one of her friends.

A small voice echoed far away in my mother's cellular, "What do you mean it's more complicated? If my son had been bitten by that dog, my husband and I would be in court demanding the dog be put down!"

"Richard adamantly refuses to consider that option," my mother countered.

"Is he insane? Does he care what you have to say?"

My mother was silent.

Her friend continued, "What do you think, Chelsea? What if other children wander into that yard? What if the dog kills the next child? Won't that be on you and Richard?"

"You're not being fair. The dog has an owner who is responsible."

"He's already shown he's not responsible."

"Richard doesn't think killing the dog is a solution, and I agree we should give its owner a chance to make things right," my mother defended.

"Make things right? The dog broke your son's arm. What if he'd gone after Don's neck instead?"

"Ginny, I don't want to have this conversation right now."

"I'm just saying."

"Fine. I'll call you later."

"OK."

I watched as my mother lowered the phone and reached to end the call. Her hand missed the precise spot on the touchpad, and she had to try again. When she finally succeeded, she tossed the phone several feet into her purse. Standing, she finally noticed me watching her from the hallway.

"I'm sorry, Donny. I don't want you to worry about these things."

"What things?" I asked immediately.

"About the dog."

When I didn't say anything, she changed tactics and distracted me with cookies and milk. It wasn't until that evening during supper, with my father on one side and my mother on the other, illuminated by the warm light of our dining room, that I remembered the conversation.

"Dad?"

"Yes, Son, what is it?" My father was eating quickly while flipping through a stack of papers he'd brought to the table.

"You're not supposed to have papers at the table."

He looked at me, then at my mother, offering her a smile that looked like a balloon that had lost its helium. "No, I'm not. I've just got an important meeting at the hospital tonight, and I need to be ready for it." He went back to the papers.

"Dad?"

"I told you I'm busy." He didn't look up this time.

"What's going to happen to the dog that bit me?"

The hand my father was using to flip through the papers stopped in midair and came back down to rest on the table. I saw him take a breath before he lifted his head. "Don, I don't want you to worry about that dog. You didn't even know he existed two weeks ago. You need to work on forgetting you ever saw him."

"But I can't, Dad. When I close my eyes, I still see him."

I felt my mother's hand warmly rest on the hand I had up on the table.

My father paused, then went on, "Sometimes bad things are going to happen to you, but you can't let them get the better of you."

"Shouldn't the dog be put down?" I parroted the words I'd heard on the phone.

My father's eyes opened wide for a second, then retreated into a frown as he again looked at my mother. "Where did he hear that?"

She defended, "Ginny called today. She's the one who said that. Not me."

The mantle clock tolled half past the hour.

"Don," my father resumed, leaning in closer to me. "Killing that dog is wrong. It is a living creature, and we should have reverence for its life." I had heard those words before. My father and grandfather often spoke of *reverence for life*. They also spoke of some great man who liked those words too. It would be years before I would connect them to the Nobel-prize-winning doctor, philosopher, theologian, and environmentalist Albert Schweitzer and his influence over them.

"But the dog hurt me."

"We're not going to let that dog near you again. You're not going to have to worry about it."

"What if he finds me?" I didn't understand why my father wasn't trying to protect me.

"He's not going to find you." He placed his hand on my shoulder. "You have nothing to worry about."

I wasn't so sure, but I wasn't going to argue with him any more. Already at that age, I understood what his hand on my shoulder meant. Tousling my hair, he then leaned back, finished the rest of his supper in record time, picked up his papers, and dashed out the door. When he was gone, my mother had two more cookies and another glass of milk for me.

But that night I had another nightmare. I was in my own backyard when the dog, black stripes and melting face, jumped over the hedgerow and bounded toward me again. When I turned to run, I tripped, falling hard onto the ground, and then the animal was on me, its jaws clamping down on my shoulder. I screamed in pain, and all went to fuzzy darkness as the dream ended and I woke up in my bed, feeling my own rapid breaths and the pain still in my shoulder.

The nightmares continued until Uncle Jack visited. My father was close to his brother even though they rarely agreed about anything. My mother would often whisper to me how funny it was that two such different people could come from the same family. While my father often wore a coat and tie, my uncle wore beach shirts and shorts, sometimes in the middle of winter. My father lived in the urban heart of Atlanta, but my uncle split his time between an efficiency apartment outside Raleigh and a beach home in the Outer Banks. And then, although my father never played video games, my uncle loved them.

Uncle Jack was the one who got me hooked. During the few days he stayed with us, he pulled out his laptop, the one he had, in his words, "tricked out" for games. At one point when my parents were busy with something, as they frequently were, I drifted to the guest-bedroom doorway to find my uncle shooting virtual skeet with a plastic gun. Thinking he didn't notice me, I watched for several minutes, impressed with his accuracy; he didn't miss a target. I drifted into the room.

"Would you like to try?" my uncle said, handing me the gun. "I've got the sensor mounted just above the screen, so all you have to do is point and shoot."

The gun was heavier in my hand than I expected.

"There are weights inside to give it a more realistic feel, though it's still plastic." My uncle smiled. "Go ahead, mate. It's perfectly safe."

I missed the first skeet, which came out ridiculously fast.

"Hold on a sec." He reached down, pulled up the menu, and bumped it down from "Insane" to "Easy."

I still missed when the next gray disk flew across the screen. After I failed to hit the second as well, my uncle stepped behind me and reached to help me steady my arm, saying, "Take a breath and concentrate."

This time when the skeet emerged, he helped me pull the trigger at the exact moment, and I yelled in satisfaction, "I did it. I did it."

"You sure did, kid."

He took a step back and sat on the bed while I focused on repeating my success. I knocked out about half of the targets before the game ended and displayed my score.

"How'd I do?" I turned around to check with Jack.

He winked at me. "You're a natural."

"May I do it again?"

I did a better job the second time around. When my score danced across the screen this time, my uncle stepped forward and accessed the menu again.

"There's another level to this game I want to show you."

He gently lifted the gun from my hand. The screen flickered and then something started moving. It looked like we were driving a Jeep in a dark jungle, large green fronds flashing by, and something was chasing us. When I saw the white teeth, I froze; something was trying to bite me. I suddenly felt cold. Yet at that moment Uncle Jack fired his gun. There was a small red flash, and as the biting thing slumped and fell, I realized it was a dinosaur.

"You OK?" I heard my uncle say. He had paused the game and was looking at me. I was breathing more heavily than usual.

"Yeah," I squeaked through a dry throat.

"It's your turn." He handed the gun back to me.

I was surprised how much I welcomed it. When he resumed the game, I jerked the gun wildly, missing my target.

"Focus," Uncle Jack said.

Someone was calling my name, but the only thing I knew in the moment was that pulling that trigger silenced the gnashing teeth before me. I kept firing.

"Donovan! Donovan!" My mother's voice sounded behind me. Then I saw her hands take the gun from mine. "Jack, while you're here, I hope you'll respect our rules."

I saw my uncle lean back. "It's not real."

"You know what your brother thinks." My mother was quiet in her anger; somehow that made it worse.

"The boy needs an outlet."

My mother walked up to him and placed the gun in his hands. "Not this." Then she escorted me out, hoping to lead me away from temptation, but I had already heard its call. That night I slept peacefully; it was weeks before I realized the nightmares were gone.

❧

Uncle Jack also introduced me to *Transylvania Nights*. Those first years he and I would have to wait for hidden moments when we could indulge in our shared interest; it would be months before I could play video games. My parents never approved of them; they said they were a waste of time and only encouraged the thought that violence was the only way to solve our problems. After the confrontation with my mother and a conversation that evidently occurred later between him and my father—Jack only hinted at it—my uncle was supremely careful in hiding what we were doing.

Yet in my teenage years, I pushed back. Teens rebel in many ways, and I think my parents finally acquiesced, realizing they had things pretty easy. I know my mother felt guilty about the amount of time they left me alone for the sake of their jobs, so they finally relented, just as long as I stayed away from the "mature" titles. Uncle Jack could finally give me games openly, and the first title was *Transylvania Nights*, a cutting-edge game, advertised as the most realistic game ever.

Uncle Jack laughed when he saw the ads, "What's realistic about a monster-hunter? They're just glad they designed a PC game."

"I thought it was for multiple platforms."

"Not that PC, but PC as in politically correct."

He was talking about the central character Brie Washington, who had African and Hispanic ancestry, who in her fictional world grew up on the streets of Durham, North Carolina. The reviewers praised how her proportions were lifelike, how her wardrobe fit her role as archaeologist and explorer, unlike certain other games that put women with exaggerated measurements into minimal clothing. The gaming studio advertised that such decisions had made the character even more popular among women gamers, while the more realistic graphics on the combat with vampires and werewolves would keep the interest of male gamers.

The game was a great success, selling record numbers and spawning sequels in succeeding years, ones I preordered and played as soon as I could get my hands on them. Each time there was a special anticipation as I explored the new plots, worked through the new mysteries, discovered which characters I could trust, put down the monsters terrorizing helpless victims, and collected the treasures they protected. The sequels were fun, but they never did equal the sensation I got playing that first game.

My father once came in on me playing it on a large wall screen with the speakers cranked up. I still remember it well. I felt self-conscious not only because I was playing as a woman character, but also because I could feel the weight of his disapproval palpably on my neck and shoulders. He never said a word, though, and after watching for a while, he walked quietly out of the room. Alone again, I shrugged, shaking off his silent censure. This was my choice. At the time I was trapped in some subterranean den with a wounded partner named Ahmed, shooting werewolves in the dark, firing again and again. There was no doubt; these monsters were not going to bite me.

4
REUNION

G ROWLING PLAYFULLY, KAN MOVED CLOSER, BREATHING in her scent, savoring it, as they brushed their faces together, licking and biting. When Lana put her weight against his shoulder, he gave into her push to tumble with her into the snow. By the time she pinned him, he was biting down a yelp from the knifing pain coming up his wounded leg. Only letting her have the advantage for a moment, though, he turned free, and she finally relented. Their play ended with each crouched in the snow, snout to snout, watching the other closely.

Kan thrilled at the recognition in her eyes. Through a low-pitched whine, he asked, *How are you?*

You don't have to worry about me.

I didn't know if I'd find you.

I'm here. She smiled.

I thought I'd find you sooner, but the pack moved.

We need to find a new home. I only lingered because I felt you would be looking for us.

A new home? Why? Kan first doubted what he heard, but then pieces started coming together. *Is it the tiger?*

You know about the tiger?

I saw the marks last night.

Prey was becoming scarce, she explained. *The tiger moved into our territory, and we lost one of the males.*

Which?

Doda.

No! The weight of the loss began to sink in, and Kan suddenly understood the signs he had seen the night before. *How is that possible?*

Doda was strong, but even he wasn't able to take on a tiger. I wasn't there when the tiger attacked; I only saw the pack running away and Etsi terribly agitated. Later I doubled back on my own and found the remains—don't worry, I was careful. Etsi grieved Doda's loss so much she pulled away from the rest of us. Most of the pack didn't know what to do. Some of the younger ones came to me, and to head off Danuwa's growing unrest, I finally stepped in and decided we needed to search out a new home. The pack followed my lead.

What led you this way? he asked.

You remember Wesa.

Yes.

She's the pack's best hunter.

Next to you.

Lana barely smiled before continuing. *I went on several patrols with her, and sometimes Noya too; we could cover ground much faster than some of the others. We went in several directions out this way away from the tiger. I preferred to stay closer to the river, and we did have some luck finding food for the pack.*

How's Etsi now?

She's tired.

Has she resumed her leadership role?

Lana did not respond, but Kan saw something in her face that made him ask, *Have you become the new alpha for the pack?*

She looked away. *It just happened. I wasn't planning on it.*

As his mind raced with the implications of her answer, he could not decide exactly what to ask next—until something struck his imagination. *Has another male been running with you?*

She looked back, and seeing the pain in her eyes, he regretted the question.

She growled, *You weren't here, and things were falling apart. You know that wasn't my fault.*

She paused for a moment and then continued, *Don't think I wasn't approached, but I chased them away.*

Who was it?

Does it matter?

He looked down and raked a paw through the snow. How could they be in this situation? Which males had approached her? He still wanted to know, but he finally decided it was better not to press the question.

I need your help. He heard the tenor of her voice break ever so slightly, a brief moment of weakness. *I don't want to do this alone.*

Meeting her gaze again, Kan asked, *What can I do?*

The pack needs order, and that means a new alpha pair.

After last night I don't know if the pack will accept me as alpha. I've got a nasty leg wound from a wolverine that surprised me.

A wolverine? The edges of Lana's mouth turned up slightly.

I know. It bit down and wouldn't let go. The leg wound allowed Danuwa to get the better of me. His voice sounded more defensive than he wanted.

The wound will heal in time. She returned to a serious tone. *You know my friends and I will deflect most of the challengers until you're back in the game.*

So I don't have much choice, do I? He did not like this new responsibility. He preferred running in the woods as they had done many times before, just the two of them. Life in the pack would change greatly now that this move put them at the center.

The pack needs us.

He saw the resolve in her eye and knew there was no arguing with her, at least not now. If this was the price to pay for having her near, he would make the best of it.

Are you hungry? she asked, and he was both frustrated and relieved to move on to something else.

A little, but I should be fine for a while longer.

We need to bring you back into the pack. She stood. *It's not going to be easy, but I think there will be enough who will be glad to see you return. If there is another challenge, then we'll face it.*

I'll manage, he growled and pulled himself to his feet.

Lana howled quickly, and within a few breaths, Noya and Sasa, the two females who'd found him in the woods the night before, joined them, tails wagging. He was glad to see them, and he did not have to wonder long whether his near loss to Danuwa had lessened his standing in their eyes, for when Sasa neared him, she rolled over onto her side, exposing her weak leg, her tail lowered in a submissive way. Kan leaned down and licked her cream-colored face.

Sasa was the ungainly one of the two sisters; sometimes she waddled like a goose and could not keep up with the others. The awkwardness came from a crippled leg, arising from a wound she had received when she was a pup. It was a mysterious situation. While playing in the woods one morning seasons ago, Kan had seen Etsi run by. He guessed she had left the pups in the care of another wolf in the pack, yet not long after Etsi passed, he heard a howl of pain coming from the direction of the den. He immediately ran in that direction and arrived about the same time Etsi and some others did. Not long after

Etsi ducked inside, Kan heard her motherly growl and then a yip from a pup.

Etsi refused to let others near the pups for the rest of the day, but the next time Kan saw the pups, he noticed Sasa had a nasty wound on her front left leg. When he asked Lana her thoughts, they came to the same conclusion, that Danuwa must have been the source of the wound. There must have been some moment when the pups were alone, when he had the unsupervised freedom to bite her so viciously, and he must have been the pup who later yipped under his mother's discipline.

The lack of coordination which resulted from her brother's attack shaped Sasa's life in the pack; she became an easy target for the role of omega female, the scapegoat of the pack, the one who frequently ate last, unless one of the other wolves found a place for her. Even though she shouldered the frustrations of all the others, she still kept a positive attitude, still wagged her tail wildly, still loved to play despite abuse from some of the ones who had something to prove. Like Danuwa. And maybe those two males who traveled with him, Kan thought.

Noya approached more cautiously, still standing, but her head and tail lowered, whining an affectionate greeting. He nuzzled in closer and let her lick his neck. Cream-colored like her sister, Noya was in the middle of the pack; she was a good hunter, having trained with Lana and Wesa. Kan had memories of hunts when Noya had made the decisive leap that helped bring down their prey. She also was a good sister for Sasa, watching over her, defending her if others in the pack ever got too rough with her. Kan knew Noya to be a quietly strong wolf, and he felt better knowing she had Lana's back too.

Lana howled authoritatively, and Noya and Sasa turned and headed back into the woods. It was time to find the rest of the pack. Lana looked back at him, before jumping after the others, and Kan followed as best he could.

He found he could not keep up with Lana, so he ran in the

rear of the formation with Sasa, who wagged her tail, evidently enjoying his company. From time to time, Lana would dash ahead with Noya but then circle around and come running past Kan from behind, nipping him playfully on the back. As she passed, he thought she was enjoying his handicap a little too much.

The trip proved to be more of a burden than he would have liked, but he tried to keep Lana from discovering how much. One time while climbing an upgrade, the early sun in his eyes, Kan stumbled in the snow and could not recover before Lana had doubled back to check on him.

We're almost there, she consoled.

I probably should rest a moment before seeing everyone again.

You'll manage, she teased.

He growled.

Then they set off again. Although he trusted Lana, Kan knew for himself they were on the right track when scent markers gave testimony to the passing of other wolves, wolves he knew. Though he could identify several of the younger wolves in the pack, he also noticed the absence of a prominent scent. He remembered what Lana had told him and began to wonder what life in the pack would be like without Doda's charismatic leadership. The alpha male had been the father of three litters; he and Etsi had watched over each group of pups, and they had even taken in Kan and Lana, two outsider wolves. Doda had been a strong leader, maintaining a firm sense of order and rank in the pack, yet devotedly watching over even the weakest of the group. How would they survive in this wilderness without him?

A howl in the distance broke his reflection, and as he searched to identify whose it was, Sasa shuffled ahead in an attempt to catch up with her sister. In a flash Lana was at his side.

Here we go, she barked. Kan heard the excitement in her

voice, saw it in her eyes, but as the scents, the sounds, and the nearby presence of the other wolves pressed in on him, he doubted again.

Then he noticed another wolf coming toward them, only a few leaps away. The gray male advanced with warm confidence, growling playfully, his tail wagging vigorously, his tongue lolling out of his mouth. The greeting was infectious, and Kan and Lana were soon exchanging licks with their friend. Kan was not surprised to see Unalii welcome them first. The beta wolf was the caretaker of the pack, watching over the others, particularly any litter of pups, making sure no one was left behind, yet also assisting in the reinforcement of ranking in the pack. Kan welcomed Unalii's licks and sniffs. Memories of hunts together gave Kan courage; he did have friends in the pack.

Unalii noticed the wound on Kan's leg, licked it once, and then ran a couple circles around Kan and Lana, his tongue lolling out playfully, expectantly.

I'm ready, Kan nodded to Lana.

As he stepped forward, Lana took a place by his side, and Unalii raced up the hill toward the other wolves, who were milling about in various places along the clearing, some hidden in shadows, some soaking up the sun of the new day.

Kan paused to take in all the details, the chill in the air, the musky scents, and the presence of all the wolves who began to converge on him. In the midst of this crowding, Kan observed his mate's smile.

I'll do this for you, he pledged.

At first he tried to follow her lead, but soon he lost sight of her as a crowd of gray fur, white teeth, and red tongues engulfed him. The barrage of warm greetings was so quick, so immediate, he struggled to identify familiar faces, but they were there in the midst of the confusion. To hold his footing, despite his leg wound, he pushed back against the large males; he endured the sniffing around his legs and tail; and he returned the affections so easily offered. In a matter of moments, it was as if he had not left; he again belonged to the pack.

When his friends started retreating, some returning to their patrols, others prancing about still caught up in the excitement, Kan noticed another wolf keeping his distance. The masked wolf stood erect, showing no emotion, giving no ground. Even after the previous night, Danuwa held onto his place in the pack. Two other males lounged nearby, and in the daylight, Kan was able finally to remember their names, Sikwa and Oni. They were indeed from the last litter, the one Kan did not know as well. They must have been the only ones who had survived. Sikwa, the older and much larger of the two, rose and trotted lazily over to join the last ones greeting Kan. When Oni saw his brother move, he soon followed. Kan immediately checked for Danuwa's reaction, but the masked wolf already had turned and jumped into the woods.

Sikwa offered no real affection. The large wolf bumped into Kan, who was prepared for the act of intimidation. Oni's greeting was submissive; he rolled on his side, much as Sasa had earlier in the day, and Kan realized Oni must now be the omega male. Not only was Oni the youngest in the pack, he was the smallest male, and most likely would remain the weakest. Although Kan leaned in and licked Oni on the muzzle in a token of friendship, Kan believed he only saw fear in the omega's eyes, not open terror, but the dull legacy of constantly enduring the dominance of those around him. In a flash, though, Oni turned and dashed after his brother, who was already tracking Danuwa's trail.

With the rush of greetings finally drawn to a close, Kan secured a quiet spot to sit and rest, and Lana, after circling the clearing, settled in close to him.

We're holding together, Lana offered. *There were some tense moments after Doda's death.*

At that moment Kan realized he had not yet seen Etsi. He raised his head to sniff.

As if she read his thoughts, Lana answered, *Etsi's out on patrol, but Taline's here, and you know how close the two are.*

He noted the mid-aged female, who was pawing at the snow a few yards to his left. Taline lifted her head several times to scan the woods nearby, eyes alert, ears standing up. She seemed unable to relax.

She's not necessarily happy about the way things have turned out, Lana continued. *She wasn't particularly close to Doda, but I don't think she can handle how Doda's death has devastated Etsi.*

Is Taline going to be a problem? he whispered back.

I don't think so. She doesn't have much choice as long as the rest of the pack supports us, and I don't think she's the type who would challenge me anyway.

Kan looked from Taline around to the other wolves and began to size up each of them, asking Lana for her impressions of their loyalties. He pulled her into a discussion of pack politics because he felt he needed to understand where each wolf stood. Assuming the life of an alpha would be a serious challenge following the successful leadership of Doda and Etsi. Kan easily identified their friends: Unalii had already shown his affection, and Noya and Sasa were still close to Lana. Yet it was all too obvious Danuwa was his biggest threat, with Sikwa and Oni potentially backing up any claim the masked wolf might make for dominance. There were several other wolves in the pack, though, and Kan did not want any more surprises.

While you were away, we also had a new female join the pack.

Really? Kan questioned.

Remember the pack accepted us.

But this is the first wolf besides us....

Lana finished his thought, *Etsi didn't give birth to. Yes, it happens. Several days ago Koga came running in with Wesa. I found it strange at first too, but if Koga could win over Wesa, then I was going to give her a chance.*

Koga?

Yes, she's a smaller black wolf. Others in the pack didn't know what to make of her, but in our last hunt, she was the one who helped corner the deer out on the ice. We wouldn't have made the kill without her.

Where is she?

I'm not sure.

He listened without comment even though the news troubled him. What could he say when he had been away? He had to trust her again, but who was this new wolf, and where would she stand? Lana seemed to think she was a valuable addition to the pack. He decided he would reserve judgment until later.

Another thought caught up with him. *Thank you, by the way.*

For what? She nudged in closer to him.

For getting Danuwa off my back last night.

Oh, for saving your life, she teased.

Aren't we being overly dramatic?

Things looked desperate when I got there.

I suppose, he admitted, recalling the feeling of pushing in vain against Dunawa's weight. Perhaps he did owe her his life.

Evidently noticing the change in his tone, she bit him playfully on the ear. *Thank you for coming for me. I've been trapped, and I've missed you.*

He rolled her, and they came up, snow on their muzzles, grinning widely.

While playing with Lana, Kan noticed Taline in the background, head down. Although she was not looking in his direction, he could tell she was watching, and he suddenly felt a little nervous, thinking of Doda. He had not been here when his packmates had learned of the death. They were still grieving and here he was playing in the snow.

He walked forward close again to Lana and whined, *How long will they grieve?*

It's been almost a moon cycle. This hit them hard. You've got to be patient.

He remained quiet.

Your return has improved the spirit of the pack, but some will grieve longer, those who were closest to him and those who just don't like change.

At that moment an image of Doda came to him, a time when the alpha male was celebrating his second litter of pups. The older wolf had been successful earlier in the day in leading his pack in the taking down of a large elk. Bloody haunch clamped in his teeth, Doda made his way to his beloved Etsi and the seven pups in her den. He dropped the meat outside and barked to get her attention. When she came out to eat, he threw his head back in a full howl. It grew in intensity, and the others in the pack that day had joined in, their excitement about the pups clearly on display. In spite of himself, Kan also celebrated that day, finding their joy infectious.

That is what alphas did. They held up pack spirit. If he and Lana were going to lead, they were going to have to lead by example, he thought.

Then very tentatively, he started a howl. It was soft and squeaky at first, much to his irritation, and he was aware of Lana's curiosity. She let out a whine of encouragement, and he tried again, intentionally pulling the sound lower. It sounded a little better.

Lana's voice now joined, and he felt a surge of exhilaration. Then Unalii added his howl, and Noya and Sasa. With each new pack member, the sound grew stronger, and in it, Kan heard the pack's pain. Their loss entered him, and he too grieved Doda's passing. That great hunter, that pack father, the one who had taken care of so many was gone, and they all felt it.

Kan also heard in this grand chorus the fear in the pack. They had been displaced. An intruder had driven them from their homeland, and they were unsure about this new territory. Their routines were broken, and life together suddenly was off balance. It was the dead of winter; food was scarce; their lives were already hard; and now they had to shoulder this terrible twist. Would they be able to survive?

As these anxious notes sounded, Kan began to worry too. His howl broke, and he lowered his head.

Lana's howl did not break. Her voice pushed from fear to hope. *We will make it. We are a pack. We stand together. We will find a new home.*

He watched her in admiration. Had she ever been more beautiful? Picking up on her tone, he rejoined the wolf song.

❧

Past midday, Lana's tone got more serious. *I don't like that Etsi's not back yet. I haven't seen her since yesterday.*

Maybe she doesn't want to see me, Kan suggested.

I don't think that's it. I've a bad feeling about this. I think I'll take Wesa and go scout for her.

I can come too.

You need to stay here and rest.

I don't want to lose you.

Wesa and I can take care of ourselves.

Her look of determination and the stiffness in his leg led him to give in. *Don't take on any tigers!*

No, I'll save them for you, wolverine-wrestler, she barked into the air while running into the woods, where Wesa was patrolling.

In the moments after she left, he wondered if he needed to stay with the pack. How long would she be gone? Should he have followed her? What if they met the tiger in the middle of the woods? He tried to push his doubts away, as he lay down to rest, but each time he put his head down, the image of the tiger would jump out of the darkness of his thoughts.

Finally he decided he was not going to get much rest, so he had better do something constructive, something to distract himself from thinking about the dangers of Lana's mission. He turned his mind toward his mate's strategy; he needed to think about the pack, about assuming the role of leadership. It was time to confer with his friend Unalii, who had largely remained to the side after his entrance, providing a calming presence for the younger wolves in particular.

Unalii stood as Kan advanced. The beta wolf was of medium height, with dark gray over his shoulders and back, a lighter gray highlighting his face, a quiet wisdom residing in his eyes. At first Kan's natural instinct was to lower his head, but remembering his new role, he tried to hold it a little higher. It was unusual to see the beta wolf lower his head. Kan pushed quickly past this formal sign of ranking to greet the beta wolf warmly. The affection was reciprocated as they licked each other's muzzles, brushed shoulders, sniffed legs and tails, whining and barking for the others to hear. Kan knew these public displays were crucial to pack loyalties; others would be watching and listening, breathing in the mixing of scents.

Kan recalled hunting with Unalii, taking down elk and deer, and running in the fields, playing tug-of-war and keep-away, the gray wolf always seeming to get the better of him. As they shared this reunion, Kan wondered what Unalii remembered. But all seemed well. Unalii showed no signs of resentment over Kan's absence.

Earlier Kan had noticed his tongue was dry, and now he decided he would try to get Unalii and some of the others to follow him down to the river nearby for a drink.

He nipped Unalii playfully on the front leg and tried to dash away, only to have his leg rebel, pain shooting up his back. Unalii offered a low growl of concern.

This is really annoying, Kan thought to himself. He could not show weakness.

Pushing against the pain, he doubled back, nipped Unalii again, and pushed off with his good leg. Unalii finally accepted the invitation, jumping at first to catch his friend, then slowing to a gentle lope beside him. Despite the throbbing leg, Kan found pleasure in the company. Not having to turn his head to look, he felt others join, recognizing the sound of their paws on the snow, their scents in the wind. Noya. Sasa. And then Askai, who was Unalii's younger brother. A group of five. Not bad for a start. Perhaps some of the others would follow later. Maybe they would even find Lana and Etsi in the woods.

But on the way down to the water, they only found Oni, who meekly lowered his head and rolled over at their approach. Kan did not know what to think of the pack's omega. Oni obviously spent most of his time with Sikwa and Danuwa, yet the small wolf did not seem to have anything to hide. He seemed to submit to whoever was around him. Several of the company greeted Oni, standing over him, until he finally fell in line behind them. As they walked forward in formation, Kan again wondered where Oni would stand in any struggle for power.

The woods were quiet, disturbingly so. He thought how the pack would be in trouble if there were no prey to hunt.

By the time they made it to the river, he was limping noticeably. Kan could not hide the effects of his wound despite his best efforts, but Unalii was still there by his side, and that gave him courage.

A general excitement spread as they came down to the water, but he noticed the other wolves were largely holding their places, higher-ranking in the front, lower-ranking in the rear. He then realized they were waiting for him. Largely to get the intense attention off of him, he went down to give the symbolic first drink. He looked up, sounded an affirmation, and watched as the higher-ranking wolves came down first; Unalii stepped forward slowly, then Noya, and then Askai, while Sasa and Oni hung back, finally only drinking after the others had their fill.

Lovely pack politics, he thought sarcastically to himself as he watched Sasa and Oni lap up the water. If he was going to be alpha for Lana's sake, though, then he would have to think more carefully about these relationships; he was going to have to watch out for these others.

At the sound of a deep thump, he discovered Askai had found a pool off to the side of the river, the water frozen solid. The pack mischief-maker was jumping up and falling down, front paws extended onto the ice. Kan trotted over to see that bubbles beneath the ice had bewitched Askai, who was trying his best to break the barrier between. Acknowledging Kan's approach only by the wagging of his tail, Askai pulled up again, coming down full force onto the ice, another thump and a slight crack, which excited Askai, sending him up into the air again. This time, when he landed, there was a louder crack, as a large chunk of ice broke free, sliding sideways in the water revealed. Lurching forward, Askai tried to grab the ice in his teeth, and it kept eluding his grip, slipping ever away.

Kan trotted forward and reached to place a paw on the ice to help Askai grab it. Once the playful youth finally had the sheet of ice in his teeth, he tossed his head back and released the ice into the air. The ice blue sheet somersaulted in the air, light glistening off of it, until it crashed on the rocks nearby, sending shards in several different directions.

Noya and Sasa joined the game, nipping and chasing each other. Not to be left out, Oni grabbed a shard, as an invitation to Askai, who immediately began to chase him down the frosty bank. Momentarily breaking off from her sister, Noya tried to pull Unalii into the play.

Pack life is also this, Kan thought. His leg was hurting too much to join in, and he wondered if that was the reason Unalii held back too, for Noya had given up on him and gone back to Sasa.

At this moment Askai came racing by with Oni close behind, yet when Oni reached Kan, he suddenly stopped. Kan felt the smaller wolf's eyes and turned. Oni lowered his head, his tail already down. Kan watched him closely. Was this a challenge in Oni's passive way? Or was he studying Kan, as if he were some strange curiosity? Kan again had a difficult time reading the omega, but then Oni fell on one side close to Kan and pawed at Kan's front legs.

He wants to play? Kan doubted for a moment, but there was something primal, simple, and genuine about this request. Kan gave in, biting Oni gently on the muzzle. Oni growled lightheartedly, then rolled and jumped to his feet, inviting Kan to chase him. Kan impulsively leaped after Oni, but the pain in his leg made him pause again. Oni looked back, disappointed, until Askai collided with him, and the two went running off in a new direction.

While walking back to Unalii, Kan felt his stomach grumble. Now his thirst was quenched, his body was telling him it needed something to eat soon. The others had to be hungry too. He wondered how desperate things would get.

He knew recreation was important for the pack, a time to pretend dangers were not stalking them, a chance to unwind and remember the carefree life they had as pups. He guessed this moment was the first they had indulged in play since Doda's passing.

So he let them. When the laps shortened, the growls softened in intensity, most of the pent-up energy spent, Kan decided it was time to go on patrol, time to explore the area, to scout for prey. Unalii seemed to understand, and the others, after leaving markers in strategic places nearby, fell in line behind them.

Kan felt he needed to learn the new territory, but the scouting mission did not yield much. From Lana he had gathered it was likely the pack would not remain there; they had settled only temporarily. The pack had to move from the threat of the tiger, to mourn Doda's death, but Lana had intentionally not gone far, knowing he would be looking for them one day. Now he had caught back up with the pack, they needed to address whether this new spot had enough prey to support them temporarily while they laid out a plan. After exploring the areas nearby, Kan was highly skeptical. The search for their new home seemed even more a necessity.

When his group was finally on its way back to the clearing, Lana and Wesa intercepted them, each showing some agitation. Something was definitely wrong.

Where've you been? Lana asked him.

Scouting. I thought it wise to get to know the area. What's wrong?

It's Etsi, she said. *We can't find her anywhere.*

What do you mean?

When Wesa and I went out scouting, it took us some time to find Etsi's scent. We did locate it, along with Koga's, so the two of them must have gone out together. We tracked their scents beyond the recent markers we've set up, in the direction of our old camp. I think she's headed back to where Doda died.

Maybe she'll return soon, he tried to reassure. *And who is Koga?*

Remember she's the one who joined the pack when you were away. You haven't met her yet. She's recently been scouting with Etsi, but it's not like them to be out this long, and there is a tiger out there.

We'll organize a search party. I'll be glad to go.

But you're wounded.

A twinge in his leg caused Kan to swallow his retort. How

long would the wound be a problem?

Worry showed in Lana's eyes, and when she spoke again, there was a tremor in her voice. *I'm afraid Etsi's not coming back.*

5
PROTEST

"**I** COULD USE YOUR HELP, AND YOU WOULD GET TO HOLD real Russian tigers," Mick tried his very best to bait me.

We were a month into the spring semester, and I was invested in my new classes and my new TA assignment, which did not have the energy of the previous semester. Mick's invitation was a welcomed diversion even though I did not know if I wanted to commit. The university was bringing two tiger cubs to campus, and the cubs' parents happened to be from the Amur region, north of Mick's hometown of Vladivostok. The administration wanted to bring the cubs in to educate students about the plight of Amur tigers. Mick advertised that he, as a graduate student in biology, would have special access to the tigers and that he was looking for someone to help corral students for the petting zoo exhibit. Nervous about the whole prospect of being that close to a tiger, even if a baby one, I was on the verge of turning Mick down when something unexpected turned up.

"We'll have the tigers out for anyone who wants to see them," he explained.

"How much help do you need?" I asked in a noncommittal way.

"One or two students. I think we have everything else organized."

"Has anyone else signed up?" I was looking for a way to back out.

"I announced it to the class I'm TAing this semester," he explained, "and I had one student show interest. She's got an interesting name—Soola, I believe."

I lifted my eyes from the scuffs my shoes were making in the carpet. "What does she look like?"

"What kind of a question is that?" He frowned at me. "She is not your type anyway."

"And how would you know what my type is?" I defended before making my own attack. "I can't imagine why she'd sign onto something knowing you were in charge."

"She is the best in my class and knows a good looking Russian when she sees one," he said, leaning back, a sly smile on his face.

"Then you can count me in." I couldn't believe what I was saying. "I've got to be there to protect her from the likes of you."

Animals really weren't my thing. After the Brazilian Mastiff had mauled me when I was five, I never did develop a desire to have a dog. On top of everything, my parents weren't exactly pet people either; my father always said he was too busy, and my mother showed no resistance to the no-pets policy—that is, until I was nine, when she decided I needed to have a cat to learn some responsibility. At the time, as I see it, my mother was feeling guilty again about how often she and Dad were away with their jobs. She, of course, said something else: she was concerned I wasn't "making any connections"—at that age

I didn't have any close friends. She didn't give me any advanced warning, or any say-so in the matter either; I just found that little bundle of fur and claws mewing in a cardboard box near the other birthday presents. When I reached in to pick it up, as my mother pushed me to do, the kitten turned in my hands and scratched me. I named him Scar on the spot, despite my mother's attempts to persuade me to try out other names. That cat always had a mind of his own, and the two of us never did grow close. We tolerated each other's presence in the house.

What was I thinking, committing myself to this tiger petting zoo? These animals were much more intimidating than household cats. I had a mental picture of Mick's poster, the jumping tiger, mouth open, claws out. But these were tiger cubs, I tried to convince myself. As I debated back in my room whether to pull out or not, my thoughts turned to Tsula. Was I that starved to see her again?

My class that semester was boring. After the first couple sessions, I tried to determine what was different, for something was definitely missing. Tsula's attention and questioning had elevated discussion throughout the previous semester. Seeing what the classroom was without her was depressing. In these early-semester musings, I entertained the thought of calling Tsula, even going so far as to look up her phone number, but doubts held me back. Was it appropriate for me to call? Would she care to hear from me?

Mick's invitation was opening another door, and all I had to do was walk through it. I didn't tell Mick, though, my suspicions about his student volunteer. In fact, I'd never mentioned Tsula by name to him before; I'd only vaguely talked once the previous semester about having a "troublemaker" in my class. He'd grinned at the time, as always when he teased me, and said I was letting a lowly undergraduate shake me up. Now I wondered how much she was stirring up his class. Of course, my intuition could have been off, but how many biology majors were named "Soola" anyway. Even though she was devoted to wolves, I could see her signing up for this assignment with tiger cubs—at least that is what I was hoping.

☙

On the wintery morning of the tiger exhibit, Mick and I waited outside the biology building, our breath visible in front of us. Mick had told his volunteer to meet us there since the actual location for the exhibit had been up-for-grabs for several days. We didn't have to wait long before a familiar feminine figure, dressed in a forest green coat and jeans, emerged over the low hill and approached us. Tsula's eyes went wide for a moment when she noticed me, and then her face settled into a gentle smile.

"Don?"

"Good to see you, Tsula."

There was an awkward second when I didn't know what to do, but then she stepped forward to give me a quick hug.

"You know each other?" I heard Mick ask in the background.

Tsula explained, "He was my TA last semester." I noticed she didn't hug Mick—perhaps she just reserved that honor for former TAs, or just those who'd given her an A.

I grinned at Mick. I didn't know how to read his expression at the moment. I presumed he was shocked, but there was something else too.

"So how do you two know each other?" Tsula asked, breaking the silence.

"We share an apartment," I offered.

"Really?" Tsula seemed genuinely surprised. "Small world."

Mick interjected, "We evidently do not share everything."

"I didn't know," I lied.

Mick was still frowning at me.

Disarming the quiet tension, Tsula asked, "So, what's the plan?"

Mick remembered his role as host and turned his charm

back on. "I'm glad you could make it," he said with a half-bow.

"Thank you for including me." Tsula smiled.

The two of them did seem to get along well.

"Let's go meet Todd then," Mick said, pointing toward the center of Duke's West Campus, where the exhibit would be.

Along the way Tsula walked primarily with him, and I quietly observed from behind.

"So what was it like to grow up in Russia?" she asked him.

Mick jumped at the chance to talk about his home country. "It wasn't easy, but I am stronger for it. Russia can be a cold place."

"Is that why you came to America?"

"Do not misunderstand me. I love Russia. I came to America to study because I wanted to see more of the world. I could have gotten my degree in my homeland, but if I had, I would not have met people like you."

You flirt, I thought.

"That's kind of you to say, Mick," Tsula said in return.

It was obvious when we were coming up on the tiger exhibit. The white truck was already there, and the banners were already set up, calling attention to the spot, a stretch of grass right off Chapel Drive. Several people were already examining things as they walked by, but Mick immediately turned toward a short man, dressed in khaki, with a closely cropped beard.

Mick introduced him to us, "This is Todd Ranier of the Tiger Conservation Association. He's the one running the show today."

While Todd ran us through a mini orientation, we watched the tiger cubs rolling around in the cage behind him. Evidently enjoying the cold weather, the two cubs were wrestling, pawing and biting one another. I don't remember everything Todd said, but he wanted to assure us the tiger cubs were old enough to be away from their mother for the day. There were petting zoos set up in malls and other public places, he explained, that did not truly care for tigers, whose practices crossed into animal abuse. He also wanted us to understand, and to communicate to the students, that these animals should not be viewed as exotic pets. Confining them to human domestication, putting them in cages or pens for most of their lives was a high form of abuse. We should respect these animals as the free spirits they were.

No trouble here, I thought.

What truly stands out to me from that morning is the memory of the cubs coming out of their cages. Todd placed the first tiger on a table in front of Mick, who eagerly came forward to welcome this "fellow Russian" to the university. Black stripes stood out against the vivid orange fur of the cub, cute and cuddly with sharp claws and teeth. When Todd asked who would be next, Tsula looked at me. I saw the expectation, the thrill in her eyes, and easily stepped back so she could hold the second cub.

Tentatively, Tsula reached out her hand for the cat to smell and then ran her hand over the cub's head and down its back. The cub shrank down and eyed Tsula's hand, unsure. Todd whispered to the cub, who eventually relaxed and started to rise to meet Tsula's rubbing.

"Don?" She looked to me.

My first impulse was to shake my head and bow out, but seeing her look at me expectantly, I stepped closer, not quite sure what to do. I didn't have any real desire to pet this tiger—there was a reason why these animals weren't pets—but the ageless impulse of boy-wanting-to-impress-girl set in, and I tentatively reached out my hand for the cub to smell. When its ears went down and its eyes narrowed, I pulled my hand back.

The cub squirmed, and Tsula ran her hand along its back and scratched around its ears. It settled back down.

I said, "Guess you've got the touch."

Tsula looked up and smiled.

We both glanced over at Mick. "He seems to have it too,"

Tsula observed, and I wondered if I had jumped into waters too deep for me.

A second later, she turned back to me. "Don't give up, Don." Although I appreciated the encouragement, I didn't reach for the cub a second time until much later.

After this first encounter, we moved the cubs over to the pen, where they could run around in the grass. We had a little less than an hour to get acquainted with the cubs. Although I enjoyed the brief interaction with Todd and countered the teasing from Mick (that I didn't know how to hold a tiger), the cubs and Tsula captured my attention. Tsula was right; there was something special about these "wild" animals. There was a will there; those cubs pushed away from us; they wanted to play, run, and explore. We had to be patient with them and still be wary of those teeth and claws, but they were cubs, babies, easily influenced, and even though we could feel muscles pushing and pulling, they were still small enough to manage. Being this close to the cubs, though, made me wonder about their mother, and what she would do if she were to see us handling her babies.

Tsula was much better with the cubs than I was even though she said she had no experience with tigers. She had a gift with animals. This was the first time I had really seen her outside of the classroom (except for that brief conversation outside the computer lab). Here we were out on the Quad, under the majestic oaks which occasionally swayed in the wintery breeze. The sunlight fell golden on her dark hair and made her amber eyes glisten. I admired her graceful movements as she crouched with the tigers and jumped to catch them before they ran away.

When the students started to arrive, Tsula was a little more reserved in promoting the tigers than I had expected, but I wasn't a great announcer either. It was Mick who excelled in this world, advertising the animals with a loud, sonorous voice. At one point I heard Tsula compliment him on his showmanship, and I thought all Mick lacked was a ringmaster's top hat. Overall, the tiger cubs were very popular that day; many students came through the mini-zoo.

Not every encounter was a success, though; there was one couple in particular who caused us trouble. Built like a football player, he was dressed in jeans and t-shirt, despite the cold, and she, slim as a ballerina, exhibited the latest pink athletic wear along with a shade of lipstick too red for her pale complexion.

She spoke first, "Hey, Kevin, look at the cute cubs!"

He grunted something I couldn't catch.

While I remained at the front table in case anyone else showed up, Tsula guided the couple to the female cub, explaining to them they had to treat the tiger with respect, she was not a pet, and they needed to let her sniff them before touching her.

The lady in pink bent down and reached out all too quickly—obviously having ignored Tsula. The cub shrank back and growled. The lady squeaked, pulled her painted fingernails back, and frowned at Tsula. "I thought you said these were tame tigers!"

Tsula answered, "If you had listened to me, I told you you needed to approach slowly and give the cub a chance to adjust to you."

The pink coed saw the insult and returned volley. "You should have warned us that your animals were vicious."

"They're neither vicious nor stupid. They respond to the way they're treated."

"You didn't just call me stupid! Kevin, can you believe her?"

Kevin had not been part of this conversation, but had approached the tiger on his own, picking it up, even as it wriggled and pulled against his hands. At the moment his girlfriend addressed him, Kevin was holding the female cub up out in front of him, trying to stare her down, though the cub, ears down, wanted no part of it.

Although he had been assisting Mick with the male cub, Todd had caught a glimpse of this devolving situation and taken a few steps in Tsula's direction. "Young man, you need to put the cub down."

Kevin immediately tossed the cub to the side, where she rolled several feet before getting to her feet, stunned, but without injury.

Tsula confronted the couple. "It's time for you to go."

The pink coed glared at her, but didn't say anything now that Todd, with his official presence, was standing behind Tsula.

Kevin grunted again, and the couple left, the pink lady cursing Tsula in a whisper we all could hear.

Another student had walked up at that moment, so I didn't get a chance to talk with Tsula immediately. When I looked her way again, I saw that she and Mick were in conversation, his hand on her shoulder. At that moment I called for Mick, asking him to come help the new "customer." After Mick escorted the student to the male cub, since Todd had pulled the female cub aside for a break, I had a chance to check in with Tsula.

"Sorry you had to deal with that."

She responded, "That's fine. I'm sort of used to it. There's always someone who comes along to spoil things."

"So you're an optimist," I said with a grin.

"A realist."

"Sometimes I wish I had the courage to tell people off."

"It can get you in trouble," she admitted.

"Oh, I've seen the kind of trouble you can stir up."

Her eyebrows came together in an expression of challenge.

"I'm teasing," I clarified. "Don't you have a sense of humor?"

"Maybe."

The rest of the morning passed quickly with no more altercations as several more students, a selection of professors, and a couple college deans showed up to promote the event. When our allotted time was up, Mick, Tsula, and I thanked

Todd for the opportunity while he carefully put the cubs back in their cages for their trip back to the zoo. As soon as I finished shaking Todd's hand, I turned back to Tsula, and on the spur of the moment, surprising myself, I asked, "Any plans for lunch?"

Tsula seemed caught off guard, looked toward Mick, and then back at me. "Mick already invited me," she said with some reservation.

Raising my eyebrows, I checked with Mick, "Really?"

"To show appreciation for her hard work today," Mick said in his flamboyant way, a wide grin spreading across his face, like the cat who'd caught the canary.

"Don did as much as I did," Tsula offered.

"Did he?" Mick teased. "Oh, he's quite the tiger tamer."

I wasn't going to argue. I knew Tsula had done more. I had been there more to watch her than the tigers anyway.

"Besides, *Tovarishch* told me he was busy," Mick continued, surprising me.

I glared at him because I had told him no such thing. Ultimately I gave in, feeling this wasn't the time for a fight. "Yeah. I forgot," I said with mock forgetfulness, not convincing Tsula one bit. "Maybe next time."

Todd broke the scene, asking Mick if he could lend him a hand. When Mick was in conversation with Todd, I took a step back, looking down, but Tsula grabbed my arm and gently pulled me under a massive oak nearby. I caught a whiff of her perfume, a subtle, clear scent.

"I was actually wondering if you'd be interested in giving me some advice on a project I'm working on," Tsula whispered.

I was speechless, but her eyes were inviting, and I finally managed, "What did you have in mind?"

"I need someone with a good video camera, who knows how to use it."

"And you thought of me?" I asked.

"I remembered one of your class presentations—you said

you enjoyed photography."

She had a good memory, but I wasn't going to let her off so easily. "Photography and videography are two different things."

"Are you saying you can't do it?" Tsula cornered me.

"I didn't say that. I've dabbled some in video editing. It eats up a lot of time."

"Anything worthwhile does." She grinned.

"It'll cost you."

"Oh, I don't have much of a budget," she apologized.

«No. No. I don't mean money."

"What did you—" her voice trailed off as she put a thought together. Was she blushing?

"You'll owe me, and I'll collect a favor of my own at the time of my own choosing."

She recovered. "That price sounds a little steep." She frowned playfully. "You drive a hard bargain, Mr. Williams, but you've got yourself a deal."

"Ah, but I haven't heard the full terms of our agreement. What is this project you're dragging me into?"

"It's about wolves."

"Surprise, surprise."

"I want to expose how the media distorts our understanding of them—how novels, films, and video games present wolves as vicious monsters, as nightmares. Then people fear them, and when people fear them, their first response is to pull out a rifle." She paused a moment, then assumed a persona, lowering her voice to a guttural growl, "The only good wolf is a dead wolf."

I smiled at the impression, but then continued, "Shouldn't people be afraid?"

"I think respect is better than fear."

"Have you picked your examples?"

"I have several best-selling books that have werewolves, and there are plenty of movies too. As you might have guessed, I don't know much about video games, though. I was hoping you could suggest some titles. I did a preliminary search and found references to something called *Transylvania Nights*. Have you heard of it?"

"I've heard of it." I'd been drawn to the bait, but now seeing the hook, I was wondering whether I wanted to swallow.

When I paused, she jumped in again. "So can we shake on it?"

I stared into her eyes. I wanted to spend time with her, but was this the only way?

"If you're not interested, I'll ask Mick. I would have preferred a subtle finesse on this project. He'll obviously work better when we get to tigers."

I looked up and saw Mick had finished talking with Todd and was walking back toward us. "Count me in," I said clearly.

"Then pick me up Friday night at seven. Bring your video camera and your critique of *Transylvania Nights*."

Before I could ask any other questions, Mick was back. "Are you hungry?" he asked, his attention solely on Tsula.

"Yes," Tsula said, her voice changing slightly.

Mick turned to me. "Thanks for the help."

"No problem."

Then I watched as Mick brushed his hand over Tsula's shoulder and they walked down the stone-slab sidewalk, past stately trees and Gothic buildings. As I looked up at the Chapel towering over us all, a winter breeze chilled me, and I pulled my jacket closer. When Mick and Tsula finally passed through a distant archway, I turned and went to the hospital cafeteria, where I ate a solitary lunch, yet pondered Tsula's invitation.

❧

I didn't want to talk with Mick about Tsula. Although I was curious about where they had gone and what they had said to each other, I decided I had to let it go. I had an idea how that conversation would have gone anyway, with Mick's incessant swagger and chauvinistic boasting. Even if it was just a polite little lunch with no serious emotional connections, Mick would have said he charmed Tsula, that she could not resist his Russian good looks. I didn't want to listen to such boasting. And if the lunch really was a romantic spark in the start of some passionate relationship between the two of them, I didn't want to hear that either.

The one thing that helped, though, was the memory of her hand on my arm, her eyes watching me, and her intimate invitation under the oak. Along with these memories, I had new pictures to reference, ones I'd quietly taken with my Reality glasses throughout the morning's events. The early light had captured her golden tones perfectly, which stood out all the more against the washed-out colors of the winter backdrop.

So I was to pick her up on Friday. I thrilled at the thought, but then my brain kicked in, and I wondered what I'd gotten myself into. What were we going to do? She'd asked me to bring my video camera and my critique of *Transylvania Nights*. What did she have in mind? What kind of video was this? She wanted me to criticize the portrayal of wolves in the game, but it was just a game, my game, one I'd played for years. These were werewolves, imaginary creatures, and I'd shot plenty of them. No one took them seriously—except Tsunami Games, who made plenty of money off of them. Yet wasn't I also going to make a career out of these images? Wasn't this going to be my future after graduation?

These thoughts troubled me over the next few days. Tsula had gotten to me again.

የ

Friday night, my heart thumping, I knocked on her apartment door a couple minutes past seven. I heard the click of the lock opening and watched as the door swung inside, warm yellow light flooding out into the dim hallway. I was immediately stunned, transfixed, unable to put together the face before me. It was a deep gray, curved highlights in black, save for white lines below the nose. Furry ears stood above her head. The feminine face was smiling, but there was something about the teeth too, the canines more prominent than usual. Finally, though, I noticed the bright eyes; they were hers.

"Tsula?" I asked tentatively.

"Do you like my disguise?" Hearing her voice brought me out of my confusion, allowing me to identify the face paint, the headband with ears, and the teeth extensions. She was also dressed in gray cotton blouse and pants, nicely accentuating her slim figure.

"My, what big ears you have?" I joked.

"The better to hear your wonderful compliments."

"And what big teeth you have?"

"The better to bite you when you misbehave."

She invited me in, and when I showed her the camera I'd brought, she said she'd trust my judgment on what would work best for the protest video.

"Protest video?" I asked, my voice cracking, to my irritation.

"Don't worry, Don. You're in good hands. Now put this on."

She tossed me a t-shirt the same color of gray as hers. I'd worn jeans and a button-up shirt, hoping it was a nice compromise for whatever she had in store for the evening. I held the shirt in front of me.

"I hope it's your size. I guessed," she said tentatively.

My hand was at my top button when she said, "You can change in the bathroom. Halfway down the hall on the left."

After I had changed, noting the wildflower theme in her bathroom, I stepped back out, looking for her, the t-shirt fitting a little snugly.

"It looks good on you," she said. "Now it's time for your transformation. That is if you're up for it."

"Transformation?"

"You need your own disguise where we're going tonight."

There are moments in life that never leave us. The sights,

the smells, the sensations, they all stay with us. That night in Tsula's apartment, she changed more than my appearance with her paints. I remember the cool touch of the sponge against my face, the impish smile playing across her lips, the soft curve of her neck. I wondered what she was doing, but she refused to hold a mirror up for me, saying I had to be patient and let the artist follow her inspiration. Rather than arguing, I closed my eyes and enjoyed the feeling of having her near, listening to her breathing.

"Are you sleeping?" I finally heard her ask.

"No." I opened my eyes to see her standing in front of me, holding a mirror at her side.

"Are you ready to see your new face?"

"You've made me wait this long. What do you think?"

She held up the mirror, and I was stunned a second time that evening, amazed at the details she was able to pull out in such a short time.

"I have some drama training," she said.

"Acting?" I asked.

"Some, but more with makeup."

"Now what?" I asked. "What do we do now that we are all dressed up? Howl at the moon?"

"We have a meeting we need to attend."

I had nothing but questions, and I was a little disappointed at the prospect of leaving her apartment and meeting up with strangers, but I was under her spell. "I'm along for the ride."

"You have your role to play," she said mysteriously.

She led me out, offering to drive. During the short trip, she explained to me the recording was to be the first in a series of protest movies her animal-rights group was going to release onto all the major streaming video sites on the Web. I felt my stomach sour as I considered the implications. She admitted university officials had not sanctioned the organization; it was a fledgling group, but she imagined the university thought it was too radical to support. These videos probably would solidify the case against sanctioning.

When we reached our destination, she parked the car, turned to me, and smiled. "You make a great wolf."

"I think you make a better one."

She got out, and I followed her up to a large, old house, white columns lit up by outside lights. Several students crowded around the spacious front door. My first impulse was to turn around and get back in the car. When I saw these students had also transformed themselves into various other animals—leopards, bears, penguins, lizards, quite the menagerie—the impulse to run only grew, but at this point Tsula had me by the hand, and I wasn't going anywhere else.

We passed inside, where Tsula introduced me to two more wolves, both young ladies beneath the paint, respectively named Carmen and Leslie. The marks on their faces were cruder, simpler, than the artistry on Tsula's face—and on mine. Tsula quickly explained to them that I was to be in charge of the filming and editing; I enjoyed her exuberant endorsement, pushing aside the thoughts that I was on the road to a lot of trouble. Tsula guided us through the crowd to a back room, where yet another wolf was waiting for us, his disguise the crudest of all. He came forward and hugged Tsula.

"Now we can begin," he said, eyeing me suspiciously, and I immediately wondered if I had another rival. Tsula introduced him as Hugh.

Hugh led us down a hallway, the old wooden beams creaking beneath, and out a large back door. When the transition back into darkness left me momentarily blind, I paused, but then I felt Tsula's slender hand grab mine and pull me forward again. I heard a few voices call to Hugh and Tsula in the darkness, but we kept moving forward.

"Where are we going," I whispered.

"We've got a bonfire out here near the woods. Hugh and I

thought it would make a good backdrop for the video."

"Are you and Hugh close?" I asked in spite of my own sense of discretion.

"We're friends, if that's what you're getting at." I sensed she was looking at me in the darkness, enjoying having the upper hand.

As I caught sight of the golden light of the fire ahead, a brisk breeze chilled me, and I realized I should have brought a jacket as my lower jaw began to shudder. Trying to regain control, I remained silent, not wanting to stutter and reveal any weakness. When we finally reached the large bonfire, in a pit dugout for it, I welcomed the warmth on my face and chest, leaning into it.

Asking the others to circle around the fire, Tsula explained to me, "This is the first element in the video. We also want to include pictures of wolves who have been killed by irresponsible hunters—people don't believe in the suffering unless they can see it. Also, a friend sent me some video of wolves in the wild I'd like to include for counterpoint. I hope that is doable."

"That shouldn't be a problem."

"Is there enough light here?"

"We'll see how the footage looks, but the camera will be able to handle firelight nicely. One of the reasons I got this model was its low-light performance."

Tsula asked her friends if they had their parts ready. They nodded quietly, a nervous electricity in the night air.

She then asked me, "What is your suggestion about the best way to film?"

"It is a Reality 3D cam, so it will open the possibilities of both AR and VR."

Carmen jumped in, "AR and VR?"

"Sorry. Augmented Reality and Virtual Reality. The first superimposes the video over your current surroundings, like a hologram, while the second creates a whole separate reality— the viewer would see this gathering mostly as we see it; there are still significant limitations on the VR," I explained.

I saw they were still waiting, so I continued, "I'll make certain to catch each of you at the best angle of the firelight; that can be a little tricky since the shadows will be heavy, but with the wolf paint, we should get some interesting effects."

"That sounds great. Just make sure you give me an idea how you want me to shoot you," Tsula said. "We want you in the video too."

My suspicion finally proved true. The back of my neck grew warm. "Tsula, maybe I should just be the cameraman this time."

"Do you want my artwork to go to waste?"

At first I didn't understand what she meant, and by the time I remembered the face paint, I had already lost the opportunity for further protest. An owl hooted in the distance. I decided to roll with the tide and try to settle the complications of my involvement later. While the others watched, I set the camera on a tripod at the edge of the pit.

"Who's first?" I asked.

"I am," Hugh answered.

Stepping over to him, I move the tripod into place, and after fiddling with the settings on the camera, I held up my hand to let him know I was ready. As I watched him in the small camera screen, I wondered how close he was to Tsula and what he thought of me. Hugh introduced their group and quickly laid out the purpose of the video: to counter destructive images of wolves in pop culture. As he spoke, I marveled at the dramatic effect of the wolf face paint, the dark night sky, and the flickering light of the flames.

When Hugh finished, I moved over and framed Carmen. She then presented a critique of some teen novel about vampires and werewolves I hadn't read, saying that the story only played off a long tradition going back to Little Red Riding Hood, of portraying wolves as creatures of our nightmares. After Carmen's critique, Leslie stepped over in front of the camera and offered an impassioned speech about a recent animated movie, geared for children, which showed the heroes running from a pack of wolves. She claimed such representations trained us from a young age to be suspicious of wolves. At her last word, there was silence, and Tsula asked me if I had my critique ready.

"I didn't know this video was such a production. I'm afraid I'm not all that polished."

"Give it your best. I'm sure you'll do fine." She moved closer. "Now show me how to use this camera."

As Tsula placed her hand on the camera, I noticed a brief reticence; her hand came close, but did not touch it.

"You've used a camera before?" I asked.

"Not really."

"Are you serious?" I studied her expression; it did not reveal much.

"Just show me," she said.

After identifying the correct button to push to start and stop the video, I jumped over to my place. With the firelight in front of me, it was difficult to see Tsula. I felt cut off, but managed to stammer through a short presentation. "Video games can also be a place where wolves are not represented fairly. Some games are only about shooting, and they need something for the player to shoot. Unfortunately, game designers often choose wolves, along with dinosaurs and zombies." Here I remembered Tsula's words earlier to me. "Such association makes them creatures to fear, not respect. If we are afraid of them, then we do not give them a chance; we do not try to understand them." And then parroting Carmen's words, I said, "Thus, video games also make wolves into creatures of our nightmares."

When I ended the weak effort, Tsula asked me, "What about *Transylvania Nights*? We all thought a specific reference would make the critique stronger."

Though I was still reluctant to go down this path, I heard the note of expectation in Tsula's voice and did not want to disappoint her, so I set up the camera for a second recording.

I repeated what I'd said earlier, this time adding, "*Transylvania Nights* is one such game that has the player hunting and shooting werewolves. There are many scenes in dark cavernous spaces or graveyards at night where these monsters can jump out and attack you, and if you don't shoot them, then they will kill your character and end the game. Excitement is built off of fear; the game means to scare you. Those who play it see wolf features twisted in nightmarish ways. These images, whether we realize it or not, probably do have a negative impact on our understanding of wolves in the real world, and we should rethink whether we should be engaging in something that teaches us to fear and to destroy what we don't understand." Then I ended with something I remembered my grandfather often said, "To the one who is truly ethical, all life is sacred."

When I stopped, my eyes focused on the sweat on the palm of my right hand, and I quietly panicked. What had I said? I tried to remember, but at the time I couldn't. I also felt the others looking at me.

"Good job," Carmen interjected.

I was waiting for Tsula, though. What did she think? When I looked, she stepped out of the shadows, smiling, but then she was all business again. "Are you ready for me?" she asked.

I was glad to end my torture and pass the torch to her. "Most definitely."

Tsula provided the coda to the video, offering a quick summary of what each of us had said and then moving into a personal story. "I was fourteen when I first had the chance to commune with a pack of wolves. My dad and I took a long trip in the summer up to the Great Lakes, and we went looking for gray wolves in northern Minnesota. We didn't have much luck for the better part of a day, until we decided to rest in a field of tall grass near a line of trees.

"We were sitting there quietly when a large female wolf emerged from the wood and trotted out into the field. Though she did not acknowledge us at first, it wasn't long before she turned and started to come near us. When she was only a few yards away, two more wolves emerged, then another, and another. Soon there were seven wolves moving about in the field, all casually going about their business. The large female came forward, her tail raised high, and I bowed low, as my father had taught me, communicating I was not a threat. The wolf sniffed me closely, circled me once, and then walked a few steps away to drop comfortably into a reclining pose on the ground.

"My dad and I were there several hours observing the wolves. They are intelligent and beautiful creatures. That female wolf cared for her pack, and they were loyal to her. These animals were not monsters. Yes, there was the potential for danger; we should not sentimentalize wolves either. They still have claws and teeth; they are the most skilled of hunters, but since my dad and I approached them with respect and care, there was a chance to share that time with them. This is how we should imagine the wolf. They are wise spirits deserving our attention; we can learn much from them, and we vilify them to our own peril."

I was skeptical about the whole project while her friends spoke, and everything came tumbling down around me when I spoke, but after Tsula finished, somehow I felt something different. It was a new sensation for me. I remembered the way she had with the tiger cubs, and then imagined how she'd been with the wolves, and I wondered what it would be like to be in the midst of a pack.

"So are we done?" asked Leslie. "My boyfriend's waiting on me."

"I feel good about it," Hugh said.

"What do you think, Don? Did you get enough?" Tsula's words brought me back to practical matters.

"I should have something to work with."

"How long do you think it'll take for you to put it together?" Hugh asked, his tone a little too forward for my taste. "We need to get moving on this."

"I don't know. Video editing is time intensive, and I've got to squeeze it into my schedule." Then looking at Tsula, I said, "But I'll try to get it done sooner rather than later."

"Then we're done here," Hugh pronounced, stepping away from the fire back toward the house.

The others followed him, leaving Tsula and me. She walked over, and I grinned again at her wolf-likeness. Somehow I found myself attracted to it.

"All life is sacred," she said.

"It's something my grandfather often said. I think it's from Albert Schweitzer."

"Schweitzer?"

"He was a doctor-missionary who won the Nobel Peace Prize decades ago."

"Well done," she whispered as she leaned closer.

Her cool lips warmed softly on my cheek, and before she could pull back, I turned my face and kissed her. When something pinched my lower lip, I drew back, my hand instinctively touching my mouth. Upon lowering my finger, I turned it into the firelight and discovered a smudge of blood.

"Sorry," she apologized.

I had forgotten her fangs.

"Beware the bite of the wolf," I said with mock drama.

She smiled, and I saw I'd smeared her face paint. The fangs didn't stop me from kissing her a second time.

6

INNOVATION

"**W**OULD YOU LIKE A JOB?"
The words caught me by surprise. Interviews weren't supposed to be done this way; at least, my experience wasn't following what my father had taught me. He'd said a job interview most likely would be a formal affair, scheduled in advance, requiring me to dress in a coat and tie, yet here I was in jeans and polo shirt, speaking to a guy in a printed t-shirt, shorts, and sandals. The man who'd just offered me a job, Justin Cranston, was not sitting across the room behind an imposing, ornate desk, but was standing next to me, leaning forward over a slim laptop computer, studying my online portfolio—a collection of my programming work which I had started back in high school, but had developed and expanded through several undergraduate projects and recent graduate work.

I started informally pitching my idea for a new gaming

interface while standing outside the company's booth, trying to make my voice heard above the dull roar of the crowds of people milling around the exhibits at the gaming conference. At first Justin was just polite, nodding his head with no real emotional response, but when I gave him a glimpse of my portfolio, he immediately suggested we move to a smaller, quieter room they'd set aside for such private conversations. Immediately after this invitation, though, he stepped to the side and consulted his phone for several minutes. A little awkwardly, I waited, looking around at the other people rushing around the conference center until Justin finally looked up and asked me to follow him.

As Justin guided me down a short hallway, another man, who seemed to appear from nowhere—I only just recognized him in the corner of my eye—shadowed us. His features and his dark hair suggested a Japanese ancestry. He was wearing jeans and a black t-shirt. What seemed odd to me was he also wore sunglasses with a mirror finish so I couldn't see his eyes. I wondered how he could see anything in the dimly lit hotel corridors.

I didn't want to seem rude, so I didn't ask Justin who the man was. Evidently he anticipated the question, though, as we approached the door to the room, and said, "He's my bodyguard." He said it with such a twist I felt he had also implied, "He's not, but you shouldn't ask who he really is either."

When we entered the room, Justin led me over to a table, where he set up his laptop for me to continue my presentation. The man in sunglasses took a post near the door, standing, resembling the bodyguard he was supposed to be.

Resuming my pitch, I argued, "Virtual-reality tech will never reach its potential as long as it relies on measuring external cues of the body. Tsunami Games has been a real contender in virtual reality, but your system still involves glasses, gloves, and a treadmill.

"The Reality glasses were, of course, a game-changer; they created a new level of immersion we hadn't seen—when paired with sensors tracking eye movements, voice modulation, facial expressions, and physical movement. There is no denying the popularity of this interface and the engine that holds it up—I've enjoyed the games too—but I keep feeling we're not pushing far enough.

"These technologies are too external; they limit the illusion. With them it only takes a small slip for a gamer to doubt the reality of the virtual experience. We see the moving feet of the magician behind the curtain; we don't give ourselves entirely over to the magic. For a genuine breakthrough to take place, our technology must tap directly into the source of those senses, the human brain."

Justin grinned slightly, "I like the reference to Oz, but isn't this what programmers have been trying to work out for years? We all want a holodeck."

"Ah, the holodeck on *Star Trek* is also external—to pull that off would take much more technology than something that tapped directly into the brain. We need to think more in terms of shaping dreams rather than matter."

"Shaping dreams?"

"Have you ever had a dream that felt like it was real?"

Justin looked skeptical. The man in sunglasses had not moved, apparently still watching behind those twin mirrors.

I continued, "It involved all the senses—sight, sound, touch, taste, and scent."

"But how do we tap into those parts of the brain? I think only a few rabid gamers would sign up for brain surgery even if we had the technology to put a chip inside someone's head."

"No, I don't think we'd need a chip. Much like our wireless technology—if we can learn to communicate with the brain in the language it understands, brain signal processing, I believe we can build these new broadcasters to sit on the outside of the head."

"So the opposite of an aluminum foil hat. It doesn't shield thoughts, but implants them," Justin joked.

"You'd have a hard time marketing that." I smiled. "I was thinking more along the lines of hiding the brain-computer interface inside the banding of a baseball cap. You could even have the branding of Tsunami Games out front on the cap."

"Nice. But I'm still skeptical that you can build the tech."

I launched into a more technical discussion, drawing on neuroscience terms I'd long heard from my dad. Growing up as the son of a brain surgeon finally proved an advantage. It was while I was in the midst of these medical terms that Justin's phone whistled, sounding like R2-D2 from *Star Wars*. When he pulled his phone out to check it, I hazarded a look at the man near the door. In the mirror sunglasses, I only saw a reflection of Justin and me. It was then I heard Justin extend the job offer.

The question caught me by surprise, for I was in the middle of an argument, still trying to convince my audience, fully expecting to resume the pitch and play it to the end. His abrupt invitation suggested he had heard enough.

Before I could answer, Justin continued, occasionally biting the thin, angular mustache on his upper lip. "It might take some time for me to work out how to get you into programming and development. I might have to start you out on a provisional basis as a level designer, but I like what you're saying, and I think the rest of our team will too, particularly if I'm behind you."

"I am very interested, but I do have a commitment we'll have to work around."

"Oh?" His eyebrows went up.

"I'm pursuing a doctorate in computer engineering."

"Really?" he said almost suspiciously.

"I think if I take the time to conceptualize it properly then the technology could be revolutionary."

He paused a moment, checked his phone again, and then shrugged. "We'll work it out."

We shook hands, and he joined the man in sunglasses. Together they walked back to the exhibit. When they were halfway there, I saw they were engaged in a conversation, but I couldn't make out what they were saying.

My mind was entertaining other thoughts, though, as Justin's offer began to sink in. I had a job! My first step away was a skip, but then I pulled myself back in, realizing I was headed into the crowd again. Several yards away I looked back at the Tsunami Games exhibit, at the large posters advertising their games, at the people who had circled around it, dressed up as different characters.

I saw one lady dressed in khaki shorts and blouse, with the boots of an archaeologist too. Her hair was pulled back in a ponytail, and she wore glasses, trim, thin ones, suggesting to me images of libraries, books, and serious study. I had seen fans dressed as Brie Washington before, but somehow that day this woman convinced me. The illusion was complete. An icon from my childhood lived and breathed before me. What would be her next great adventure?

I suddenly realized I might have a hand in shaping that story. In joining Tsunami's team, I was now going to be part of this legacy. I would share in the influence these games had over the lives of untold millions. The thought made me giddy as I turned to leave. I had to share the news with someone. I thought about my parents and wondered how they would react.

My father had often pushed me. Frequently he reminded me, whether he intended it or not, how I did not measure up to his plan for my life. I always got the feeling he wanted me to become a neurosurgeon just like him, to sacrifice my life in the service of the needs of others.

He often told me, "If you're going to do something, then you should become an expert at it."

The problem for him was I did listen; I just didn't want to do what he wanted me to do. I wanted to be a computer programmer for a gaming company, and I was going to be the best one I could be. I was going to become an expert at virtual reality, creating a system that would so fully encompass people's senses they could not tell the difference between it and the real world around them. Through high school and college, when I spoke with my father about the human brain, I concealed my secret plan. He, of course, loved my interest in his specialty and still held out the hope I was going to turn around and move into medical school.

I did have one conversation with him when I was home from college when I tried to suggest my plan to him.

"Dad, what do you think of the prospects of neurogaming as a therapeutic treatment for depression and anxiety?" I was trying to legitimize my interests with language he'd understand.

"I think there is some potential for children with ADHD and veterans with PTSD—as long as these 'games' are not substitutions for reality. Patients must always be aware they are playing a game; otherwise, we would be stepping over into all sorts of psychoses."

"But what if the answer is a break with their reality? What if they just need to try something else for a while, to step out of their lives for a few hours? Isn't that what many people do now with books and movies and role-playing games—and others do with alcohol and drugs?"

"Yes, but when you start communicating more directly with the human brain, tapping into the source of our senses, the means by which we understand the world around us, then you make the illusion too inviting, and there will be dire consequences." My father's gaze was strongly directed at me, and I knew I had not fooled him. He knew what I was thinking, and there was no doubt what his answer was.

So I did not talk with him anymore about my plan, yet I

did continue to question him about the human brain and what current research said about how it worked. I learned more in high school and college, from conversations with my father, about the human brain than many doctors learn in medical school, so I knew enough terminology to impress your average person, and my vision was evidently infectious enough to convince Justin Cranston too.

Justin did eventually come through on his offer. Following up on that gaming-conference conversation, I had sent my resume out that evening after polishing it some. That was the March of my second year of graduate school, and though I acted quickly, I did not hear from Justin until late May. In the meantime I had been forced to commit to the teaching assistant position.

I didn't actually start working for Tsunami, though, until the fall, the semester I met Tsula. Walking into their office for the first time was an intimidating and inspiring moment. There were various posters of their different releases, and I paused before the now dated cover art for the first release of *Transylvania Nights*. While I was looking up at it, I heard someone come walking up behind me.

I turned to see a man about my height. He had a goatee, shaved head, and a wide-grin, his white teeth and red shirt standing out against his chocolate skin.

"That was a winning formula," he said.

"Yes," I responded.

"Sorry, my name's Trevor. I'm one of the designers on the *TN* team."

"Oh. I'm Donovan Williams. Mr. Cranston asked me to drop by."

"Yes, you're the new blood. He said you had an innovative take on VR."

"I've been thinking about it for a long time," I said.

"Long time?" he asked. "You look like you're only about 21."

"Soon to be 25 actually."

"I've got you by about a decade, Donovan."

"'Don' will be fine. *Transylvania Nights* is one of my all-time favorites."

"Well, if you work here for long and ever get on the team, you may never like it again."

"Why's that?" I asked.

"It depends on the job, but we spread around the grunt work. If you're a programmer who's rewritten a section of code for the thousandth time, or a designer whose supervisor has yelled at you for taking too much creative license on designing a character, even a background one, or a game tester who's played the game every day for hours trying to find all the bugs, the drudgery of it all may stamp out all the joy you once had for these games."

"Man, that sounds jaded."

"I'm just trying to let you know what you're in for. We're all code monkeys. That's not to say these jobs don't have their moments, but most people misunderstand what the life at a gaming company actually is."

A guy on a scooter zipped by, almost hitting me, and continued down the hall, the fluorescent lights glistening off the shiny floor. Trevor smiled again, "You've got to watch yourself."

It seemed like a rough beginning, but Trevor Jenkins took me under his wing that day. I wasn't able to see Justin until later, and though his greeting was warm and he made a big announcement about my joining the team, my time with him was brief; he had some business he needed to work out. It was Trevor who supervised my orientation, showing me to my station and computer, and who broke the news that Justin had assigned me to work as level designer on *Cloud Kingdom*, a franchise game whose target audience was elementary-school girls. The assignment meant I'd be immersed in a land of fluffy animals with plenty of pinks, purples, and pastel blues.

"Sorry," Trevor apologized, "but that's the bottom rung on the ladder. We've all got to put in our time. We all thought we could sign on to the big-name games when we walked in the door. But don't despair. I probably shouldn't tell you this, but I've never seen Justin as excited as he was when he was telling me about your VR ideas. I'll be sure to take you down to our lab later today. Maybe sometime soon you'll get to work in there."

As a consolation prize, he said he'd try to get me in to meet the *TN* team, but because a few members were out that morning, I'd have to wait. Meanwhile, he could show me around and introduce me to a few people. I heard several names and saw many faces that day, but only one or two sunk in. I had been aware of the long list of names in the credits of the games I'd played, but now I was actually able to see these were real people, some crouched over their computers with glasses, squinting at their screens, while others insisted on standing before elaborate desks built for better posture.

After lunch Trevor was able to deliver on his promise. We were able to head down into the basement lab, where he introduced me to the development team, led by Mark Winter, a tall, thin man in his 40s, with a whisper of blond hair on top of his head and around his face in the impression of a beard.

"Nice to meet you," I said after Trevor introduced us.

"So you're the new guy?" Mark asked suspiciously, like a preying mantis defending his territory.

"Today's my first day." Caught off-guard, I could only state the obvious.

Trevor jumped to the rescue. "Justin asked me to show him the VR lab."

Mark left his station, his mouth tight and his eyes down. We followed him over to a tall, rectangular box. Although it was made out of plastic and looked more like a shower stall, I did for a moment have a vision of a large refrigerator box I decorated as a spaceship when I was a kid.

"Here's our VR booth," Mark said with as little emotion as possible.

Trevor stepped forward and opened the door. "Let me anticipate your first question, Don. No, we don't have time for you to try it out today."

"How'd you know?" I smiled.

"It's what I would have asked."

"Are you sure you can't bend the rules?"

"I've got a deadline," Mark interrupted.

"I've got this," Trevor responded, and as soon as the words were out of his mouth, Mark nodded and returned to his station.

I mouthed my surprise to Trevor, but he secretly shook his head and then returned to showing me the chamber. "You probably already know about all this stuff, but you strap yourself into the stand so you can use the treadmill below, which allows for a full 360 degrees of mobility—you can go in the direction you want to go. There are surround sound speakers hidden at different levels, and jets that spray selected scents into the air around you. There is a built in air conditioning and heating unit. Once you're in place, you don your Reality glasses and the haptic gloves. It's the latest tech streamlined into as simple an interface as our engineers could design."

"It's nice," I said with genuine excitement, a boy with the latest toy. "But it's not simple."

"No, I guess not." Trevor smiled.

As he had admitted earlier in the day, Justin had already told him about my plan. When he smiled, I dared to hope I'd earned an ally in that venture. Mark certainly wasn't going to welcome the change, though.

Overall, the first day was a success, and I couldn't wait to settle in even if I was working on a lame game. Over that fall semester, as I took courses at the university, struggled with being a new teaching assistant, and played *Transylvania Nights VII* in my decreasing free time, I also worked for Tsunami

Games, gradually becoming enmeshed in their system. As the weeks passed, I got to know most of the developers and programmers and met many of the writers, audio experts, and producers also involved in the creation of a game. Though I did establish working relationships with some of the others, my strongest friendship was with Trevor. I only talked with Justin on occasion, but from those brief encounters, I felt he was pleased with my progress.

I also came to discover the importance of the mysterious guy in sunglasses. It was mid-November, a few months in, and I had mostly forgotten him. Justin had asked my team to come in early one morning because we were nearing an early deadline for the game's development. After I had parked and was walking toward the building, I noticed a man, across the parking lot in one of those prestigious spaces up front, stepping out of a royal blue convertible; he was in black slacks and black oxford shirt, more sharply dressed than probably everyone else at the company. He still wore the sunglasses even as he walked into the building. I slowed my pace, so I would not overtake him.

When I got to the conference room, I asked Trevor about the man in sunglasses.

Trevor smiled. "So you've finally noticed him."

"Well, the sports car did stand out. I couldn't decipher the make and model."

"We think it's custom designed and built. He has flair," Trevor whispered, "but he's also a bit of a recluse. I can count on one hand the number of conversations I've had with him, and I've been here for some ten years. His name is Kenji Sadayoshi."

"So who is he?" I interjected.

"You've been thinking probably that Justin runs this company, but once you've worked here for a few years and you keep your eyes open, you start to notice Justin never makes any important decisions without consulting his phone. We think someone else is pulling the strings, sending him texts, telling him what to do. We all suspect it's Mr. Sadayoshi, though Justin won't talk about it, and Sadayoshi is never present in any meetings. We also don't usually see him; some speculate there is some secret exit he alone uses. Every once in a while, he comes through the main door; we're not quite sure what's different about those days." I thought back to my interview and remembered the text Justin received just before offering me the job. I had judged it a distraction at the time, but was it something else? I had not seen Sadayoshi move an inch in that interview.

"That's weird," I said and immediately regretted it.

"Be careful," Trevor whispered again. "If Mr. Sadayoshi is never present at the meetings, then how does he know enough to make important decisions? Several of us think there are secret cameras in strategic places throughout the building."

"Is that legal?"

"It's his company." Trevor grinned. "You've just got to be on your best behavior."

"What's with the sunglasses?" I asked.

"Our theory is they're like see-through mirrors, so he can watch others without their knowing whether he's really focused on them or not."

"That's—" I bit my tongue.

"You're learning."

Our conversation ended as the meeting started and we got back to work. Later I tried to ask more questions, but Trevor said with a shrug of his shoulders, "I can't help you. You'll just have to settle into the mystery of it."

That wasn't my nature, but at the time I didn't have any recourse. I was also distracted, for at this point in the semester my thoughts were growing increasingly toward Tsula even while I was at work. In the end I had to shelve my questions. It would be several more months before I learned anything else about Mr. Sadayoshi.

Since my team met our November goals, Justin was very accommodating when December brought deadlines for my projects in my classes, the end-of-the-term grading for my TA commitment, and the break I needed to head home to Atlanta. When I came back in January, I was hoping there might be some change to my situation, that Justin would finally say I could now officially join the *Transylvania Nights* team, to help with the design of the werewolf lairs. Justin did announce that Tsunami was green-lighting work on an anniversary edition, which would update the original game in light of new graphic capabilities and a revised game engine, but there was no special announcement for me. I had to return to the land of pastels.

I began to wonder why Justin—or Mr. Sadayoshi—had hired me just to sideline me on this game that was destined for bad reviews and moderate sales, and would eventually pass out of everyone's memory, except the few who made it the butt of their jokes. This work had nothing to do with what I pitched to them. Part of me began to resent being pigeonholed with other new designers. If my ideas were revolutionary, if they truly excited Justin as Trevor had suggested, then why were they wasting my talents on a game that had no future?

This resentment had just started to worm into my thoughts the week I found myself editing the protest video Tsula had masterminded. In the days following my filming of the "council of wolves," which was how I referred to it, there was a part of me that felt like the night had all been a strange dream, but when I went to my computer, the footage confirmed the council had been real. Even as I tried to hold onto memories of face painting and first kisses, sensations not captured by the camera, I found myself drawn to this video of Tsula. While I listened to her story again in the process of editing, I found myself wondering what I would have done that day in the field with the wolf pack. The most likely scenario was I would not have been there at all, yet if some twist of fate had brought me to that place, the wolves would never have emerged; they would have kept their distance, and I would have preferred it that way. Hearing the passion in Tsula's voice, though, I considered what that moment with the wolf pack meant to her and what I had witnessed the morning we shared with the tiger cubs. Was I missing something? Charging into my memories, though, was the Brazilian Mastiff who bit my arm and would not let go. I recalled the wild, fierce eyes. Would wolves not do the same?

In the editing process, I finally came to the footage with me in it, or so I had to reason, for on first glance I did not recognize the person speaking, transformed as I was under the artistry of Tsula's hand. Early that night I'd only seen a brief reflection of my face in a handheld mirror, and then later I'd stared with bleary eyes at the face paint before I washed it off and headed for bed. Now I had the leisure to study it, the dark lines around my eyes, the dark nose, the whiskers, and the foreign grayness dominating my face. I admired Tsula's work; she had reshaped me, but I did not know how to receive or interpret that gift.

Once I moved beyond the initial disorientation with my image in the video, my main concern became whether anyone would recognize me under the makeup. If I had such a time identifying myself, would it be difficult for someone else, particularly someone over at Tsunami Games, if this video ever were to come to their attention? Tsula wanted me to post the video to all the current streaming sites, and with all those tech-savvy people at Tsunami Games, there had to be some who trolled these sites for any references to their releases, especially such a flagship as *Transylvania Nights*. Maybe I was being paranoid, but I didn't want to jeopardize my dream—even though the position of level designer for Pastel Land was not actualizing that either. I sought for ways that would disguise my face and voice, but on the first run, the blur factor made my image stand out too starkly from the others in the video, as if I had something to hide—which I did, but didn't want to highlight. Finally I chose a slight blur, which worked well with the shadows, and an audio filter which lowered my voice just a bit. Although the changes did seem to obscure my identity sufficiently, I chose to put the video aside and delay the posting of it.

The next week I had a bad day at work. Justin came in and for the first time criticized an element in my design—not an unreasonable complaint now that I look back on it, but it stung at the moment, and I came away disgruntled and vindictive. I didn't want to be working on that game anyway, and there he was belittling my work.

That night Tsula called. I was glad Mick was out. We had not talked about our potential competition for Tsula's affection, so he did not know of my potential "betrayal." I was not going to volunteer any information either; I thought Tsula would take care of that on her end if there were anything to address.

When she called, she naturally asked about the video. "How's it coming?"

"I'm almost finished with it."

"You're not having cold feet about this, are you?"

"I was amazed again at your painting skills," I dodged.

"You're trying to change the subject."

"You did a great job. I'm not so sure about what I said."

"All the pieces fit together. It wouldn't be the same without you," she encouraged.

"It'd be better."

"We need your expertise."

"We?" I asked. "I don't think the others were convinced I added much."

"Carmen was."

"Was she?"

"And I was," she said suggestively.

"How convinced are you?"

"You could come over, and I could show you."

I hadn't seen her since that night. Although we'd talked on the phone several times, we hadn't discussed what had happened between us, so this invitation was key. I jumped at it cautiously. "I could be persuaded to come over if the reward is compelling enough."

"I'll make it worth your while."

"OK. I'm headed your way. You best be prepared."

"I'll be waiting," she said in a way that lingered after I put my phone down.

I immediately went over to my computer and downloaded the final edit of Tsula's video. While I was at her place, I'd show it to her, and then we could use a dummy account on a university server to post it to the Internet. I wasn't going to employ anything that could be traced back to me, of course, but I was going to post it. It was a gamble whether the video would ever show up on Tsunami Games' radar, whether anyone would notice me, whether Justin or Mr. Sadayoshi would even care, but it was a sure bet the video would impress Tsula, and as I exited my apartment that night, rousing her admiration was my chief concern. I had finally decided to throw the dice no matter how they landed.

7
LOST

I NEED TO GO WITH YOU, KAN ARGUED.

Your leg will be a liability, Lana countered.

I managed taking a group out scouting.

You know this will be different. We'll be tracking for miles. There's no telling how far Etsi and Koga have gotten by now, or what we will find when we reach them. And if we run into the tiger, what then?

I'll find a way. I can't just sit here. If I'm going to be the alpha like you want, then I've got to do this.

Although he heard and measured her arguments, he thought about how he felt with the pack behind him. He knew how discouraged they had become at Doda's death, but pack morale was beginning to change. Askai and the others had shown that playing with the sheets of ice. Even if the pack could adjust to the alpha male staying behind, Kan felt like he needed to push against this challenge, not play things safely.

I'm going, he said finally, expecting no further discussion.

I hope we don't regret it, she growled, turning away from him.

At the instigation of Kan and Lana, the pack gathered at the center of their current territory, the slight hill offering a commanding view of the forest nearby. Now was the time to select a smaller group of wolves to take the longer journey to track down Etsi. Her noted absence was not helping the spirit of the pack, and Taline's frenetic pacing and whining was beginning to put the other wolves on edge.

This is another setback, Kan thought. Too much instability. We have to settle this so that the pack can move on.

Moments before, Kan and Lana had conferred on who should go; now they entered the ritual of publicly identifying the ones they had selected. Kan followed as his mate walked forward through the crowd until she found Wesa. Lana had argued Wesa was the most careful hunter of the pack, often noticing details others overlooked, and since she was also the beta female, helping enforce pack hierarchy along with Unalii, she demanded respect in the pack. As Lana licked Wesa, Kan wondered about this choice. One side of him would have preferred to take Noya, but he knew they had to leave some of their most trusted allies behind too. Noya and Unalii, in particular, would maintain the pack's structure while the scouting party looked for Etsi. So Wesa was a sound choice.

For the present Lana deferred to Kan. His first instinct, of course, had been to select Unalii, but he soon decided against that, in favor of Yona. It would be helpful having the tallest member of the pack along. He was a good strong choice, yet there was a moment of doubt in Kan's mind. He looked over at his two rivals, Danuwa and Sikwa. These two males milled about, restless, stirring up the tension in the pack. At that moment, when Oni did not move out of the way quickly enough, Sikwa bit his younger brother's snout and pulled him to the ground. Danuwa growled and put a heavy paw on Oni's back. Kan wondered if they would cause trouble while he and Lana were away.

If they were going to win over those who doubted the transition of leadership, they would need to include them in important tasks. So, on an impulse, going against his agreed upon pick of Yona, Kan loped over to Sikwa, who released his grip on Oni and raised his head slightly. He is keeping his head low, Kan thought, as he licked Sikwa's snout. A few whines of surprise sounded around them. Kan's gaze met Danuwa's, the masked wolf ever so slightly barring his teeth.

Turning back around, Kan checked on Lana. She evidently wanted to stick to the wisdom of their original plan, for she approached Yona and licked him too.

I wish that were it, Kan thought. *But we can't leave Taline behind. She is a liability either way; she's too close to this complication.*

Lana did walk to the edge of the circle toward pacing Taline. Of the wolves in the pack, Taline was closest to Etsi. Also, since she had watched over Etsi's second and third litters while the alpha had devoted herself to taking care of the pack, several of the younger wolves still shared special bonds with Taline. Kan noticed, though, Taline's recent agitation had distanced her from the others; they did not know how to behave in front of her when she turned away from their nudges and kisses. Kan thought it a bad sign when Lana's lick did nothing to console Taline.

As soon as Lana turned toward the center of the pack, Kan joined her along with Wesa, Sikwa, Yona, and Taline—a scouting mission of six. The rest of the pack huddled around. Kan and Lana started another chorus of howls in an effort to lift spirits. These were trying times, and they needed to do all they could to hold the pack together. A series of bad choices could lead to the breaking of the pack.

As the howls died down, Unalii's strong voice sounding last, those who were not going brushed up against the six in the center, sharing their scents. Kan appreciated the signs of affection and hated the prospect of leaving again so soon upon getting there. He did not know whether it was wise to follow Etsi. The pack probably would be better off if they just moved on. There would be a clean break. But then there was this Koga. He did not know anything about her; he had to trust Lana and the rest of the pack that she was worth the effort too.

When Unalii licked him, though, he felt a little better. We are leaving the pack in your capable paws, Kan thought. He gave Unalii a playful push, then turned to receive Askai's earnest farewell.

Lana barked above the growls and whines. It was time to go. Kan jumped back over to her side, and the other four fell into formation behind them.

❧

It had been a full day, and he had only gotten in the slightest bit of rest. As he moved forward through the woods, Kan discovered Etsi had followed almost the complete reverse of the trail he had passed the night before. He did not think he would see this ground again, particularly this soon, and if he were not traveling with Lana, he would not have had the energy to retread this path. Despite her presence, though, the snow felt cold beneath his paws.

Having to travel past where he had fought with Danuwa did nothing to improve his mood. Kan barely recognized the area in the orange light of early evening, but he could still smell the mix of his and Danuwa's scents, and Sikwa made it clear he still remembered by marking the base of the broken tree. Though he would rather forget it, Kan knew his role as alpha required certain actions; he could not let such a challenge go unanswered, so he trotted over to the spot and marked directly on top of Sikwa's scent. The younger wolf only watched, then grunted and trotted off after Wesa.

As the party made its way through the woods, Taline proved an annoyance, nervously pushing toward the front of the group. Once when she passed Lana, the white wolf nipped her on the tail to reinforce pack hierarchy. Though Lana's exercise of authority did not quiet Taline's obsession, Kan noticed it kept her from running ahead again.

Wesa was always close to the front, leaving Sikwa and then Yona to bring up the rear. Kan did not like having Sikwa where he could not see him, but he felt better about the formation knowing Yona's eyes and teeth were back there to hold the troublemaker in place.

Kan cursed his wound several times along the way. It certainly would have been easier if he had stayed behind. He could be resting now instead of chasing after this old she-wolf. But he kept these thoughts to himself; he did not want to face an I-told-you-so from Lana. When the pain became particularly sharp, he ground his teeth together and focused on favoring his other legs.

It was easy to track Etsi, for her scent was dominant, Koga's only lingering in the background. Etsi had done nothing to hide her passage, and she had favored marking in all the old places. Kan imagined she was finding comfort in anything connecting her to the past. At one of the markers Wesa had uncovered beneath a thin layer of snow, Kan breathed in the scent himself, and memories of his recent night quest—running, wounded and uncertain—softened him. *Can I blame her? I have an idea what this journey is like for her. But what would I do if Lana were gone?*

Glancing up, he saw her waiting for him, her white fur taking on a bluish tone in the shaded light, the wind tossing snowflakes onto her ears and shoulders. *Ready?* she asked.

He realized again the others were also waiting. *I don't have much privacy anymore, do I?*

She barked in amusement as they set off again.

☙

Running under a sense of urgency, the wolves quickly made their way back to the territory they had been forced to abandon. Just as the sun approached the horizon, they finally neared their former home, and Taline, unable to contain herself, dashed sideways first, out of Lana's reach, and then leaped ahead. Kan watched as Lana picked up her pace to follow, leaving him behind. Wesa quickly filled the position at his side, and he knew she only held back out of respect for his position.

A screeching yowl from up ahead broke his concentration. What was that? Moving beyond the initial shock of it, he realized the voice was Taline's. He tried to run harder, but his back leg crumpled under him, sending him chest and snout first into the snow. When Kan finally stood, snow cold in his mouth, Wesa was way ahead; evidently her concern for Taline dominated now.

Kan felt Sikwa nearing, but Yona was right there too, coming in closer, nudging him encouragingly. Thank you, he thought. There are advantages to running in a pack.

The three male wolves resumed their pace and caught up with the others in the clearing they once had called home. As he pushed past the last brush, Kan caught the odor of carnage in the air and located the three females gathered together several yards ahead. Lana looked back, terror in her eyes. Kan noticed first red stretching out into the snow at Lana's feet, then the horribly twisted gray shape beyond Taline's whimpering head. As he neared, Kan identified Etsi, or what was left of her. Something larger had torn into her, ripping her flesh, exposing her blood, ending her life.

He neared Lana, and they each bowed their heads, brushing against each other, eyes closed. In the darkness he could not banish the image of Etsi's torn body, but Lana's breath warmed him even as Taline whimpered in the background.

Lana shifted, and he heard her howl, raw and chilling in the cold air. Taline quickly joined in the sounding of her fallen mother. Kan joined, and even Sikwa added his voice. Yona sounded, his howl deeper than the others.

The only one who was not sounding was Wesa; she was sniffing around her mother's body, head popping up frequently, ears erect, eyes darting. Noting her nervousness, Kan lowered his head and, pushing past the horrible sight, tried to focus on the smells beyond Etsi's blood.

A strange, ominous scent in the air and memories of the scratch marks on the pine brought back a sense of danger. The tiger that killed Etsi could easily still be nearby, and if Wesa was on alert, there was an even greater chance. He lifted his head, breathed in deeply, and scanned the tree line around them. He felt a chill on his back. How could he face a tiger with a bad leg?

We've got to get out of here, he whined.

Lana stopped her howl and looked at him.

We can't stand up to a Siberian, he argued.

How can we leave her here like this? she asked.

I think the tiger is close. Look at Wesa.

Wesa was looking to the far side of the clearing. Now focused on the same general area, Kan caught the sound of the slightest shuffle, and then there was a movement in the dark woods. A shadow emerged, moving quickly toward them.

It was a wolf, her fur as black as a cave at night.

As Lana ran past him, he heard her yip, *That's Koga.*

Lana intercepted the approaching wolf, and Kan watched as she and the black female quickly sniffed each other and exchanged licks. Kan noticed Koga did not relax; she stood alert, as if she could dash away as quickly as she had appeared. Although he was curious about Koga and what Lana saw in her, Kan felt he could not afford this distraction, not when the severe reality of Etsi's exposed corpse gave testimony to a great danger roaming in the woods nearby. The tiger could already be moving toward them.

Lana, we need to retreat to a safe distance. You can catch up with Koga then.

Lana glared at him, but a moment later she began to trot back to the others, Koga by her side. Although Lana did as he asked, Kan felt she was taking too long; he needed to be decisive, so he turned and walked back the way they had come. He had to consider the safety of the pack.

After only a few steps, he heard a humming purr that seemed to come from all directions at once, and then he saw in the corner of his eye a large orange and black form emerge from the tree line. The movement was swift and graceful, and the tiger was already well into the clearing, closing in on the wolves near Etsi's remains, before Kan could jerk to his left and bark a warning. Wesa was already barking as well, placing herself between her fallen mother and the tiger. Kan felt Sikwa bolt past him into the woods and watched Yona place himself nearby, between Kan and the tiger.

As the tiger paused at the barking, Kan realized Lana and Koga were on the other side; he could not join them without crossing the tiger's path. He saw in Lana's eyes she realized the same.

Go! he barked. Lana hesitated. Would she be stubborn to the last?

Immediately the tiger turned and looked in his direction. Kan stood transfixed by the terrible beauty of the great feline, exposed in the light of the setting sun. He was too near the tiger; he did not know where to look. His sight pulled first toward the bright orange snout in the center of the face, then to the cavernous mouth guarded by four bone-colored fangs, then to the radiating, fanlike pattern of orange and white blotches and black swirls in the fur running from the mouth. Kan forced himself to locate the two golden-green eyes inside the hypnotizing mask, and there he saw the tiger studying him and

Yona, a probing intelligence, as if the tiger were trying to decide who was the greater threat.

The tiger suddenly uttered a deep, guttural growl.

Kan felt a cold rush run behind his head and down his back. He heard a chilling threat in that growl.

But something broke the trance, and the tiger roared, whipping back around toward the others. Kan saw Wesa running away, evidently having nipped at the tiger's rear haunch. The tiger's paw swept through the air after Wesa, but she outdistanced it and joined Lana and Koga.

The tiger did not pursue Wesa, though, for Taline, now barking wildly, was closest. She alone refused to leave her mother's side, and even as the tiger turned toward her, she did not run. Kan felt frozen in place. He watched as Wesa from her new position tried to jump the tiger again, but the hunter was running now, having finally selected its prey. To Kan's horror the massive beast leapt into the air, muscular arms extended, finally to land on Taline, pulling her into its deadly embrace, enveloping and muffling her bark and then her last piercing cry of pain.

He felt Yona's insistent nipping at his side and also saw Wesa was already escorting Lana and Koga in their escape. Though he was disgusted he was running away from his mate, and from poor Taline, he pushed off with all the strength he could muster, and he felt the snow shifting under his paws. Guided by a strong sense of self-preservation, he covered the open space and jumped into the brush of the forest.

The first thought was they had to get away—escape, not caution. The forest was growing darker, and the air was getting colder now the sun had slipped away. With Yona running beside him, Kan pushed despite the stiffness in his leg. How far could he run? How far should he run before they stopped and looked for Lana and the others?

He knew he was running in the direction of their new home,

but Lana, Wesa, and Koga had been headed in the opposite direction when he last saw them. How far would they go before they could turn and swing a wide arc past the tiger's territory? He felt the urge to stop and look for that arc, but he did not know which side they would choose. It would be dangerous for him to go blindly searching for them even with Yona by his side. How could he confirm she was safe? He did not dare howl. Not only would that give his presence away to the tiger, but it would also tempt Lana into doing the same. He would be painting a greater target on her.

Should they even worry about the tiger if it was gorging itself now on Taline? The thought sickened him, those bone teeth bloodied, ripping into his packmate. What did she do to deserve that? She had been faithful to the end.

Kan realized Yona was nipping him again, pushing him forward. Kan had a responsibility to him too. They had to put some distance between them and the tiger; they would have to save the reunion with the others for later. He would have to trust Lana to Wesa's care. Kan hoped he was making the right decision.

Moving forward, Kan picked up Sikwa's scent; here was unfinished business. That coward did not have any trouble running. How was Kan to govern such behavior? How was he to discipline Sikwa for abandoning his pack? Yona evidently picked up the scent too, for he looked back at Kan expectantly. When Kan nodded, Yona trotted forward, snout close to the ground. After several paces through the woods, it was obvious Sikwa was on a path straight back to their new home, no deviations. They pushed on after him.

Several markers later, Kan finally stumbled, his leg throbbing. Yona let him stand this time unmolested, apparently thinking they were a safe distance away.

Kan noted there still was no hint of the others—no scents, no sounds. Where was Lana? Where would they have run? Wesa would have encouraged her to head back this way, but Koga was a wild card. What would she have done? How would her presence have affected what Lana did? Kan regretted following Sikwa's path. He felt like he should double back to find Lana. Yet when he turned and took a step back in the direction they had come, Yona suddenly jumped in front of him, barking, forcing Kan to focus on him. Finally considering Yona's loss, a mother and a sister, Kan felt the larger wolf's desire to head home.

Despite his worries Kan finally stopped trying to get around Yona; he did not have the desire to fight. Besides, with the confirmed loss of Etsi and the additional death of Taline, they did not have any reasons left to risk being anywhere near the tiger; maybe Lana and the others, who would pass much more swiftly through the woods, were already ahead of him and Yona, well on their way back to their pack. Perhaps they took a different path, thinking this well-marked one was too risky.

As he stood there in the darkness of night, facing off against Yona, Kan wondered how he had gotten there. These woods were to be a place of retreat, but now this tiger had turned it into a hunting ground. What was it doing there anyway? Why had it turned on the wolves? What did it want? How far would it come? Would it continue to be a threat? How far did the pack need to go to escape its creeping presence? If he and Lana were to lead the pack, they would need to make some important decisions soon. The pack needed to move farther away, to find food, to find safety.

Yona whined, and Kan focused on his packmate again. He needed to make a decision. Yona obviously did not even want to wait. Kan thought again of Lana, though. He remembered the night before and the quest to find his mate. He had worked too hard to find her, and now she was missing again, now facing another threat.

Kan barked and twisted his head toward their current home. Would he be able to convince the tall wolf to go on without him? When he glanced at Yona, he saw the indecision in his friend's eyes; he knew Yona did not want to abandon him, just as Kan did not want to give up on Lana.

Kan growled and barked again. Yona finally lowered his tail and trotted past, headed back toward the pack. A few steps away, Yona paused. Though Kan did not look over his shoulder, he could feel his friend look back. A heartbeat later, Yona was gone, and Kan found himself alone.

He wondered if he had made the right decision. Should he have gone back with Yona? Perhaps Lana and the others took the long way around and were already back since they could run circles around him in his current condition. She would be worried about him if she saw Yona come back alone. She would run out and find him, scolding him for sure.

But that did not feel right. A tiger was running in the night. They could not outmaneuver him that easily, and there had been no sounds. Lana or Wesa would have risked a howl when they felt they were moving into the land the pack patrolled. Kan had heard no such signal.

Kan imagined what Yona would find on his return. Unalii, Noya, and Sasa would warmly greet him, sharing tokens of affection, wagging tails around, but then there would be the whines and yips as the others tried to discern why Yona returned alone.

Then Yona would spot Sikwa and growl at the coward who by now was probably already stretched out casually on the ground somewhere, resting. Kan remembered the loss of Taline and the loss of Etsi; the image of Sikwa lying safely at home turned his stomach.

And what was he doing? Kan thought as he found himself sitting in the snow. He was resting there in safety while Lana was out somewhere in danger. He needed to go help her.

He stood and made some stumbling steps, his leg not cooperating. How much good would he be to her? She had not wanted him to go on the mission anyway.

Another option presented itself, though. If he could not find her, maybe he could send her hope. He threw his head back and offered the strongest howl he could muster. He was hoping to hear her voice in return, a sign she was safely away from the tiger, but if she could not sound her position, she could at least hear his voice, could stop worrying about him, could draw strength to face the challenge before her.

Only silence followed his howl. Some alpha he was.

Another wolf howl finally did sound in the distance. It was not Lana's, though. It was Yona, and then Unalii's voice joined in, and Noya's and Sasa's too. They were coming toward him. So Yona had made it back and had secured reinforcements.

Unalii and Noya arrived first, soon followed by Yona and then finally Sasa. Kan was glad to see them and he welcomed their licks. After the initial surge of excitement at his friends' arrival, Kan noticed he still keenly felt Lana's absence. His worries rushed him again.

I have to go back. I have to find her.

Thinking he had rested long enough, Kan took several tentative steps forward, but both Yona and Unalii overtook him. They barred his passage, and even stood their ground when he bared his teeth and growled. In fact, they pushed him back, and he did not have the energy to resist these two large males. What were they doing? Did they not realize what he had to do? They could not make him stay. But even as Kan thought that, Unalii gently and firmly pushed him to the ground. Although Kan felt this was no way to treat an alpha, he finally acquiesced.

Sasa came over to lick him, and he closed his eyes for a moment. It did feel good to give in. He felt Unalii and Yona retreat quietly. When they were yards away, he opened his eyes to watch them meet up with Noya, and the three of them went off into the woods in the direction he wanted to go. They had left Sasa to care for him. Kan guessed Yona had convinced the other two to go with him to scout the three missing females. He would find his sister Wesa. Kan felt better, but he could not banish the thought that he needed to be out there too.

Despite the fatigue from running, the trauma of finding Etsi's corpse and witnessing the tiger's pounce on Taline, and the ongoing struggle with his leg, Kan continued to fight sleep. Sasa's licking was soothing, but she was not his mate; he could not rest until he knew what had happened to Lana. He felt he could overpower Sasa and run after the others, but when he looked in her direction, he saw the devotion in her eyes. If he bit her, it would be an act of betrayal. Yet could he get away from her without at least a nip?

Kan pushed to stand, but before he had gotten halfway up, he heard Sasa growl. The sound surprised him. How could she be growling at him? Her challenge was not fierce; she still knew her place, but it was a reminder of the will of the pack. They wanted him to rest. At that moment Kan knew Sasa would resist, and the thought of fighting her unsettled him. Kan knew Sasa held onto a deeper strength. Whenever the pack faced challenges, whenever tensions rose among the ranks, someone would always go after Sasa; she was the pressure valve. She shouldered the acts of aggression; she let others have places of privilege because she had fallen into this role. The pack could not cohere without the strength of her submission.

Kan did not want to fight her, so he settled back down to consider another possibility. Sasa resumed her attentions. Maybe he could rest a little while and give off the appearance of acquiescing. He could look for the moment when he could make a break for the woods; his wound would be a liability, but Sasa had her own limitations, the legacy of a deeper wound.

Settling down temporarily, Kan searched for his moment. He let some time pass, waiting for the point when Sasa would feel satisfied she had done her job, when she would let her guard down. She had just pulled back to scratch her side with her back leg, and Kan was getting ready to spring, when an unexpected vibration in the air startled him. He jumped up. What was it? The sound again tickled his ears, the unmistakable crunching of snow behind him. He realized too Sasa was growling softly in his ear. Kan did not have to turn his head to recognize the confident, yet careful, gait of another wolf approaching. The scent in the air confirmed it was Danuwa. What was he doing out here? Had he followed the others out of curiosity?

Kan thought about the night before, about Danuwa's challenge. Was the masked wolf back to finish the job? Suddenly a whole new set of thoughts stirred in Kan. Noya, Unalii, and Yona were all out in the woods with Lana. How far had they gone? How long had he rested? Could he call them back? Danuwa was thorough; he had chosen his moment well. Kan realized his strongest allies were missing; the rest of the pack was far away. He and Sasa were on their own. He felt a chill as he noted Sikwa's approach from the other direction. His rivals were closing in.

8
SUMMER OF
THE RED WOLF

"SOMEONE SHOT HIM," TSULA SAID, HER VOICE DISTANT. Walking forward, I put my arm over her shoulder and looked down again at the animal we had been tracking all morning. The canine was lying motionless on its side, its legs outstretched as if it were caught mid-leap, its eyes open in an eerie stillness. I scanned from his black, furry tail along red haunches, side, and shoulders, to the terrible gash in its chest, the cream color of the fur there now overrun with blood red.

When we entered the woods that morning, we were afraid something like this had happened. The rangers put trackers on the red wolves, and whenever the signal stopped moving for more than a day or two, they'd typically send out a small flying drone to investigate, but this time, since the drone was down for repairs, Tsula had volunteered, and it was a testament to how she'd earned their trust so quickly that her supervisors let her go out alone. I had surprised Tsula by dropping by that morning; I came because I'd noted her concern the night before when she'd discussed the wolf's lack of movement. As I was walking into the ranger station to find her, I found Tsula rushing out, and she invited me to tag along. Several hours later, following the signal into a remote section of the swamp, keeping in contact with the rangers, we finally found the wolf we were tracking.

"Maybe the hunter thought it was a coyote," I said and then regretted speaking. The words somehow profaned the moment.

Tsula was quiet. I saw her bow her head. When she stood, I saw the anger in her face.

She called her supervisor to report the death. The ranger came out with a team, who took pictures of the area and then lifted the wolf carcass onto the back of a truck. There would be an investigation.

Tsula got it into her head she was going to find who was responsible. So over the next several weeks, along with her usual responsibilities, she started doing research into hunting permits. She started driving around the nearby neighborhoods and farms. That hike changed our summer from the quiet celebration I wanted to something more complicated.

Back in the spring, the rangers had chosen Tsula for a highly selective, though temporary, post at the Alligator River National Wildlife Refuge. When I learned she would be so close to the Outer Banks, I quickly worked on convincing my uncle to let me stay the summer at his beach house in Nags Head. My mother wasn't too happy about my choice, but I promised I would run home when I could—though we both knew the drive was a long one. My uncle asked for a modest rent, largely at my father's prompting, so the beach house finally did become my home for the summer. I looked forward to spending some time with my uncle too since he would be popping in just about every weekend.

Despite being tied up with my graduate studies and my work for Tsunami, I still had several opportunities to check in on Tsula even if I had to drive several miles to see her. I was always impressed with the row of crepe myrtle blooms in Manteo in the summer; they reminded me of fireworks—and they lasted much longer. Tsula had made contact with a widow who had a room to let, so by the end of the summer, I knew the way to Mrs. Moore's cozy house well. We shared some happy times, visiting the lighthouses—Bodie, Duck, and Hatteras. We swam in the ocean and visited the Lost Colony on Roanoke Island.

The road I also learned well was the long way to the wildlife refuge. Tsula saw our situation as an opportunity to pull me into the outdoors. As she began to learn the layout of the refuge, hiking through the acreage that was passable on foot on a regular basis, checking the progress of the red wolves there, she would pass these lessons on to me. Lovely white cypress trees grew out of the water and the swampy, boggy section we had to navigate around. I had never seen anything like this landscape, and the beauty of it stunned and intimidated me. There was something wild about it, despite the tourists who came to visit. There was a force, a presence—you may think me superstitious—in that refuge. It was a perfect place for the red wolves. When I first heard their howls, I paused at the otherworldly nature of their calls. Tsula, despite her mountain background, reveled in this wetland wilderness, and I grew to love her for it.

But the red wolf shooting, two weeks in, sucked the innocent discovery out of our exploration of this landscape. One afternoon, a few days after we discovered the dead wolf, Tsula convinced me to go driving around with her onto roads I'd never seen. Of course, I'd only been on the main highways leading to the Outer Banks, and I knew the beach roads very well, but I'd not done much exploring on Roanoke Island and the surrounding areas.

"Tsula, are you sure this is a good idea?"

"Why?" she asked, an edge to her voice.

"It's not like we can blend in with the locals. We're going to stick out. And do you really expect the person who shot that wolf to be bragging about it? The one who did it might not even know what a red wolf is."

"I don't think he should have been shooting at coyotes either."

"So are you going to report anyone who admits to shooting a coyote?" I followed up.

"You're not being very supportive."

"Are you going to knock on doors? What authority do you have?"

"I have knocked on a few doors already. I get their attention by mentioning the reward," she said and ran her hand from her forehead back through her hair.

"So you hope to stumble on a snitch?"

"Do you want me to take you back?" she asked, her eyes fixed on the road ahead.

"No."

We drove in silence for a while until we came to a spot where a dirt road branched off the paved one. Tsula turned down it, and I wondered how dirty her truck would get as the dust flew up behind us. After the road turned, we saw a makeshift fence out of wood and wire, and beyond it, a pasture with some twenty or thirty cows bunched in a corner. We drove farther and saw a couple trailers and an old farmhouse behind them. Tsula decided to pull up to the house.

She turned to me. "Will you, at least, make yourself useful? Could you knock on the door, and if anyone answers, tell him there has been a red wolf shooting and the Fish and Wildlife Service is offering a reward for information leading to the capture of the culprit?"

"Tsula, I'm not good at this."

"Just give it a try."

"What are you going to be doing?" I asked, suddenly feeling that I might rather have her job.

"I'm going to have a look around."

"Is that a good idea?"

"How do you propose we catch the one who shot that wolf?"

Not having a good answer for her question, I reluctantly got out of the truck, observing that Tsula slipped out her side, crouching low, using the vehicle as a shield, closing her door about the time mine slammed shut. Recovering some, not wanting to give Tsula away, I focused on the farmhouse in front of me. It had white boards and a wrap-around porch. I tentatively placed my foot on the first rickety step leading onto the porch; when it held me, I continued up. Upon reaching the front door, I allowed myself one look back over the yard and could not locate Tsula.

Remind me never to play hide-and-seek with her, I thought.

Although I felt like returning to the truck and driving away, I turned back around, lifted my arm, and gave the door a good series of knocks, not wanting to face Tsula's questioning without some results.

There was no answer, so I knocked again a little harder. I then heard some movement inside and footsteps drawing nearer. After the clicking of the locks, the door opened, and I saw a large man with silver hair and stubble, dressed in a snug white tank and blue jeans cinched up with a belt that disappeared slightly beneath his belly. The air in the house was warm and stuffy.

I stammered, "D-d-did you hear about the sh-shooting?"

"Shooting? What are you talking about, son?" the elderly man spoke in a crackling, raspy voice.

"The shooting a few days ago."

"Who's been shot?" I saw the confusion and frustration in

his eyes.

"We found a red wolf shot in the woods almost a week ago."

"A red wolf?" Understanding came. "Why are you knocking on my door then?"

I wasn't prepared for his question and didn't respond quickly enough for him.

He said again, "Do you have a good reason for bothering me, son?"

"My fr—," I started and caught myself. "I-I've been driving around telling people in the area. There is a reward for information leading to the location of the shooter."

"So what's so important about this red wolf? Isn't it like a coyote? I don't want him eating my chickens, messing with my cows, fighting with my dogs."

"It's endangered," I defended. "Critically."

"And what am I supposed to do about that?" He swayed a second, grabbed the doorframe, and righted himself. "Look, son, you can either come in and sit down, or you can go and leave me alone." He turned and walked back inside, leaving me at the door.

Glancing over my shoulder, I still could not locate Tsula. It seemed to me I had not given her enough time, so I took a few slow steps inside, giving my eyes a chance to adjust to the dim light. Something musty in the air made it hard to breathe, and then there was the overpowering smell of cigar smoke. Ahead I saw the silver-haired man reaching to sit down on his couch, the television on, loudly blaring some game show.

I went to the well-worn brown couch on the other side of the room, noticing the paintings of hunting dogs on the wall above. On another wall I saw the pictures of wild birds.

While he was catching his breath, I decided I needed to carry the conversation. "So you're a hunter?"

He hit the mute button on the remote control. "That depends on whether you are going to arrest me for the wolf shooting," he said with a wry grin, then reached down, grabbed a new cigar, and proceeded to light it. After the first puffs, he looked at me and must have seen my dislike, for then he said, "You're in my home."

I didn't say anything, and the quiet in the house sat heavily on us. The roof of the room was also shorter than normal, and the walls were a dark-wood paneling. The one window in the room had a shade drawn down over it.

I thought about Tsula wandering outside looking for clues and then realized the old man was studying me.

"So do you work for the government?" he asked.

"No." And then I realized the points he was connecting, so I chimed in, "I'm a volunteer."

"You're not from around here, are ya?"

"No, I'm from Atlanta originally, but this summer I'm staying in Nags Head."

"Figures. A city boy." He said almost to himself as if confirming some secret knowledge.

"Did you grow up here?"

"Been here all my life. Unlike the transplants the beach has brought in."

"Like me." I couldn't resist.

"You don't seem as bad as some of 'em. I've seen the license plates. New York. Pennsylvania. Ohio."

"Have you always been a farmer?"

"No. I spent some time with horses."

"Horses?"

"Barrels. Racing. Rodeo."

When I didn't comment, he continued, "I had one horse no other could beat when he was in his prime. I've got a shelf full of trophies we won." He went on to describe how he bought the horse from a friend, how his horse won several competitions, how others kept asking to buy the horse from him, and finally the sad day of the horse's death. As he told his story, his eyes glazed some, and I felt he was looking keenly into the past.

I tried to bring the conversation back. "Have you been hunting recently?"

"I don't make it out much now, but I've still got my dogs. And my grandson and his friends sometimes take them out and run them for me."

"Have they," I started.

He cut me short, "I'm not going to let you accuse them either in my home."

"I'm sorry. I probably better go." Then feeling I was being a little abrupt after his hospitality, I added, "I enjoyed the stories."

He stood and reached out his large hand; it enveloped mine when we shook hands. His eyes, though tired, watched me closely, and I felt them on me as I walked back to the front door and closed it behind me.

Outside, the sun seemed too bright, and I squinted as I stepped off the porch, almost missing the step, my left foot sliding off it and coming down hard on the ground. The jolt ran up my leg and hit my back. Hoping Tsula didn't see my mistake, I tried to shake off the stiffness on the walk back to her truck. I was surprised to see she wasn't there.

I considered different possibilities. Was she expecting me to wait for her here at the truck, or did she want me to drive on down the road so she could catch up with me? Had she stumbled into something, or had she gotten caught up in her own conversation with a local? I was divided until I remembered I'd left her keys in the ignition. After cranking the engine, I drove slowly away from the farmhouse down toward the two trailers.

As I approached, Tsula came out from behind the closest of the trailers, sliding carefully along the wall until the truck passed and she could open the door and jump inside in one fluid motion. I picked up speed once she was in.

We both spoke at the same time, and then I let her go first.

"What did you find?"

"An old farmer, who's also been a horse trainer and a hunter," I reported.

"Has he been out in the woods lately?"

"He said he hasn't, and he doesn't look like he's in the shape to go very far, but he said he has a grandson who runs his hunting dogs. I don't know if he's the one we're looking for. What'd you do?"

"I looked around the trailers. From tire tracks it looks like a large truck often is parked there—perhaps the grandson. But I also found a spot where it looks like they've skinned some deer—and perhaps a coyote."

"How did you discover that?"

"My dad has hunted some, and I know my animals."

As we were nearing the end of the dirt road, we saw a large red truck turn off the highway onto the road in front of us. Since the road was narrow, I tried to hug the side as closely as I could, wondering if we could clear the truck. As we passed, I noticed there were at least two people inside and that the driver was a broad-shouldered young man with a buzz cut. He frowned at us, turning his head to follow our passing. In the rear-view mirror, I saw the silhouette of the gun rack.

It's probably not wise to mess with them, I thought.

Tsula said, "I think we've found the culprit."

"Aren't you jumping to conclusions?"

"It's my intuition."

"So what are you going to do? Go arrest them?"

"I might."

"Where's the proof?" I asked.

"No one said this would be easy."

&

We had dinner that evening, and though I tried to get her to talk about other things, I could tell her "detective work" was still bothering her. And it continued to occupy her thoughts over the next week or so. She told me she had conversations with the rangers, who were not all that prepared to act on her hunch. In fact, one of the rangers was clearly upset Tsula had taken matters into her own hands. Fortunately he wasn't Tsula's direct supervisor, but he did put pressure on the woman who was.

Tsula told me the reward had brought in some phone calls, but no solid leads. It looked like there was going to be no resolution, that this killing would fall into the unsolved cases. This time there were too many variables and no foolproof way to locate and punish the one who shot this critically endangered animal.

♨

"You mustn't let it ruin your summer. This may be a once-in-a-lifetime opportunity," I tried to convince her one Saturday evening when she came over to the beach house and my uncle had gone out with some friends.

"I know," she said in a resigned way.

"Think about the success you've had with the other wolves."

She turned from me to sit sideways in the sofa chair and stare out the window at the ocean. My attempt to cheer her up seemed to have the opposite effect.

Trying a different tactic, I said, "Would you like to go for a swim?"

"Not really." The tone in her voice told me not to ask a second time.

A dark cloud had invaded our carefree summer.

I walked over to her, placed my hands on the sides of her shoulders, and leaned down to brush my nose against the back of her neck behind her right ear to tickle the soft wisps of hair there. "You've given it your best."

She didn't say anything. When I leaned in further, kissing her neck below the ear, she pulled away from me, shaking a little. In the months I had known her, I had never seen any tears. She was always in control. Her quiet crying so surprised me I stood there dazed for several moments before finally sitting down next to her and putting my arm over her shoulder, pulling her in close. She didn't resist.

"Is there anything I can do to cheer you up?"

When she didn't answer, I just held her and appreciated the warmth of having her near.

My mind raced, and I considered suggesting that we go hunting for some more clues. But my second thought was, what would that solve? More snooping wasn't the answer. We wouldn't find anything, yet again; we'd be tempted to break the law ourselves, and she would come back to Mrs. Moore's home more frustrated. Sometimes bad things happen, and there is nothing we can do to fix them.

I felt her twisting to sit up. She was wiping her eyes. "I'm okay."

"How 'bout some ice cream?"

She nodded, and I went to freezer, scooped out the white-chocolate raspberry swirl, and by the time I came back with the waffle cones, she was out on the porch. The stars were just starting to come out, and the evening breeze was coming in off the ocean.

"It's a great evening to look at the stars," I said, trying to lighten the mood. "Wish I had a telescope."

Tsula, though, took things in another direction. "Do you believe in God?"

Still holding the ice cream, watching some running down the fingers of my left hand, I stumbled over the question and her serious tone. "What?"

"Do you believe in God?"

"Why do you ask?"

"It's an important question, don't you think?"

"Does it matter what I believe?" My voice sounded harsher than I intended as I handed her her cone.

"I was just asking." She sounded hurt.

Silence. I struggled to find a way to soothe the burn.

"I'm not sure." I stared out at the moonlit spot on the ocean, feeling she was measuring me again in some way. "What does that question even mean?"

"Belief in God relates to other questions. Why are we here? What's the purpose of life? How are we supposed to live? Will we be held accountable for our actions? Surely you've thought about these things."

"Yeah, but which god are you talking about. I took an Intro to Religion class. We studied Buddhism, Hinduism, Judaism, Christianity, and Islam—even a little bit about tribal religions." She didn't look impressed, so I continued. "I'm not convinced they are all talking about the same Supreme Being. The professor tried to get us to define the word 'religion,' but I was just as confused at the end of the semester. The only thing that really stuck with me was his recommendation we identify the context whenever someone said 'god.' He said too many people say, 'god,' and then assume you understand what they mean."

"And what does the name mean to you?"

"I don't understand it all that well. How would you define it?"

"God is a Being beyond our comprehension."

"Isn't it convenient to say we don't understand?" I asked.

"Isn't most of the universe beyond our understanding?"

"Science teaches us more each day."

"But there is mystery. Look up at those stars." She pointed up with her left hand as the wind whipped her hair behind her. "What do you feel before such beauty? God is the source of beauty, life, all that is good."

"Others who look at the stars see an overwhelming expanse."

"Many find comfort."

"Are you projecting that hope? I remember studying a German guy—Feuerbach, I believe—who argued our concepts of God are visions of what we hope life is about."

Her amber eyes locked on me. "Is that what you believe?"

"I don't know. There's a lot of bad stuff in the world. Perhaps, Freud was right, saying religion is a security blanket, comforting those unable to face reality." When Tsula frowned, I backpedaled, "But I don't think all the religious people in the world are messed up either. What's wrong with a little religion? We still tell stories of Santa Claus to children even though we know it's all make-believe."

"Sounds like a safe academic answer, Professor."

I grinned at her sarcasm, but then felt her comment was more serious. "And Marx helped us to see religion often keeps us from facing the unjust distribution of wealth."

"But what about you? What do you believe?" she continued to press me.

Sensing a growing dissatisfaction in her, I softened my response. "I guess I'd like to believe in God."

"'Believe in, as in Santa Claus?"

"Maybe," I said.

"But is that belief?"

"Well, what do you believe?"

"We're talking about you now. Don't dodge the question, Professor."

"I don't know...."

"Did your parents ever take you to church?" she asked.

"My mother took us to an Episcopal church some when I was a kid. We celebrated Christmas and Easter, and sometimes we said a blessing before a meal, primarily at Thanksgiving. Since I had a close friend in high school who attended a Methodist church, I went on some youth trips and learned some Bible stories."

"And what'd you think?"

"I always found the Old Testament confusing and dark—all those stories about armies and fighting and death. I like the stories about Jesus better, but the crucifixion always bothered me, especially when preachers said it was a good thing."

"Is there no sacrifice in love?" She was looking out over the ocean.

"Sorry?"

"Is there no sacrifice in love?" she repeated.

It seemed to be a Catch-22 question. "Probably," I said. Then in the silence that followed, I decided I could finally turn the questions away from me. "What do you believe?"

"I believe in God," she stated plainly with no antagonism. "I believe in love—there is a purpose in this life; we were created to do good things. A Great Spirit watches over us, judges us, loves us like a parent. I have felt God near. I grew up going to my uncle's church—he's a preacher." She paused a moment and looked down at the dunes directly in front of us, then continued, "I believe there is evil in this world and that we need to fight against it. We struggle, and we sacrifice, and we do our best not to hurt others. Though there is much suffering in this world, love will win in the end."

"That's a nice thought," I said curtly, feeling the conversation sounded too much like my father's quoting of Schweitzer.

"Are you making fun of me?" Her question was quick, her voice no longer reflective.

"I wasn't being sarcastic," I defended.

"Yes, you were."

"Thank you for telling me what I meant." I did not like having my motives questioned.

"It's all in your tone of voice. I was trying to share something important with you, and you turned it into a game," she said, turning away from me.

"That was not my intention," I shot back.

Her questions ceased, and she stood there quietly, leaning against the rail, looking up at the sweeping expanse above us, and the stars just starting to shine. As the waves crashed and hissed into foam in the background, I felt I had hurt her, but did not know what more to say. At that moment I did not understand her faith. She argued it was genuine, and all I could offer was I thought religion was a comfortable blanket that made people feel better when they got a little down about life.

I thought it would be fine to say I didn't oppose her faith either. There wasn't enough evidence to declare there was no such thing as God either. Yet my answer did not satisfy her; she had said I was taking the safe way out.

Although I offered a bed for her to sleep on for the night, she insisted she was fine. Not able to dissuade her, I watched her headlights pull out of the driveway, and her taillights fade into the darkness. We had seen two firsts that night: her first tears in front of me and our first fight.

&

A couple days passed—no calls, no texts—before I saw her again. As soon as I picked her up for lunch that day, I noticed she was reserved. Our conversation at the restaurant was courteous and a little forced, nothing mean, but there was a divide. She ended the outing early, saying she had to get back to work.

This lunch was our last visit before I was to head home to Atlanta for the Fourth of July. Originally I was going to invite her to come with me, but now I saw she needed some space. She had turned from me, and I didn't know how to make things right.

The long drive and the visit home helped provide some perspective. After hours of reflecting on my argument with Tsula and dealing with traffic, I pulled into my parents' neighborhood. Although many in their social circles had chosen fancy suburban neighborhoods with gates and fences, my parents had picked a house in one of the more historic sections of Atlanta, a "house with character," as they liked to say. My father loved history and my mother loved the architecture of the early part of the twentieth century, so their interests met in this white columned house and yard of stately trees. I knew I was home when my mother came out to greet me before I even got out of the car.

After we hugged and I gave my report about the trip, she said, "Just a heads up. Your father has a risky surgery planned in four days. A patient with a brain tumor, and the prognosis is not good."

"No holiday time for surgeons."

"I've taken a few days off." She smiled. "We'll find something fun to do."

As we stepped inside the house, I smelled freshly baked cookies, and I knew my mother had pulled her tools out to temper my father's stress. He came from the hallway into the library and threw his arm around my shoulders.

"Good to see you, son!"

We sat down and caught up. I gave them a quick update on my graduate-school work, noting Dr. Stanley's recent approval of my progress. I also told them about Tsula's quest to find the mysterious hunter who had shot the red wolf. My father was particularly interested in hearing how this situation would play out.

Then my mother changed the subject, "How are things with your job?"

"I'm enjoying it," I said simply, knowing this was a sore subject with my father, who now was silently staring out the window—a boy on his bicycle was riding by.

When I had run through my updates and the conversation lulled, I turned the attention to my father. "Mom tells me you've got a bad one coming up."

"Anthony Rook. A lawyer. It's taken too long for him to get to me through the referrals. The tumor is enmeshed in the frontal lobe. It will be a difficult surgery."

"Sorry."

"He's a good man. Lots of *pro bono* cases. He became symptomatic in the courtroom; the judge held him in contempt for an outburst of anger, but it was Tony's wife who pushed him to see a doctor. I told him there's little chance I can get it all, but he definitely wants the surgery."

I saw the redness in my father's eyes, the drooping mouth. He must have been having trouble sleeping again.

"Maybe we could get a game or two of tennis in," I offered.

"I'd like that." My father smiled.

I mostly enjoyed my visit home. My parents and I learned not to talk about certain things, but the weight of Rook's cancer and the impending surgery weighed on my father, and I took on some of the stress. After my recent conversation with Tsula, this story hit me hard. I'd watched my father wrestle with difficult cases before, but this time somehow I felt more was at stake. What was it like to get cancer, to learn your life would be shorter than you'd planned? Why did a good man get cancer? What could my father do? Why did Dad torture himself over it?

The surgery came at the end of the week, and my father came home exhausted. When I asked him how it went, he shook his head.

"I had to tell him the truth. The cancer will probably return in a year or so. He'll have to live with that however long he has."

My father slept all the next day, and I was glad of that even though it meant I did not have much more time with him before I had to head back to Nags Head. He and Mom put together a big breakfast for me the morning I had to leave, and then I got on the road, alone with my thoughts.

Life seemed so random. How did one navigate around such suffering? Was there any purpose in it? What did I believe? My thoughts returned to my argument with Tsula, and I wondered where my life was going. I'd enjoyed that summer with Tsula. Had she not shown me there was beauty in the world too? What had I experienced on the beaches of the Outer Banks and in the wildness of the Alligator River Reserve? Was all that just an accident?

During that long drive, I also wondered if Tsula would welcome me back. I knew she had a general idea when I'd be in, but we hadn't talked all week. So, about halfway through the trip, I tried to call her; I was quite nervous, and when her voicemail answered, I hung up and sent a quick text, asking her if she'd like to have dinner with me that evening. An hour later I got a text saying she would.

When I finally reached Mrs. Moore's yard, I saw Tsula sitting on the doorstep. She jumped up to greet me, to my relief, with a smile on her face. "Did you miss me?"

I walked forward, slipped my hand round to the small of her back, pulled her in gently, and kissed her. *Let Mrs. Moore watch*, I thought.

Tsula was a little taken aback. I celebrated the rare moment, catching her off-guard.

"I've got something for you," I said, and I turned back to the car for the roses.

After she ran them inside, we set out for supper. Sitting at our little table, looking out over the sound as the sun set, our conversation was a little forced at first, but both of us were committed to getting connected again. There were two themes in our reconciliation. Tsula introduced the first.

"I've decided I won't be able to catch the one who shot our red wolf."

"Really?" I was genuinely surprised.

"Even if I know who did it, there's just not enough evidence to convict. We could put a little pressure on them, but our hands are tied. The North Carolina law allowing for the shooting of coyotes muddies the water."

"I know the whole situation has frustrated you," I consoled.

She half-smiled. "I'm only going to be here for a few more weeks, so I've got to leave it to the authorities who will be here for the long haul."

Later in the conversation, after telling her about my father's cancer patient and impossible surgery, I introduced the second. "I need to apologize for the way I spoke to you the evening you shared your faith."

I paused at the effort, and she looked quietly at me, waiting, so I continued, "I'm too much of a skeptic for my own good. I should have listened more and spoken less."

When she still didn't speak, I said, "I want you to know that I'm open to exploring the spiritual. I won't pretend to understand faith, but I'll take you seriously when you talk to me about it."

She responded, "I won't ask for more."

After our meal was over, we did not dawdle; I told her that I had something to show her back at the beach house. She asked what it was, but I told her she had to wait. While I was away in Atlanta, I had done a lot of thinking.

When we climbed the steps to the beach house, I started to explain my thoughts to her, "You know I've not really been an outdoorsman. Growing up in Atlanta made me a city boy. Now, though, because of you, I've discovered that I've been missing something. I've found something out here in the wetlands."

"That sounds absolutely spiritual," she teased.

I nodded and continued, "You've also gotten me to think more about what we are losing when building projects overrun these habitats."

I took her hand and led her out the back door. We took the steps down to the beach, the sand already cooled by the night. Clouds above obscured the stars, and a wind blew humid air in. Lightning flashed far out over the ocean.

"What is it?" she asked.

I had a long speech prepared, but all I got out was, "Since you've come into my life, I feel I've become a better person. I feel my life might mean something more, if you'll be by my side." I reached into my pocket for the little burgundy felt box, opened it, and placed the ring in her open palm in the dark. "Tsula, will you marry me?"

There was a long moment of silence. Was I supposed to say something else? What was she thinking?

"Don?"

"What is it? Am I moving too fast?"

"We're not ready for this."

"What? Why?" I stammered.

"We need to be honest with each other."

"Honest? What do you mean?"

"I'm not sure I know you." Her voice was a distant whisper.

"I'm right here. What do you want to know?"

I could just see her frown in the darkness as she asked, "When were you going to tell me about Tsunami Games?"

9
DISCOVERY

"WE'D LIKE YOU TO ASSIST LAUREN HAYES AND HER team in the level design of *Transylvania Nights, the Anniversary Edition*," Justin said while adjusting the wireless earpiece in his ear.

Although I was thinking, *It's about time*, I instead said, "I'd be glad to help."

"You would still need to bring *Cloud Kingdom* to an end, but if all works out with you and the *TN* team, we should be able to transition you over by early fall."

So this was going to be a slow process. When he had called me into his office, I wasn't quite sure what to expect. I spared one thought about the possibility of promotion, but then shot it down because eight months of punching code for Pastel Land had deadened my hopes for a change in situation—exactly as Justin had warned.

"I'm almost finished with the last of the *Cloud Kingdom*

edits and should have them to you by the end of the week," I assured him even though I probably still had several hours of work. I was going to put in the crunch time so that I could finally be rid of the project.

"I'd like for you to go down and meet with Lauren and lay out a plan."

"Sure thing."

When I didn't move toward the door, he looked back at me. "Anything else?"

"There is one other thing I'd like to ask you."

"What is it?"

"You've hinted that we didn't have to come into the office as regularly if we could get our work done at home." Noticing my throat was dry, I swallowed and continued, "My girlfriend will be moving to Manteo for the summer, and my uncle has a beach house in Nags Head."

Justin stared me down, showing no apparent emotion. He wasn't going to help me.

I finally got my request out, though. "Would it be possible for me to spend most of the summer there, teleconferencing with my team?"

"I thought you were going to put in more hours over the summer months when you didn't have classes."

"I will, though I'll still have research responsibilities with the university too."

"I'll leave the decision up to Lauren."

That wasn't quite what I wanted to hear, but as I exited Justin's office, I thought, *At least he didn't say, "No."*

I ducked into the men's room, splashed some water on my face, and ran my fingers through my hair before going to look up Lauren. On the way I passed Trevor in the hall; he held up his hand for a high-five.

When I obliged, he said, "Congratulations, man! I know how much you wanted this."

"Thanks, but why am I always last to know?"

He winked. "You're still new kid on the block." After a chuckle at my expense, he resumed his errand. "Don't worry. It won't last forever."

When I finally caught up with Lauren, I found her at her station, and she spotted me while I was several feet away. Her red hair stood out immediately, particularly against her green blouse; no one else in the office had that natural color.

"I've been expecting you," she said with a wide smile, and there was a twinkle in her blue eyes, behind the purple framed-glasses.

"You have?"

"Justin asked me if I'd take you under wing a few days ago."

"He just told me."

"That's the way things work around here. So how'd you enjoy *Cloud Kingdom*?" she said with a playful smirk.

"Oh, it's the best game ever."

"Now that you've worked on it."

"You should see the changes I've made."

"I have been looking over your work actually, and it's passable. We don't want to inflate any egos around here." Her eyebrows went up in a quick comical look.

"So how long have you been on the *TN* team?"

"About four or five years."

I let slip, "I'm envious."

"There's a lot of pressure working on a flagship game. After a few weeks, you may wish you were back on *Cloud Kingdom*. It's still all code in the end."

"I've had my fill of pastels, thank you very much."

"You'll be trading them for a host of darker colors—blacks, browns, and grays."

"What's the first assignment?" I asked.

"We've made a first run through the chapters in the game, but have decided to go back and add some. It's easier when you're doing an anniversary edition. Most of it is just updating the original design in light of changes in our gaming engine. I'd like for you to work on the level design of Chapter 3. It's after the plane crash. Brie is in a wilderness, lots of evergreen trees around, trying to save two wounded characters, one a pilot, the other a passenger, from a pack of wolves that has gotten the scent of blood."

"Sounds exciting."

"That's the drama of it. Now let me reveal the work behind it."

When she invited me to pull up a chair to show me how to access the drive where the files were kept, I noticed her rose perfume was strong, but I jumped at the chance to take on the new project, and we spent the next hour or so studying the code. By the end of the day, I was feeling much better about my job at Tsunami. It was also then that I risked asking Lauren about my plan for the summer.

I explained the situation, and Lauren smiled, unlike Justin.

"I understand," she said with a wink. "As long as you check in with me every weekday to confirm you aren't messing up the game, and you make each of the bi-weekly team meetings in person, then I'm fine with it."

I smiled in relief. "Thank you!"

Her tone changed. "Just be careful, Don. Remember these jobs aren't easy to land."

"I'll do my work. I promise you that."

Back at my car, I celebrated the change that had finally come. I now had a taste of my dream job. There was still room to grow—I wanted to get into tech development—but this was *Transylvania Nights*! This was my game. On impulse I reached for my phone to call Tsula, but then caught myself. She still did not know. Over the past couples months, we had grown closer and were spending more time together, but I never lost the feeling she'd disapprove of the gaming job. Since my hours at

Tsunami were during the week, times when Tsula had her own commitments on-campus, I didn't have too many complications.

I had to tell someone, though, about my new assignment, so I dialed Uncle Jack and left a message on his voicemail. Since I was living in the Triangle, I was able to see my uncle about once a month. He continued to be a source of encouragement.

The phone call was not enough of an outlet, so when I got back to the apartment, I ended up bragging to Mick too.

"Guess who's now working on *Transylvania Nights: Anniversary Edition*?"

"Not you?" Mick seemed genuinely surprised. I'd shared my earlier frustrations with him about my job at Tsunami, so he didn't think I was going to move beyond Pastel Land either.

"I'm not officially on the team. I'm just helping out, but at least this is progress."

"So are you finally going to show them they need tigers in the game?"

I laughed. "So a certain tiger expert can be a consultant?"

"But, of course. I am glad you asked." Mick was sitting at his desk, working on something. He looked back at the screen. "So what can you tell me about the new game? Is it as good as the others?"

"An adventurer-archaeologist named Brie Washington goes into the castles of Eastern Europe looking for fabled treasures carried there after the fall of the Byzantine Empire, but along the way she finds werewolves."

"That is the first game, you troll," he said with irritation.

"It is the anniversary edition."

"So there is nothing new?"

"Mick, you know I can't tell you anything. I signed a confidentiality agreement."

"But you can trust me," he purred.

"I haven't seen enough of it yet, but it looks awesome."

"This means if the game stinks, then I can blame you."

"Even good games can spoil in the hands of a mediocre player," I shot back.

"Only you would know."

"From seeing you play."

"Not everyone can recognize genius." He paused a moment, looked back at his screen. "So what does Tsula think?"

We hadn't talked much about her; I knew it was a sore subject. The brief conversation we'd had when he discovered Tsula and I were dating had gone better than I'd thought it would—he'd just warned me to watch out, that she was intense. Since then, I'd steered clear of the subject, not wanting to press my luck. I couldn't afford an apartment on my own, and I didn't want to scuttle my friendship with Mick either. So his question immediately made me cautious.

"I haven't told her yet."

"Really?" One of his eyebrows went up; it was a strange expression.

"Am I supposed to tell her everything?" I asked. The words came out more defensively than I'd intended.

"I don't know. Are you?" He was studying me again.

"I'm waiting for the right moment," I finally said over my shoulder as I headed to the kitchen to find something to eat, leaving Mick to return to his screen.

꧁

Lauren proved to be a great supervisor, and I had no problems working with her that summer.

"I'm just a big softie," she said one day in mid-June. "You can have a couple more days."

"I want it to be my best work. I promise you won't be disappointed." I smiled, hoping that'd help smooth over the delay.

"Do you think you could have it by Friday's meeting?"

I had temporarily forgotten about the meeting. "I'll shoot for it."

"That'll be good. I'll see you then."

After we closed the video conference, I checked my calendar. She was, of course, correct. The summer sun must have dazed me, for I'd let the date slip up on me. I had only two days left. Thinking ahead, I quickly typed an email to Mick to let him know I'd be in Thursday and Friday evenings. Since it was a three-hour drive to the Triangle and my meeting at Tsunami was early Friday morning, I'd decided it made sense for me to check in with Mick and get some rest before driving back to the beach on Saturday. While I was looking at my calendar, I decided to send another email, confirming a meeting with my advisor on Friday afternoon.

Once I'd squared away those details, I returned to my design work of the alpine forest, the crash site, and the approach of the wolves. Although the connection speed in the Outer Banks wasn't as fast as Tsunami's network, or even the university's, I knew Uncle Jack had the fastest available connection installed in his beach house, and I was able to access Tsunami's servers through my laptop and do passable work, which I checked with my Reality glasses in a dark bedroom on the landward side of the house, where my uncle did most of his gaming when there. Though I found the programming challenging, these designs immediately felt different from the work I'd been doing over the past nine months; here the code connected me to fond memories of previous versions of the game. Several hours in, my eyes were sore, but I felt satisfied.

That night I swung by Mrs. Moore's to pick Tsula up for supper; we were going to try out a new seafood restaurant.

"So how was your day?" I asked, a little concerned since I hadn't heard from her.

"The rangers aren't very optimistic about catching the shooter."

"Is there any evidence?"

"We've got a bullet," she explained, "but it's not going to do much good unless we can obtain access to the rifle that shot it."

"It doesn't sound like much can be done."

"I'm not going to give up," she said quietly, but firmly.

I turned my head quickly to look at her, then back to the road. It was bothering her. I struggled for something to say.

She spoke before I found the words, "What are you doing Friday?"

"I'm sorry, Tsula. I've got to go back to campus for a meeting with my advisor."

"Oh."

"Why?" I asked. "What were you thinking?"

"I want to do my own looking around." She paused. "Why do you have to drive back to campus? You tech guys are always talking about the advantages of teleconferencing."

"My advisor still likes to meet in person. I'd have expected you to understand that."

"How often?" she continued.

"I'm not sure. Maybe twice a month."

"Don't professors take off some during the summer months?"

"Sure he'll be on vacation the first week in July, but the rest of the summer he likes to keep tabs on his graduate students." I didn't tell her Dr. Stanley was going to be on another trip for three weeks in July and August, extending his stay in Los Angeles after a conference.

"Can you reschedule?" she asked. "I could use your help."

"I've got a deadline, Tsula."

"Deadline?"

"What's the rush? I could help Sunday afternoon."

"I don't want the trail to go cold," she interjected.

"Trail?"

"I feel like the longer we wait, the less chance we'll have of finding the shooter."

"I promise to help, but I can't this Friday."

"Okay," she acquiesced.

Tsula was a little distant the rest of the evening and the next day, so I was a little reluctant to leave Thursday evening. I questioned my duplicity during the drive, but the meeting at Tsunami went well, and my second thoughts evaporated. When Lauren prompted me, I gave a report on my code work. The other programmers and designers watched, their faces relatively blank, the coffee only just kicking in for some of them.

Afterwards, though, Lauren smiled and said, "You came through. Good job, Don."

Justin, who'd sat in on the meeting, walked by and nodded his approval.

So I left feeling upbeat about my progress. It looked like I'd have a solid job when I graduated.

My meeting with Dr. Stanley also went well. Since I'd gotten a positive response that morning, I showed him a modified form of the work. I couldn't discuss it openly because of my confidentiality agreement with Tsunami, but I was going to use a video game simulation that looked very similar for my dissertation project, developing a brain-computer interface that would read and write in the language of the brain, electrical impulses. Dr. Stanley found the simulation promising, but he said I needed to work more on the interface design since that was the crux of my doctoral studies.

The visit with Mick also went well. We spent most of our time playing games.

In one moment of camaraderie, after incapacitating a group of terrorists who'd kidnapped a group of diplomats, I extended an invitation, "Why don't you come visit the beach house for a few days?"

He pushed his glasses back onto his head and looked at me. For a moment I regretted what I'd said. I'd, of course, thought about it earlier, but rejected the idea, feeling it would put my relationship with Tsula too much in his face.

"It would be rude not to ask," he said, "and rude not to

accept your offer."

"My uncle has a sweet setup. You can have your VR on one side of the house and your spectacular view of the real ocean on the other side."

"I cannot pass on an ocean view. I will see whether it measures up to my view back home."

"It's always a competition with you," I chided.

"There is no other way, *Tovarishch*."

❧

When I got back to Nags Head, Tsula pulled me into her investigation. It was only days after I met the old hunter, whose grandson was probably the shooter, though we couldn't prove it, when Mick called me to say he was coming for a visit. I was hopeful his coming would be a nice distraction for Tsula from her developing obsession.

Tsula seemed happy. "Hey, Mick, it's good to see you," she said when we picked her up at Mrs. Moore's.

Mick had just gotten in an hour or so before, and we were meeting up with Tsula and then grabbing supper at the seafood restaurant which had become our favorite place. Mick stepped closer and hugged her, holding her a little longer than I expected, but I discarded it as a Russian thing.

As we drove to the restaurant, Tsula was in the passenger seat, and Mick sat in the back behind me, so I really couldn't see his face. Since I rarely talk when I drive, Tsula and Mick carried on a conversation, natural when two biology majors get together. He asked a lot of questions about her work at the Refuge, and Tsula delighted in telling him about the red wolves.

When we got to the restaurant, Mick curiously asked for a table, but the hostess said they only had booths available. She led the way, and there was one awkward moment. Tsula sat down first and slid to the wall. Mick was ahead of me to the side, and he looked back at me, his face obscured in the dark, the bright booth lamp behind him. Since he waited, I took that as the sign to step forward and sit next to Tsula. Mick finally sat across from us, and I noted a slight frown on his face.

"Everything okay, Mick?" I asked.

"Sure. It is just my leg is little stiff after the drive. I pulled something last week when I was out running, and it is taking me time to shake it."

I enjoyed the conversation that evening. I was glad to have someone to distract us from the frequent discussion of finding the culprit behind the wolf shooting. Although Tsula mentioned it to Mick, she didn't spend more than a few minutes describing how much it was haunting her thoughts.

Mick spoke about his work with some zoologists back in Russia and of the black market in tiger parts, things he'd told me previously, but when Tsula asked him about his childhood, I noticed some subtle differences.

"My father died in a logging accident when I was eleven," Mick related, his voice suggesting a deeper sadness than he'd ever shown around me.

"I'm so sorry," Tsula consoled.

"It was a deep burden for my mother. She had to find a job and sent me and my brothers to stay with her sister when she couldn't watch us. I didn't particularly like my uncle. He didn't know what to do with us. Since we'd lost our dad, he treated us differently, avoiding us as if we were diseased. But one of my dad's friends watched out for me, especially when my mom had her breakdown." For the first time, I saw vulnerability in Mick.

"Is your mother okay?" Tsula asked.

"She had a mental breakdown and went into a state institution. I couldn't care for her. She didn't last long there."

"That must have been rough on you."

We were silent for several minutes.

"You haven't told me about your dad's friend before," I finally interjected. "What'd he do?"

When Mick saw me looking, he straightened up before

continuing, "He worked for the government, investigating and exposing those who smuggled tiger parts to other countries, especially China."

"So is he the one who inspired you to study tigers?" I said with a mixture of seriousness and playfulness.

"Don?" Tsula sounded surprised.

There was a flicker of another frown across Mick's face. "No, I read *Jungle Book* when I was eight and wanted to meet Shere Khan," he said, looking at me with a smirk.

I knew he was alluding to an earlier conversation I had with him, twisting my words. I was the one who'd read Kipling's story as a boy and was curious about the tiger. Acknowledging the point, I grinned back, deciding to be more on my guard.

I think all three of us enjoyed the evening. When it came time for us to drop Tsula off back at Mrs. Moore's, Mick stayed in the car as I walked Tsula to her door. I thought it a little strange, and it made things a little awkward. Because I felt his eyes on us, and I think Tsula did too, we didn't kiss each other goodnight as we had begun to do. After telling me she hoped I enjoyed Mick's visit, we exchanged quick goodnights.

Walking back to the car, I wondered what I'd find inside, but Mick seemed his old self again. He turned his attention back to our work together, and he asked how the simulation was coming, so on the drive to the beach house, I told him a little bit more about my recent programming.

Back at the house, he showed some more interest.

"Have you shown Tsula yet?" he asked.

"No, not yet. I'm not sure whether she'll like it."

"Why?"

"She doesn't have much interest in computers."

"Could I see what you've got?"

Swearing him to secrecy, I started the simulation. When he had played with it awhile, he asked jokingly, "Where are the tigers?"

"Is that all you can say?"

"The wolves aren't bad. Kind of scrawny like you Americans."

"We can't all be robust like you Russians."

After some more banter and a few hours of gaming, we turned in. The next morning Mick went over to the Refuge. Tsula had arranged with the rangers a private outing for Mick; she said it wasn't difficult once the rangers learned about Mick's studies. One ranger, in particular, was very curious to talk with Mick about the state of tigers in Siberia. Since I'd received an email from Lauren the night before—I cursed the timing of it—saying our deadline had been bumped up, I stayed at the beach house to complete some final programming. I caught up with them in Manteo for a late lunch; they had gotten some sandwiches for us and found a shady spot for a picnic.

When I drove up and saw them sitting in conversation, a flight of my imagination made my pulse jump and my face burn. What were they discussing? Would she ask him questions about me? What would he tell her?

When I neared and heard them discussing the anatomical differences between red wolves and gray wolves, I breathed out, feeling my face cool.

Tsula turned first and smiled at me.

Mick looked up. "Here he is."

"So how'd it go this morning?"

"Mick wowed my bosses. I think they'd like to lasso him and keep him on their staff."

"What can I say?" Mick asked, raising his eyebrows in a grin.

"We missed you," Tsula said. "Mick told me you had to do some last-minute programming work." She paused as if she'd asked me a question.

"Yeah. Trying to get some work to Dr. Stanley before he goes on vacation."

"Glad you could join us for lunch," Mick said with his

characteristic grin.

"Me too."

We settled into some casual conversation while eating our sandwiches.

The rest of his visit went smoothly, and that afternoon he headed back. He'd pulled us out of the doldrums of the fruitless search for the wolf shooter, and for that I was grateful.

❧

I didn't know Mick's visit would have lasting repercussions, though, until the night I asked Tsula to marry me.

"When were you going to tell me about Tsunami Games?"

Since I was not prepared for this question, I stumbled, "What?" The hand holding the ring drifted to my side.

"That you worked for them."

She knew. That thought broke the dam of secrecy and several other thoughts flooded forward. I latched onto one quickly. Was she playing with me? "How long have you known?"

"That's not the point." She took a step back, looked out at the ocean, then back at me. Her eyes narrowed. "I don't demand to know everything, but isn't this important enough for you to tell me?"

"I knew you'd disapprove," I defended.

"Were you ever going to tell me?"

"I didn't want an argument."

"So you thought it was better keeping a secret from me?" she asked.

"It just sort of happened."

She crossed her arms and turned from me, offering no reply.

"Did Mick tell you?" I thought back to the morning they had shared without me.

"Why are you bringing him into this? The problem is you didn't tell me."

"Did Mick tell you?" I repeated.

"You were the one who had to go back for meetings."

"So he did."

"I figured it out myself."

"From something he said?" I pursued.

"I promised not to say anything."

Realizing she wasn't going to tell me what Mick had said, I shot back, "What's the big deal if I do work for Tsunami? It'd be a great job."

"You know that company contributes to the widespread misrepresentation of wolves."

"Lighten up, Tsula. They're only video games. People don't take them seriously."

"And to think, I defended you against my dad!"

"What?"

"He said you were soft and selfish."

"Soft? Selfish? What are you talking about?"

She looked away and did not answer.

"I thought your dad liked me." I couldn't resist the feeling I'd been betrayed.

"I think he likes what you could become."

"What does that mean? I'm not soft. I exercise."

"He means you've spent your life indoors. You need to experience all that is wild."

"What have I been doing all summer?"

"You're making progress."

"Progress. So this is what you think too? That I'm selfish?"

"You tell me."

I stewed quietly in my indignation, looking for the right words. She waited with arms crossed.

"So your love comes with strings attached?"

"Love hopes for the best. Papa warned me people seldom change, but I defended you."

"I don't want to hear it. I am who I am. I make my own choices."

"I wouldn't have it any other way."

"That's not what this sounds like. You're telling me what to do," I responded.

"Why did you keep it a secret from me?"

"Because I knew you wouldn't approve."

"You assumed I wouldn't."

"Well, you don't!"

"I feel you're meant for greater things." She watched me closely in the dark.

"Greater things? Really? Do people talk like that? You sound like my parents. What greater things?"

"Don, I think you know."

"Helping others? That's what mother would tell me."

"That could be part of it."

"But wouldn't I be offering the best to them—a ticket away from this reality?" I asked.

"That's the problem, isolating you from the world around you."

"We've been here before. You didn't learn anything in my class."

"Learning doesn't demand agreement."

"It seems we've reached an impasse." My tone was colder than I intended.

She dropped her arms, studying me again. I felt the fire in her eyes. "Do you remember what you said for our video?"

"Your video," I corrected.

Shock momentarily replaced anger in her face. Within seconds she was stomping back up the beach toward the dunes.

"Tsula, wait!" I said, jumping after her, my fist clamping around the ring, the box snapping shut inside my hand.

At first she ignored me, and I tried to pick up my pace, feet slipping in the sand, but as she reached the dune, she turned to face me, looking down, dark clouds in the sky behind her.

"I can't trust you anymore. If you kept this from me, I don't know what else you haven't told me."

"I'm sorry." I looked her in the eyes. "I love you."

"Do you?" she asked, turning again, clearing the dunes, headed back to the car.

Registering she was at my mercy to get her back to Mrs. Moore's, she commanded, her voice cold, "Take me home."

"Tsula."

"Now."

I opened the car door for her and then got in on the other side. The silence in the car weighed heavy on my shoulders as we drove down the road. I wanted to break it, to see the lively, beautiful Tsula again, but I could think of no words to bring reconciliation. We'd argued before, but I knew this time the situation was different. I'd violated her trust. I wondered if I'd ever earn it back.

And then I thought of Mick. What had he said? Tsula said she'd figured it out. What had he let slip? And then the seed of another idea grew. Was it an accident? Or had he known just what to say to seduce her imagination? I'd been careful. Mick had to be the source of this problem.

Tsula didn't say anything the entire drive back. When I pulled the car into Mrs. Moore's driveway and turned off the ignition, Tsula quickly hopped out, but before closing her door, she glanced back into the car, not really at me, and said, "I don't think I can do this anymore."

When I realized what she had said, I rushed to open my door, and by the time I got out, she was already at the house.

"Tsula?"

She disappeared inside, the door quickly closing behind her.

I pulled out my phone and sent her a text. *I'm sorry. I should have told you about Tsunami, but I feel you should have trusted me to make the best of it. I could change the industry from within.* When she didn't respond, I got back into my car and drove back to the beach house, my vision blurring until I wiped my eyes with the side of my hand. All the way back, I rehearsed the conversation and wondered if I could have handled things differently. Some part of me knew this had been coming. I had been way too lucky to have Tsula's devotion.

When I got back to the beach house, I checked my messages on my phone to see if there was anything from Tsula. There was nothing from her, but a familiar name stood out, and I had to push aside the evening's drama. It was an email from Trevor, my friend at Tsunami. The text was short, just one question: "Have you seen this?" And then there was a link that seemed strangely familiar. When I clicked on it, I found the video Tsula and I had uploaded to the Internet months before. Another secret was out.

10

RIVALS

IN THE DARKNESS KAN COULD BARELY SEE DANUWA, BUT the scent in the air, the timbre of the growl, and the gait of the approaching shadow left no doubt which wolf this was. Danuwa's scent had always been strong, yet now it seemed Danuwa had done something to increase the power of that smell. Had he dug up some rotting remains to roll around in them? Kan felt the sting of the stench in his nose. Danuwa was announcing his arrival. The loud growl confirmed the open challenge; the masked wolf did not approach in silence. The shadow strode confidently forward, shoulders hunched, tail defiantly elevated.

Kan studied the shadow until he could just make out Danuwa's crooked teeth, exposed in an aggressive grimace. The dim image lacked details, but the shape suggested another, sharper image in Kan's memory, the first time Danuwa hunted with the pack. Danuwa's muzzle dripped blood as the masked wolf lifted his head from the opened carcass of the pack's fresh kill. Kan noted a fire in Danuwa's eyes that day. Earlier Kan had witnessed Danuwa's fierce charge toward the elk's throat. At the time Yona, in his brief time as beta, was assisting Doda in supervising the younger males in the hunt—Unalii, Danuwa, and Askai—as Etsi and her females drove a panicked elk into the pack's trap. Although Doda and the other males grouped in a formation to take down their prey, Danuwa broke rank and leaped past Yona, taking the place of privilege in the kill, grabbing the elk below the jawline, his jaw clamping down, choking the life out of the larger animal. Doda and Unalii knocked the animal off its feet, and Kan and Askai joined in the pinning as Danuwa ripped away at the throat. Kan felt killing was a necessity, but he saw something different in Danuwa's eyes when the masked wolf finally came up for breath from feasting on the kill.

Kan saw those eyes focused on him now, saw the same flame, the same charge. Danuwa thrilled at picking the moment of weakness. A sick feeling ran through Kan, and he wondered if Danuwa would take this rivalry to the point of death. He recalled Danuwa's weight from the night before, and the darkness that had come so close to claiming him. But Lana had been there to knock that weight off.

Where was she? Had she escaped the tiger? What challenges had she faced? He could not count on her now; he would have to brave this attack on his own even though it was her ambition that had put him in this position. He and Danuwa had ignored each other before, but this recent attention came because of the passing of Doda, the breaking of the pack's leadership. Danuwa wanted to be the new alpha, and if Kan had not returned to the pack, the masked wolf would have assumed dominance largely unopposed. However, Kan had returned and discovered Lana's compulsion to take on the responsibilities of leadership. She believed the pack needed her. In swearing Kan into the companion role as well, she had made him Danuwa's rival.

Although Kan did not want this conflict, he could not locate an escape. For Lana's sake and for his own survival, he had to make a stand, but Danuwa would make it a costly one.

When he felt warmth from the other direction, Kan shifted his stance so that he could also keep Sikwa's shadow in view. A few heartbeats later, Sikwa grew close enough for Kan to identify him clearly in the dark. The large, round grey wolf approached casually, yet steadily. He was always present for his share. Now Sikwa had latched onto Danuwa's aggression to grab his own position of power. Earlier that evening Sikwa had abandoned his packmates; he had been first to run from the tiger. Evidently the coward had run immediately to Danuwa on his return to give his report. Kan's two rivals now were doing an excellent job keeping his attention divided; he could not predict who would charge first.

Sasa was whining beside him. Even as her whine increased in volume, transitioning into a plaintive howl, Kan decided it best to keep his eyes on the approaching males. Lifting his head in a howl would add to the chances Unalii and the others would hear, even though they had to be long committed to their search for the missing she-wolves, but it would also leave his neck exposed for a quick attack. Kan also did not know if he wanted Unalii, Yona, and Noya to turn back. Lana needed them more. She faced a tiger. He and Sasa alone would have to fend off the attentions of Danuwa and Sikwa.

At least he had help, he thought as he felt Sasa brush up against him. He heard her shifting paws in the snow next to his. She had witnessed the first fight he had with Danuwa, and she knew Danuwa's ambitions personally. Kan wondered how much she had endured under the paws and teeth of her brother. Would this moment be another weight to bear, or would it be a time of revenge, her chance to release the pent-up rage of years?

Danuwa paused several leaps away. Then he stretched his front paws forward, lowering his head, while keeping his tail high in the air. Danuwa's eyes were always locked on his. Kan had seen such a bow made by other wolves while they were playing. Sometimes the wolf would tuck its snout between its paws in anticipation, waiting for another to respond to the invitation to give chase. If there was any play in Danuwa's bow, Kan thought, it was one of twisted irony. Those who are about to kill you salute you.

The distraction succeeded, for Sikwa hit Kan hard on his right side, spinning him sideways in the snow, causing him to trip over Sasa, who rolled under him. He hit the ground hard on the other side of her. He felt, rather than saw, Danuwa's jump. Kan had to get to his feet before his rival reached him.

He stood and lifted his head in time to see Sasa had locked her teeth on Sikwa's chest, inches from his throat, holding him back. Kan also had time to jump slightly before receiving Danuwa's charge. Jumping was a mistake, for he felt his rear leg buckle as Danuwa pushed him up. Panic surged in him as he felt himself going backwards. He hit the snow on his back, and Danuwa landed on top of him, teeth gnashing toward his exposed throat.

Kan thrashed wildly with his front paws to keep Danuwa from hitting any soft spots. He raked the claws of his right paw across Danuwa's nose and up past his eye. He missed the eye, but tore a gash in the middle of the mask. The wound did not stop Danuwa, but only enraged him, multiplying his savage energy even as blood flowed down into his eye.

When Kan felt his forelegs giving way to Danuwa's onslaught, he twisted his head swiftly to his left, so that the moment Danuwa's lunge succeeded, the masked wolf got a mouthful of snow. A sharp sting in his cheek told Kan that Danuwa had not missed entirely; a tooth had torn into Kan's upper neck. Still largely pinned by Danuwa's weight, Kan bit hard on his opponent's forepaw while twisting in the wet snow, turning the back of his head toward Danuwa's snapping teeth. He felt the biting pressure on the back of his skull as he managed to break free from Danuwa's hold.

He was relieved to have his belly facing down again, but relief only lasted for a second before a sharp pain shot up from his leg. Danuwa's teeth were locked into Kan's wounded leg. Kan howled, then tried to twist back and bite at Danuwa, but the masked wolf shifted, pulling his leg each time. Under the knifing pressure, Kan panicked again.

Then mercifully the pressure ceased, leaving only the sharp sting. He turned to see Sasa was jumping and biting, having drawn Danuwa away. How was that possible? Where was Sikwa? Kan then saw in the distance another wolf was wrestling with Sikwa. The scent in the air quickly told Kan it was Askai. Good ol' Askai. Come to their rescue.

But Kan did not have time to spare. He had to help Sasa. While he struggled forward on three legs, another scent caused him to turn, and he saw another wolf, a small one, bounding back and forth in a line several jumps away. It was Oni. Did Danuwa have reinforcements too?

Something was strange, though. Why was Oni pacing?

Sasa's yelp brought Kan back to Danuwa. The masked wolf had knocked his sister onto her side and was holding her down, biting viciously around her head. At the smell of blood, Kan struggled forward and snapped at Danuwa, who quickly returned the bites, yet refused to let Sasa go. Kan pressed harder; he had to get Danuwa away from his sister. Lifting his bad leg and pushing off with the others, Kan jumped into Danuwa and thrilled as Danuwa finally gave some ground, falling back. Kan, though, found himself tripping over the unmoving Sasa. He scrambled, realizing he had lost the initiative, just as Danuwa came lunging back. Danuwa came in close quickly, and Kan felt his rival's weight bearing down on his neck as he felt the teeth jabbing into his shoulder. Kan knew this was the attack that would expose his weak leg. Danuwa's scent flooded Kan's breath, nauseating him.

Kan felt himself falling as his leg gave way; he swam in darkness until he struck something hard, cold, and wet. In the next second, he could not breathe; a great clamp pressed down on his neck. He no longer could see anything. A terrible silence held him, and he felt the blood rushing in his head. Danuwa had him in a stranglehold; he would not last long. Trying to twist himself free, Kan felt a searing pain in his neck as Danuwa's jaw held. Pressure built in his lungs. He could not think of anything else. He did not want to die this way.

In the darkness of his mind, Kan had a vision of Danuwa as a spirit dog running through the woods, a shadow filled with rage, twice as large as any normal wolf. Kan floated above him and witnessed a path of destruction. Wherever Danuwa's spirit ran, the plants withered, and whenever he encountered another wolf, the packmate fell lifeless to the ground. Danuwa's restless raid on the forest brought only death. Kan despaired as he saw his friends fall. Noya and Sasa. Yona and even Unalii. And then Kan watched in horror as Danuwa's spirit locked onto Lana. The white wolf ran swiftly and gracefully away, but every few leaps Danuwa's spirit gained on her....

A solid jolt above pulled at Kan's neck, and the vision vanished. There was intense pain and then finally release.

Kan sucked in air, and it came rushing back into him, cold and fresh as the morning dew. He breathed out and in again in a loud rasp. Then again. Thought returned. He opened his eyes. Where was Danuwa? His eyes focused on the shadows wrestling before him. Other scents touched his nose, and realization came. Oni and Danuwa were fighting.

Kan pushed himself up, the spinning in his head slowing. He stumbled and righted himself, the world straightening.

Danuwa had Oni pinned. How could Oni, the littlest of the pack, the omega, have attacked Danuwa? Did he not always fall in line behind his brother Sikwa? Kan knew Oni could not last long against Danuwa. He had to make a decision.

He looked around and saw Askai and Sikwa, evenly matched, still grappling with each other several leaps away. Kan turned and saw Sasa was still lying where she had fallen. Not a good sign. He wished he could check on her, but the sounds of Oni's struggle with Danuwa pulled him back. He owed his life to Oni; he had to answer Danuwa's challenge.

Still breathing heavily, Kan braced his shoulders, lowered his ears, and moved toward the fight in front of him. Danuwa's head swung up with a deep guttural growl. Oni nipped up at him, but Danuwa kept his eyes on Kan. No sneak attack this time. Kan studied the situation. In his weakened state, he did not think charging in was a great idea, but the times Danuwa charged, particularly that last one, Kan had failed miserably. How am I going to defeat him? How am I going to survive?

A yowl sounded. Kan recognized the voice as Sikwa's and saw the momentary shift in Danuwa's eyes. Kan immediately jumped into his rival, jaws open, aiming for Danuwa's right shoulder since Oni was under and to the left. The moment before Kan's muzzle landed, Danuwa pulled his head back, ready to receive Kan's attack. Kan felt Danuwa's teeth scraping above his left eye as his own jaws snapped close to Danuwa's neck. Kan tried to keep his own face and throat away from Danuwa's bites while he tried to push the masked wolf back off Oni.

Suddenly Danuwa's head whipped down, and Kan heard a muffled yipe. He did not wait to find out how Oni had distracted Danuwa, but lunged forward to sink his teeth into the exposed side of Danuwa's neck. When his jaws locked, Kan realized he had a secure hold. Danuwa twisted violently beside him, but Kan knew he could not let Danuwa break his grip. Oni had sacrificed to give him this one advantage. If they were going to defeat Danuwa, now was the moment. Danuwa bucked and kicked, Kan feeling each jolt thunder through his head and down his back. As Danuwa slowed, Kan reasoned from his rival's limited movement that Oni must have a hold on him from below.

Kan again heard the ominous crunching snow of Danuwa's initial attack, remembered the sensation of strangling under Danuwa's hold, and felt the horror of the Danuwa's spirit chasing Lana through the woods. Kan could end this struggle here; he held in his jaws the power over his rival's life. As he felt Danuwa's pulse against his tongue, though, something else stirred in Kan. He remembered his own panic, his own grief at the possibility of going out this way. Danuwa was a packmate, and Kan did not want to kill him. The moment Kan began to relax his hold, Danuwa immediately pulled free, bit down at Oni, and jumped away.

Breathing heavily, Danuwa paused several leaps away to turn and glare back. Kan could feel the heat of Danuwa's fury and tensed in preparation for another attack. At that moment Kan regretted having let Danuwa go, for now his rival was going to kill him.

Danuwa, however, did not charge. He stood his ground, dark gash across his face. After a quick flick of the eyes, he circled in place twice before trotting back into the woods, disappearing into the darkness.

Kan felt Askai licking him. So Danuwa saw reinforcements and reconsidered. Kan barely believed the fight was over. His muscles were still tense. As he returned his friend's affection, Kan realized he would not have survived without Askai's help.

Kan then turned his attention to Oni. The smaller wolf was on his feet again, but he smelled of blood. Skipping forward, Kan licked Oni all over the muzzle. A gash ran across Oni's face, across one of his eyes. Kan felt the swelling, tasted wolf blood, and knew the sacrifice Oni had made. He would be dead, but for Oni. How had the younger wolf changed? What prompted him to risk his own life to protect Kan? Had those moments of play earlier in the day meant so much? Kan searched for some way to honor Oni's pledge of loyalty.

But then Kan thought of Sasa and quickly turned back to find her still on her side, eyes closed, breathing heavily, a nasty gash in her chest. Whimpering concern, Askai tended the wound. Kan leaned in to lick Sasa's muzzle, knowing she was wounded because of him too. Sikwa and Danuwa were free, but she was there lying in pain. It hurt to see her suffering—here was a wolf who rarely caused anyone trouble. Kan hated the violence that brought Oni and Sasa down. He would do all he could to help them recover.

Looking down at Sasa, hearing her wheeze in pain, Kan doubted his choice to let Danuwa go. Was Sasa going to die? She had already shouldered a life of being partially lame because of Danuwa, and now he had spilled her blood. Danuwa's attack was vicious.

Yet was Sasa not lying there, Kan thought, because of him? Why should he be alpha? He should just give the post to Danuwa and be done with it. He could not sacrifice Sasa to hold onto leadership of the pack. And Oni was suffering too. He may have lost an eye in this cause. Askai too surely had wounds. They had only just survived. Danuwa came so close to winning, so close to killing Kan. Danuwa knew the moment to attack when Kan's allies were away. Sikwa had told him about the tiger, and Danuwa knew Kan would be distracted and fatigued from the running and the stress of it all. Why did he let Danuwa go? Danuwa would have killed him, but Kan let the masked wolf live.

Kan remembered the hold he had on Danuwa's neck; he remembered the struggling. If he had just held on longer, tightening his grip, he might have been able to kill Danuwa. Kan had participated in pack hunts before, and he had shared in the killing of elk and deer, felt the last of life pass out, breathing stop, eyes going blank. The pack needed to eat; they had to take life for food. Yet the killing of another wolf was something entirely different. While he knew it was possible, Kan had never seen one wolf take the life of another. Danuwa seemed willing to cross that line. Kan felt the soreness in his own neck where Danuwa's teeth had been. Had he made a mistake? Would Danuwa keep challenging him? Would Danuwa kill him next time?

As Kan leaned down and rubbed his muzzle against Sasa's, he asked for her life to be spared and then vowed no other wolf would be hurt because of Danuwa's bid for dominance. Kan had to do something, but how could he outmaneuver the masked wolf?

❧

Even though Unalii's howl gave Kan the first signal of their return, it was Yona who first appeared with Noya and Wesa. All three wolves were breathing quickly, tails wagging.

Kan jumped to his feet. He, Askai, and Oni had huddled around Sasa while they had rested. Night had lengthened, and morning was approaching.

Noya ran over to him, licking him, but her tail dropped as she brushed past him to join Sasa. Whimpering, Noya licked her sister vigorously around the ears. She paused and sniffed the wound at Sasa's chest, then fell to the ground next to her, rubbing her head against her sister's. Kan looked away.

Quietly approaching and greeting Wesa and Yona, glad to see them, Kan soon whined a question—where were the others? Yona looked behind him back into the woods.

A howl sounded close by; it was Unalii's. Kan swung his head up to listen. The tone was hopeful. After limping forward down the hill toward the call, he spotted Unalii first. As he exchanged quick greetings with his old friend, he caught sight of Koga and then Lana. Tension gave way to relief, and Kan jumped toward Lana, briefly noting Koga pulling back awkwardly. He did not know how to greet Koga either.

Instead, all his attention turned to Lana. They collided, licking, nipping, and yowling. Joy surged through him, seeing her again, knowing his mate was safe.

But there was something else. She was still agitated; she refused to relax.

I didn't want to leave you.

She must have smelled Danuwa's scent on him, for instead of responding, she pursued her own thought. *Danuwa? Did he attack you again?*

We held him off. Sasa and me, and then Askai and Oni joined in.

Are you hurt? Her voice sounded tight with concern.

I'll heal. The one to worry about is Sasa. Danuwa ripped into her pretty badly. She's been unconscious for hours.

Show me.

Kan watched her pull her shoulders back. She needed to rest, but he knew she would not until she had checked on Sasa, so he led her back to the others.

The pack was standing in a circle around Sasa and Noya. Kan followed as Lana pushed her way forward. When she reached Sasa, she crouched low to the ground next to her, then slowly licked her along the muzzle. Finally she placed her forehead against Sasa's, remaining perfectly still for several heartbeats. When she lifted her head, Lana stretched to lick Noya too, who quietly leaned into her alpha's attentions.

Lana stood, lifted her head, and howled softly. Unalii, Wesa, and Yona soon joined, each voice adding depth to the sonorous sound. Kan started a howl, but it broke. He was just too tired to keep it going. Instead he closed his eyes and listened to the pain of the pack. One of their own was suffering, and too many of their pack had fallen recently. Doda. Etsi. Taline. Were they to lose Sasa too? They did not want to let her go. There was resistance in the howl. They would stand together; they would survive. They called to Sasa to return to them.

Kan realized Lana was brushing up against him again, and he opened his eyes. While the others continued their song, he slipped quietly to the side with his mate.

Will you finally tell me what happened to you? he asked.

I'm afraid it's not good news.

I didn't want to leave you. I didn't know which way you would go.

You didn't have any choice, she consoled. *We were all running for our lives. We knew we had to get away from that tiger after it took down Taline too.* She shuddered slightly. *I hate we lost her.*

I can't believe it's taken three of us. I don't understand.

I've got something else that doesn't make any sense. She looked nervous. *When we were running from the tiger you saw, I decided to turn to the right and circle around it to catch up with you and Yona. Since we were on the opposite side of where we needed to be, I knew we had to move quickly because the tiger could try to cut us off if it discovered what we were doing. Not long after we started in this direction, though, Koga tackled me. I nipped at her as I stood, but I discovered she wasn't trying to hurt me. She stood in front of me and kept barring my progress forward whenever I tried to get around her. Finally I stopped and studied the path ahead, and that's when it hit me.*

What?

The tiger scent was strong again. Since we were running away, the smell should have been getting weaker, but it wasn't. Koga pushed Wesa down, and the three of us crouched closely together under the low branches of a spruce. The wind blew against us, so we smelled the second tiger before we saw it.

Second tiger?

Yes. I caught sight of it weaving through the trees in the woods. It has more white on it and golden bands running down its front legs. This one was a male and is larger than the female who killed Taline. We held our breaths as it passed several paces in front of us. We thought we were safe, but it lifted its head, breathed in deeply, and turned to look in our direction. And then the strangest thing happened. I swear it said something.

What?

I smell you. I know you're there. She paused, then asked, *How is that possible?*

He frowned. *Are you certain you heard those words?*

Lana's face tightened. *I know what I heard.*

I don't know what's going on. What happened, though? How'd you get away?

I was measuring our options when Koga dashed out of our hiding place. She was halfway to the tiger before I could react. Wesa and I jumped out. Before we could join her, Koga turned around, barked at us, and changed direction, running now well in front of the tiger. Wesa caught on faster than I did and started running back the way we had come. I didn't like leaving Koga, but if she was sacrificing for us, I knew we had to take the opportunity to get away.

But Koga's here. And as Kan spoke those words, he came to realize the black female, seated on the side of their circle closest to where they had discovered the tigers, was watching him. She did not look away, but merely lowered her head, resting it on the ground.

Kan heard Lana's voice and turned back to her. *I thought we'd lost her too, but she found us later. I'm so grateful she was with us. Otherwise, we could have easily run right into that male tiger.*

I'm glad too. He said, checking on Koga in the corner of his eye. She was still watching them. Kan felt both relief and irritation at the same time.

Circling the other way around the female tiger seemed risky to me, but we didn't have much choice. We did swing a little wider out away from the spot where we saw her, but at one point Wesa made a move like she was going to go back and face the tiger again. Taline was her sister, and I know it must have been tough for her to abandon her. It was my turn to distract her and keep her running.

Yona did the same for me. I was going to turn back to search for you.

She nudged her muzzle against his. *I'm just glad we survived.*

Kan swallowed his questions. He wanted to find out more about the tigers, about Lana's journey, and about Koga. He appreciated the black wolf's risky move, but something did not seem right. Koga's eyes were too observant. Since she had joined the pack when he was away, she was still a stranger to him. Where had she come from? Why had she joined this pack? What drew her to Lana? And why was she watching them so closely?

He instead stated the obvious. *Me too. We are going to have run from these tigers. They are too great a threat.* His words slurred as he relaxed under the warmth of her tongue. It had been such a long night, but now she was safe. They were back, and he could rest.

We can talk about that later, she said as if she were reading his mind.

He considered her words. *We can talk later.* So much had happened. They had marched out in hopes of finding Etsi, and they had found tigers instead. The separation from Lana and the fight with Danuwa had distracted him, but Lana's story of the second tiger unlocked a memory of that moment when the female tiger surprised them, the wolves still reeling from the discovery of Etsi's torn body. The tiger swung her head in his and Yona's direction and uttered a challenge. Kan heard it clearly, but then Wesa's attack opened the chance to run, initiating a chain of events leading finally to this exhausting point.

Kan looked at his mate. She needed rest; she needed him to

be her alpha. He could not tell her the female tiger had spoken to him. He could not repeat to Lana the haunting words he had heard. *We are going to kill you all.* He could not tell her what he suspected. He would shoulder this burden alone, for there were things she did not need to know.

11
MOUNTAIN FUNERAL

UNCLE JACK STARED ME DOWN. WE WERE SITTING ON his back deck looking out over the ocean in the late afternoon, the intensity of the sun just drifting away. Since he had come in the evening before, I had been trying to put on a good face, enjoying diving into a new mission with him in the Congo in *Cobalt Blue*, but I couldn't keep up the front forever, particularly under his experienced gaze.

"Woman trouble, eh, mate?"

"That obvious?" I asked, hazarding a glance at him.

"Are you forgetting this is Uncle Jack?"

"No."

"You haven't mentioned her once since I got in, and you haven't checked your phone either. I knew something was up, and you just confirmed it."

"You should have been a lawyer."

"I once considered it for a hot second, but joined the Navy

instead." He stretched his legs out in front and placed his hands up behind his head. "So tell me what happened."

I leaned forward, rubbing my hands together, studying the grain of the deck boards at my feet. "You know she doesn't like video games."

"Yeah, I wondered about that, but she's not the first woman I've met who doesn't. That's not a deal-breaker if she doesn't try to keep you from them."

"Well, she really doesn't like games that have werewolves in them. She says they contribute to a widespread misunderstanding about wolves, that they transform them into the beasts of our nightmares."

"So she loves *Transylvania Nights* then."

"I didn't tell her about my job at Tsunami Games, and she feels like I was lying to her."

"Relationships are built on trust."

"So why'd you never marry?"

"I came close once, but when I was in Australia, she married another man."

"Ouch."

"Long-distance relationships are nigh impossible."

"How'd you deal with that?"

"It wasn't easy, but there are other fish in the sea. I know that's a cliché, but I mean it in a naval way." He winked.

"A girl in every port. That's not my style."

"You're at the beach, mate." Uncle Jack nodded toward the ocean, and I looked down.

A young woman in a sports bikini, black with highlights in neon green, was running the edge of the surf with a skimboard, her arms extended, catching the angled sunlight. She skillfully guided the board into the water and rode a wave back, exiting with a cute hop onto the sand.

Uncle Jack grinned at me. "I'm just sayin'."

"I don't know anything about her."

"Ah, but you do. Most of the attractive young ladies have left by this time, finished with their sunbathing, so this one must either be a local or a fanatic about water sports. You can clearly see she is graceful and determined. Even if she is a natural, you don't get that good without some practice."

"So what am I supposed to do, just walk up to her? She'll think I'm a creeper."

"Not if you offer a genuine smile and compliment her."

Looking down at my feet, I admitted, "I tried to do something like this yesterday. I was looking for girls who were reading, thought that might give me something to talk about, but so many had books with shirtless muscle men. I did find one with a legal thriller, but when I made eye contact with her, she turned her back to me, and a second later her boyfriend joined her."

"So she wasn't the one. You shrug it off and look for the next. It only takes one to smile back."

When I looked up again, the bikini-clad wave-skimmer was gone. I leaned forward to discover she was already a speck retreating down the beach. "I guess I'll just resign myself to being single the rest of my life."

"So you're just gonna mope? Well, I know what you need then. Even though I've enjoyed seeing you, it's time for you to head home. Your mother won't ever believe I said it, but few things break a mope faster than a trip home."

Uncle Jack knew me well, and my mother had been pushing for me to stay all summer. So those last weeks before school resumed, I did spend in Atlanta, and my father and I did get our games of tennis in. It did him and me both good.

Of course, I still had work to do for Tsunami—it turned out my place there was not in jeopardy, for Justin had only sent me the link to the video as a curiosity. When I called him to test the water, he said, "Can you believe these kids?" I grinned and shrugged off the tightness in the chest I had experienced dialing his number. Lauren continued, to my relief, to be a great supervisor, allowing me to complete my work from Atlanta.

The visit home was a good time away, but when the semester started back in August, it was difficult walking around campus without Tsula. Those first weeks back, I logged a number of hours on the couch watching action movies with the surround sound turned way up, or in my chair in my bedroom, staring out the window at the tops of evergreen trees at the perimeter of the apartment complex. Mick accused me of moping and tried a few times to get me interested in a new war game he had gotten to distract us from our studies. When deadlines started to appear at Tsunami for the anniversary edition of *Transylvania Nights*, and at school for my doctoral project, I finally woke up a little and poured myself into my work.

Although Tsula refused to answer the texts or the one or two calls I made, I did find some hope in the fact she did not delete me from her social media accounts. She was not the most faithful in keeping these accounts up-to-date, and most of her posts were about wolves or the plight of endangered species, but occasionally I might learn something about her semester. I did see some comments from the activist friends I had met, and I wondered if they had made other videos with Tsula.

It was in early December when I saw a post that made me pause. At first it didn't make sense, and then when it did, a chill ran through me. *My mother died today. I'm going to miss her.*

Tsula's mother wasn't that old. What had happened? I thought about Tsula in pain, and immediately wanted to find her. I checked the date of the post and discovered a day had passed since she had written it. So she would already be back in Cherokee. My mind flew through different possibilities. How could I see her? I would have to go. It would not be trouble to rearrange my week's commitments. What did I need to pack? I grabbed a black tie and jacket and some other things. When I finished packing, I pulled out my phone, checked the path to

Cherokee, and then headed out the door with my luggage. Since Mick was not there, I did not have to explain myself.

Within moments I was in my car, driving west along Interstate 40, and it was then, when I was alone with myself, that doubts rained on me. I'd be driving over four hours, headed into a place I didn't know. I'd visited once when I was a boy, but only had vague images of the tourist side of Cherokee—a distinction I'd learned from Tsula—nothing that would help me now. It was late afternoon, and I would be coming in after dark. Where would I stay? Surely there'd be a hotel I could afford. What if Tsula didn't want me there? I didn't want to think about her turning me away, and I didn't want to add to her pain at this time, but something within me told me I had to be there even if she did decide to shut me out.

I'd never met Tsula's mother; the one time we were supposed to meet, something fell through and she didn't show up. I'd only heard brief stories about her.

❧

"Mama and I haven't always gotten along," Tsula said during a lunch we shared back when we were dating. We were sitting across from each other, tucked away in a dark booth in a Mexican restaurant we frequented.

"I'm sorry." I looked down and ran my finger along one of the tiles on the table.

"One day when I was ten, she walked out the door and didn't come back that night to tuck us into bed. She and Papa had been having problems. My sister and I had heard them yelling, but we didn't understand how bad it had gotten."

Something in her voice made me look up.

"She didn't come back the next couple days either," she continued. "Papa tried to comfort us, but every day my sister and I asked about Mama."

"Where'd your mother go?"

"We didn't hear from her for about a week. It was strange

hearing her voice on the phone. We asked where she was and when she was coming home. She said she'd gone to visit her parents in Tennessee, that she'd see us soon, that she loved us. When she cried, I told her not to be sad, but then she was gone again."

"I can't imagine."

"The next months were tough on me and my sister. One day Mama came and got us. Papa had left us in the house to get some groceries. Mama came in like a wildfire, telling us to pack quickly. She scared Inola and me, but we grabbed our dolls, and she threw our clothes in a large bag. Then we jumped into her car and were gone."

"She kidnapped you?"

"It depends on how you look at it. Papa felt that way."

"What happened?"

"Mama took us to an apartment, and there was another woman there with a baby boy, who couldn't walk and cried a lot. We shared the second bedroom with Mama and slept on the floor. She said this was only temporary, that she'd soon take us to Tennessee. We'd been waiting to see her, but now Inola and I kept asking about Papa. I remember one time she told us to shut up and stop asking about him. Today I suspect she'd been drinking, but then all that mattered was I felt like she'd slapped me. I didn't understand what was happening to our family.

"On the second day, Mama left us in the apartment with the stranger. It was Monday, and we should have been in school. We watched TV until there was a knock at the door. We saw the woman come running and stumble; she smelled funny. The knocking came again, and she managed to open the door.

"There was a man in a blue uniform on the other side, asking if a Mrs. Watie lived there. The funny-smelling lady said our mother wasn't there, but when the officer saw us, he asked the woman to let him in. He came over to us and asked us if we were okay. My sister said we were glad we weren't in school. The officer asked us to go with him."

"Really?"

"Inola cried for Mama, but we knew we had to follow him. It's the only time I've been in a police car. He took us to the station, and Papa came to pick us up."

I nodded concern as Tsula continued.

"The next months we didn't see Mama, and Papa had to leave us several times. We do remember he told us not to worry. Inola and I did spend a lot of time with our grandparents. I'm particularly close to Enisi, my grandma. My sister and I didn't understand what was going on then, but when we were older and asked, Papa told us about the court case, how the judge granted him custody since Mama had acted recklessly and kidnapped us and intended to take us out of the state, and more importantly out of Cherokee."

"What happened to your mother?"

"She decided not to move back to Tennessee, but to stay in Cherokee. We were allowed to see her several times a month."

"Did you ever understand what the problem was between your parents?"

"Neither one of them ever went into great detail about it, but I think Mama was upset when Papa decided to give up his job and tried to make money with his woodworking instead."

"What job?"

"One of the stores had him dressing up as an 'Indian' to draw customers."

"Dressing up?"

"The stereotype. Large white headdress. They had him standing in front of a teepee and a stuffed bear on wheels. My dad, though, finally decided he'd had enough. The image wasn't Cherokee, and the shop wasn't selling crafts from here, but cheap stuff made in China."

"Why'd your mother get so upset?"

"The job paid well. The woodworking didn't—at least, not at

first. It took my dad a few years to establish himself as a mask-maker and storyteller. Mama couldn't take being the primary wage earner for the family."

"How'd your dad get custody then?"

"Mama said it was because he cried in front of a woman judge, but I think the fact she left Inola and me with a woman who was using meth was the kicker."

"What's your mom's name?"

"Summer Gordon. She went back to her maiden name."

❧

I found a listing for Summer Gordon in my obituary search. I had pulled over at a gas station outside Winston-Salem and decided it would be best to check if I could find a listing for the funeral. I left my apartment in a hurry, just with the feeling I needed to see Tsula, but now the practical side of me demanded a plan. I breathed a sigh of relief when I saw I had not missed the funeral. The family had planned the service for the next day at two o'clock. I read the brief life summary and discovered Tsula's mother had died from complications resulting from a car wreck.

Getting back on the road, I wondered what had happened. Where was the car wreck? How had it happened? Who else was involved? When did Tsula find out about it? What was this long drive like for her? Was her mother already dead when Tsula started her drive, or was Tsula desperately trying to make it back home in time, her mother fading in the hospital? My mind raced with imagined possibilities.

As I neared Cherokee, I also thought about Tsula's dad. Was he involved in the wreck? Was he hurt in any way? How would he react to his wife's death? How would his grief burden Tsula? And would he be willing to receive me? I hoped there wouldn't be a problem. I had met him while Tsula and I were dating, and I came away unsure where I stood with him.

❧

Tsula had invited me over for supper for the official meeting. A man in jeans and a button-up shirt answered when I knocked on her apartment door. He had a weathered look of one who had been outdoors a good part of his life. He had the same dark hair as Tsula, though his eyes were a dark brown, and they met me, strong and questioning.

"You must be Don." His voice was deep.

"Yes, sir."

When we shook hands, I noticed how pale my hand was next to his.

He offered, "Tsula's in the kitchen," as he stepped aside and motioned me in.

A rich, yet unfamiliar, odor danced enticingly in the air of her apartment. Tsula stepped around the corner, and I noticed the table beneath a soft light, places already set in a rustic way.

Tsula, in a dress of oranges, browns, and reds in an intricate pattern, greeted me with a radiant smile. "I'm a little behind, working on finishing up the cornbread. I'm sorry. I wanted to be there when you and Papa met." She turned to him, "Papa, you remember I told you Don was my TA last semester. He was also the one who helped introduce me to two majestic tiger cubs back in January."

Her dad looked at me. "She told me a good bit about that class. So you're in computers?"

"Yes, computer engineering to be a little more exact. We engineers like to say it's much more demanding than computer science."

He listened, no change in his expression.

"And I'm specializing in constructing virtual environments—how computers can communicate with the human brain."

"And where does that lead?" he asked.

"There are all sorts of applications, from video games to

simulations for the military and the medical professions. The more realistic we can make the simulations, the better the programs will be able to train soldiers or doctors or..." I defended.

"Tsula mentioned something about video games."

She smiled guiltily.

"My project right now does share more with video games. I am drawn to telling a good story as well as creating a believable environment. I want my work to have a wider appeal."

"I see," her dad said as he moved to sit down and suggested with a nod of his head that I should also sit.

Tsula ducked back into the kitchen. Dropping down on the couch across the room, I found that the cushion gave way easily and a hard crossbeam below greeted my thigh—college furniture.

"What do you do, sir?" I sought to turn the attention away from me. I had also read Dale Carnegie and knew people often had a more favorable impression of a conversation if they are allowed to speak more.

"I'm a storyteller."

"Are you a writer?"

"I write some, but storytelling is important to the tribe. We gather together and hear the stories told. Stories about our ancestors. Stories about who we are as a people."

"Cherokee?"

"Yes, mostly, but also as Americans. I am one of the elders who are entrusted with preserving the stories of our people. You might call me a historian of sorts."

"I believe Tsula said you helped at a museum."

"Yes. Have you been to Cherokee?"

"When I was a boy. I liked it, but I don't remember much," I confessed.

"There is a side to Cherokee that is for tourists. If you pick up a drum or a bead necklace, you'll most likely find a label that reads, 'Made in China.' It is tough, because it is easier and cheaper, but I want my people to preserve their own crafts. If you know where to go, you can still find authentic Cherokee art."

At that moment Tsula returned, announcing that supper was ready, and we moved to the table.

In the middle of the dinner conversation that followed, Tsula surprised me. "Don, I was hoping you'd share your dream with my father. He's pretty good with interpretations."

The night she had painted my face, the night I'd become a wolf, the night we'd first kissed, I had shared my dream of walking in the woods with her and of the dark presence that pursued me like a wolf. I'd thought she'd keep the dream just between us; it seemed too private to share with anyone else. Sitting there at that table, I did not know what to expect from her father.

"It's nothing," I dodged, watching her father at the corner of my eye.

"Don, please," Tsula insisted.

At her second prompting, I worked to relate the specifics of the dream, the shape of the woods, the timbre of the wolf howl, the moment of Tsula's disappearance, the terror in being pursued and falling into darkness, and the comfort in the bright feather. When I spoke, her father listened closely.

His voice became reflective. "The dream world is a mystery."

Tsula said, "It seems to be a wolf dream, Papa."

"Yes, it does, but the darkness troubles me."

"But the feather?" Tsula countered.

I felt like an outsider even though it was my dream they were discussing.

Her father continued, "The wolf is a wise spirit, Don. It comes to certain people at important times in their lives. These dreams are not common. You should take it seriously."

Though confused, I nodded. There was a moment of silence, and I tried to think of something to say to steer the conversation away from me. Mr. Watie, though, had another idea.

"You have shared a story with me. Now I will share one with you." He pushed his chair back a little, stretching his legs out in front of him.

"Ages ago there was a hunter who caused his tribe much grief. From the time he was a boy, a dark cloud thundered through his life. Whenever someone asked him to do something for the tribe, he would grumble and stomp off. He did not show respect for his elders despite the warnings his parents and friends shouted back at him.

"The dark cloud followed him into the woods when he went hunting. He no longer saw death as a sacrifice for the animal spirits. He only saw hunting as a means to get food to satisfy the hunger in his belly. The animal spirits took note of the danger he presented to them.

"Once when he was slinking through the forest, the eagle came to him to warn him, but the hunter foolishly shot an arrow at the majestic bird, which missed the eagle and landed in the brush beyond. The eagle sounded a haunting warning as he flew off.

"The hunter continued through the forest until he came upon a wolf sleeping. It is only in this way that he could have caught the wolf. Despite the shame of attacking a sleeping animal, the hunter raised his spear and jabbed down, stabbing the wolf through the heart.

"The hunter magnified his disrespect by omitting a prayer of thanks and then by dragging the body of the wolf back to the camp. Those in the tribe who saw him coming were horrified at what he had done. Many told him to camp outside the village, knowing that curses would follow from the hunter's folly.

"He mocked them, saying, 'This is only a dead wolf. Nothing more.'

"Because his friends turned away from him and it had been a long day, the hunter delayed in skinning the wolf and went to bed early that night. In his dream a large wolf, twice the size of the one he had killed, chased him through the woods. With the wolf right behind him, the hunter (in the dream) thought that he could escape the wolf by running into a cave. Many steps into the cave, though, the floor gave way, and he fell in darkness.

"When the hunter woke up from the dream, it was late in the night; no moon shone since clouds covered the stars. Spooked, he looked around and could not find the body of the wolf he had slain. Suddenly he became very angry and started to rage through his village even though it was the middle of the night.

"One of the village elders, rising from the side of his wife, confronted the wild hunter, who claimed someone in the village had stolen the wolf from him. The elder said the hunter needed to go home and rest. While they were talking, a loud howl sounded through the night and another and another.

"The elder warned the hunter, telling him the murder of the wolf had brought the wolf spirit down on him. The hunter would find no rest until he had asked this spirit for mercy.

"The hunter spat in the elder's face and turned away.

"The next morning, the villagers could not find the hunter. Some of his fellow hunters went out into the woods that day, looking for him. Out in the woods, they discovered his spear stuck into a tree, and on the ground in front of it was a darkness in the earth that looked like blood. The hunter did not return that day or any day after, and stories grew that justice came down on the hunter who refused to be a part of his tribe, the hunter who killed a sleeping wolf."

When her father finished, I looked to Tsula and saw she was waiting for a reaction from me, so I smiled. I did not want to spoil the moment by saying something empty.

She pushed me.

"I think your father is a gifted storyteller," I said at last, and I meant it. I was out of my element, though, and I didn't know why her father had told me that story. Was he trying to tell me something?

Mr. Watie looked at me closely. "Don't worry about interpreting the story now. Let it sink into you. One day, when you need it, the story will speak to you."

After dinner we sat and talked some more, but the rest of the conversation is now just a warm blur in my memory. When it came time to go, I shook her father's hand again, and Tsula walked me to the door.

"Thank you for the evening. It was a great gift," I said.

"It was time for me to return the favor," she explained with a smile.

Tsula and I parted on a positive note, but her father's words troubled me. His story kept turning around in my head. What was Mr. Watie trying to tell me? Did he want me to identify with the hunter? Did he think I was being disrespectful of his culture, Tsula's culture? Was I dishonoring the wolf spirit? I wanted to speak up and object. Had Tsula's father passed sentence on me? I didn't feel comfortable talking with Tsula about it, so I let the mystery stand. In the end I didn't know which bothered me more, my own dream or Mr. Watie's story.

⁋

The sun was setting when I reached Asheville. Since I felt it best not to drive mountain roads in the dark, particularly without a place to stay the night, thinking it best not to crash in on Tsula's house even if I could find it, I decided to pull in to the closest motel.

It was a bare-bones place, cars parked right outside the rooms, super-thin carpet and industrial walls inside. Some spots were not as clean as they could have been, but after changing, I dropped into bed and immediately felt my muscles relax as I took a deep breath. First hurdle down. I had a place to rest for the night, but it took me an hour or so to fall asleep, for my thoughts were all on the coming day. What would I find?

The church was smaller than I expected, a beautiful collection of mountain stones decorating its outside. The gray of the stones and the white of the steeple stood out before the muted rusts and grays of the hills behind them. Those who had built this church had chosen a perfect spot, the open field around the building offering a greater view of the mountains.

When I first spotted the church, though, my impression was more of relief than awe; getting there had been a little challenging. If you haven't driven in the mountains, it's a bit difficult to explain the experience. You have to be there to feel the car struggle on the climb. If you're not familiar with the area, you struggle against the urge to gaze out at the natural wonder around you so that you can keep your eyes on the winding road. From time to time, though, you can't help yourself. You glance out at the great expanse of sky and trees and then realize you are studying the tops of trees and wondering how far below you'd have to go before you found the ground that held them up. A city dweller like me also gets a queasy feeling in the pit of his stomach at the mental image of his car shooting out into that open space and falling, plummeting down into a field of twisted branches.

Coming into Cherokee was a relief. As I looked for the side roads listed in the directions on my phone, I noted the tourist shops lining the highway; only a few cars were pulling in and out. I made a wrong turn once and had to double back. So when I finally located the church still twenty minutes ahead of schedule, I was relieved. After marveling at the beauty of the place, I observed the cars in the parking lot and the people who were walking toward the church or standing out in front of it, but I couldn't find Tsula or her dad.

I parked the car at the edge of the lot and used the moment to fix my tie and finish some last-minute grooming. Several other cars were driving up when I got out of the car. As I stepped out, the crisp mountain air struck my face. It was colder than I'd expected, but recovering, I breathed in deeply. I was determined to make this work. When I walked up to the church, I saw the other people watched me, so I hurried to get inside.

A woman handed me a program as I entered. Since the back two rows were already mostly filled, I made my way down the third pew to the outer aisle beneath the window. Sitting down, I ensconced myself in the corner, feeling comfortable enough now to look around the sanctuary. The dark wooden casket stood in the center aisle beneath the pulpit. There was the reality I'd only guessed at from a few words on a social media site. Since the casket was closed, I wondered about the woman I'd never met inside. Who had she been? She was important to Tsula, and now whatever had happened to her was bringing Tsula great grief.

More people followed me in the next minutes, finding their places, some in front of me, and an older couple sat in my pew at the other end. As the hour neared, a door on the opposite side of the sanctuary, to the left of the casket, opened, and a man in a suit asked us to rise for the family.

I saw Mr. Watie first; he entered with his head down. Tsula followed closely behind him, and I forced myself to take in a breath. She looked washed out, except for her eyes, which were dark. She leaned into her father, and Inola—I'd only seen Tsula's sister in pictures—entered, holding Tsula's trailing hand. They filed into the front pews reserved for them, never looking at the congregation. Though I wanted to help Tsula, there was a part of me that felt out of place. Did we need to witness this family's pain?

I don't remember much about the service, though I did note the minister was Reverend Watie, Tsula's uncle, her dad's brother. I had attended a few funeral services before that one, but not enough to feel the least bit comfortable. Mercifully, Reverend Watie kept it short, and he did have some of the same charisma as Tsula's father—though he smiled more. He spoke about having hope in the midst of grief, about the promises of Jesus, and the influence Tsula's mother had on the community. He said she had been a hard worker and her death was a tragic mistake. Despite the pain the family was feeling, they should find comfort in the knowledge that Jesus was in the business of turning tragedies into triumphs.

I wondered how you could turn a drunk-driving fatality into a victory.

And then the service was over. I watched as the family started to exit down the center aisle, but then dropped my gaze when I saw their grief. They did not see me, though, and I exited with the rest of those gathered, in a solemn silence despite the minister's words.

Outside, the crowd followed the family and the pallbearers and casket, processing across the field to the plot in the church cemetery. Tsula and her family sat in chairs while the rest of us gathered around. I kept my distance, not wishing to intrude in these private moments. The graveside meditation and prayer were even shorter than the memorial. When they were over, Reverend Watie invited the rest of us to come and show our respects.

I held back, but Tsula eventually stood to turn and help her father. In the process of steadying him, she glanced up and spotted me, and I observed a flash of recognition. She looked down quickly, ran a hand over her ear through her hair, and whispered something to her dad, who turned. I nodded to him. When Tsula started slipping through the crowd, I moved to intercept her, and we met at the crowd's edge and took a few more steps away for a measure of privacy.

"You came?" she said, her voice wavering, new tears in her dark eyelashes.

"I wanted to be here for you." I reached to hug her, but when her gaze shifted away from me, I hesitated.

"Tsula?"

She looked back as I leaned in, despite her uncertainty, to hug her. She was tight and tense, but while I held her, her muscles thawed, and she seemed to relax.

I whispered, "I'm so sorry." She cried briefly into my shoulder, then pulled back and wiped her eyes.

"How'd you know?" she asked.

I smiled and held up my phone. "Technology, my dear Watson."

"You saw my post."

"What—" I was going to ask what had happened, but caught myself. When she waited for me to continue, I said, "Nothing."

"Come speak to Papa, and I want you to meet Inola."

I don't remember what I said to them. It was a surreal blur, and I stumbled through it. I stood with the family after this awkward exchange. As I wondered what to do, I felt Tsula's hand slide warmly into mine.

❧

When the creek came into view, he motioned for me to sit down on the rocks nearby.

Now seated, Mr. Watie removed his shoes, rolled up his jeans, and placed his feet in the water. Glancing over, he saw me sitting, unsure of myself, and invited me to do the same. Not wanting to disappoint him at this crucial moment, I would have done just about anything, so tossing my shoes to the side and placing my own white feet into the chilly water seemed fairly simple. The mountain stream was quite cold, however, and I wondered how long I could keep it up.

He examined the river down below. "Years ago there was a skilled hunter. He respected his place in his tribe, and they celebrated all his efforts to support them. He was good friends with the elders of the tribe, and the chief elder helped arrange his daughter's marriage to this skilled hunter."

I listened quietly, a little annoyed at another story. Where was this going?

Almost as if I weren't there, Mr. Watie still watched the ripples before him, a little fish darting near us. "One day when the hunter went out, he found no deer in the woods he often visited, so he went farther away from the village than was his custom. At one point he thought he saw a glimmer of movement and picked up his pace. Emerging from the trees onto a rocky ledge, wet from a recent rain, the hunter misstepped and fell. Trying to catch himself, he managed to stop from falling off the high ledge, but instead twisted his ankle as he landed on a patch of briars.

"With hands bleeding from the cuts, he tried to stand, but realized that his ankle could not support his weight. Shaping a brace with some sticks, he was able to reinforce the injured ankle enough to take some slow steps back into the woods. Dusk was falling, and the woods were getting darker. He had told no one where he was going, and he had no hopes of getting any distance on his bad ankle. So he had to settle down and rest, embracing the coming of night.

"Several hours later, listening to various animals scampering through the woods around him, he grew tired and wondered if he would sleep. Suddenly there was another presence in the darkness. The hunter heard a low, deep breathing, and a short, soft growl. When all became quiet again, he doubted whether he had heard it at all.

"A voice then broke the silence, startling the hunter even as it asked him if he needed help. The silhouette of a man approached, towering above. The hunter explained his predicament, and the stranger came near, lifting the hunter from the ground and supporting him as they took steps through the forest back toward the village.

"With some stops for the hunter to rest, the two of them finally made it back to where the hunter's brother was scouting in the woods for him. The hunter showed his gratitude to this stranger, who seemed to have silver hair in the moonlight, asking him to come back to the village, where they could reward him.

"The stranger said there was no need for such trouble. He needed to return to his home. Seeing the resolve in the stranger's eyes, the hunter relented and let him return to the darkness from which they had just emerged.

"Asking his brother if they could rest a moment, the hunter looked back. He thought he saw a flash of white between the shadows. A moment later a howl sounded clearly, strongly.

"The hunter's brother asked if they had seen or heard any signs of a wolf in the woods. When the hunter said that they had not, he paused and wondered.

"He made it home safely that night. And he offered prayers of thanksgiving for many months after. Whenever he went into the forest as dusk approached, he would remember the stranger of the silver hair and amber eyes and the sounding of the wolf howl."

Mr. Watie stopped there, and I wondered whether he was going to tell me what this one meant? That would be too easy, though, wouldn't it?

He finally looked at me with that worn face and those thoughtful eyes. "Before you can marry her, you've got to know the wolf."

I was caught entirely off guard. In the silence that followed, I grasped for understanding. What had he said? I'd come to help Tsula through a funeral and now her father was talking about a marriage. How did that follow? I was caught pondering a story about a hunter lost in the woods and wondering how it had anything to do with marriage, Tsula, or me.

The only thing I knew to do at the moment was to copy his behavior, so I looked away from him and into the mountain water, my feet chilled and numb. I did not understand; I was not a Cherokee, but here I was a guest in their land. I owed him something.

"She is changing me. Her passion for life challenges the way I've looked at the world. She makes me feel like I've been lazy, and now it's time to do something."

I checked him in the corner of my eye. He made no motion, so I continued, "Did she tell you about the night she transformed me?" Silence. "She asked me to help her with a video protesting the way wolves are portrayed in different media. I didn't know she was going to paint my face like a wolf's. She pulled me into her project, and that night I heard about her first experience with wolves, the time you two went out in the woods of—Minnesota?"

He nodded. "She had seen a wolf before, but that was her first experience with a pack."

"I've had trouble. When I was little, a Brazilian Mastiff mauled me, and I've been suspicious of dogs ever since. I don't know if I can ever become that close to wolves."

"There are dangers in the world that can cause great harm, but we shouldn't let them keep us from the wonders. Tsula sees a lot in you, and I think that is enough."

The trees above me seemed to lean in as I responded, "I hope so. I really do."

12
VISION

"CAN YOU GIVE ME A REASON NOT TO FIRE YOU?"

It was late November, and I was sitting in Justin's office. Moments before, I had been watching the clock, anticipating the end of the day—so I could head home for Thanksgiving—when Justin had called me in.

"I don't understand," I stammered.

Justin spoke to the wall screen behind him, and the protest video started playing: Hugh, Tsula's friend, in his wolf makeup, was introducing our critique of destructive images of wolves in pop culture. The video I'd edited drew me in, but there was Justin standing in front—the juxtaposition disoriented me.

"Do you recognize this video?" he interrogated.

"Yes," I said hesitantly. "Justin pointed it out to me a couple months back."

"Is that all you know about it?"

I considered my reply. How much did he know? Was this a

test? Why was he making such a big deal about it now? The last time I checked there was record of only a few hundred viewers; the video had not made much of a splash. Finally I said, "It just looked like a group of harmless college students."

He was pacing, but now he paused to look at me closely. "It's created more of a stir than that. Some hunter in California has shot some wolves, and now an activist-journalist there is making mistreatment of wolves a hot topic nationally. So a journalist here in Raleigh now is trying to feed off the attention and has pulled our company into the fray. I still don't get the connection. We don't need this negative press just on the heels of the release of our big game. Do you want to reconsider your answer?"

When I didn't say anything, Justin turned to the screen, fast-forwarded to my section, and let the video play. "Anyone look familiar?"

Evidently I didn't answer quickly enough because he turned and opened a second window next to the first. While my wolf face remained frozen in the background, the face of a woman in her 20s, blonde hair up in a tight bun, with rectangular, black plastic glasses, started to speak about the recent release of *Transylvania Nights Anniversary Edition*. Though she started by laying out the game's popularity and influence over the last ten years, there was a sudden turn in her commentary; she was saying not everyone was happy with the game. To prove her point, the reporter referenced a group of college-age protestors who had exposed the dangers in Tsunami Games' portrayal of wolves.

Then the video cut to an interview. I immediately recognized the background in the video; it was Duke's West Campus—and there was Tsula. The reporter asked her about the popularity of *Transylvania Nights*, and Tsula recounted her party line about how the media has been distorting public opinion and creating more trouble for the cause of wolf survival.

When the blonde reporter commented on the video, how effective it was, Tsula said, "I couldn't have done it without the help of the others: Leslie, Carmen, Hugh, and Don, especially Don."

Justin paused this second video, so there on the wall behind him I saw Tsula and wolf-faced me. The words "especially Don" seemed to echo around me.

Then I realized Justin was speaking. "Especially Don. I wonder which Don she means. Surely not Donovan Williams, programmer for Tsunami Games, part of the team that put together *Transylvania Nights*! Surely not that Don! Wouldn't a reporter love to get a hold of that story?" He sat down and pushed back in his chair, biting his thin mustache with his lower teeth.

The object of Justin's hostility, I felt tightness in my chest and neck. Was there any way to save my job at Tsunami? I'd worked to get there, pushing through the *Cloud Kingdom* assignment for almost a year, earning Lauren's trust over the summer, and my name would be in the credits for the *Anniversary Edition*! Lauren had just that morning hinted she'd soon be taking me down into the lab so I could talk with Trevor Jenkins and Mark Winter about my ideas for a more immersive interface. I was on my way to realizing a dream I'd had for years; I would be a major player in the legacy of Tsunami Games; my work would touch the lives of thousands of people.

Justin's glare, though, threatened all of that.

But what shaped this moment? Hadn't I let Tsula draw me into that project, and didn't Justin ask a legitimate question? Which Don was I? Two different paths stood before me, the one promised in the images frozen on the wall, the other threatened by the uptight executive yelling at me. Which life would I choose? And how much choice did I have?

❦

"I'm sorry about your mother," I finally said when the

silence became too uncomfortable.

We were out in the middle of the mountain forest, presumably following one of her favorite trails. She had not told me much, just grabbed my hand and pulled me out of the house, then left me to follow her as she skipped ahead and disappeared past a hemlock. After the funeral she had retreated to her room with an intense headache, and while she rested, her dad had taken me down to the river for our talk. On the walk back, he eased my worries by offering me the couch for the night if I didn't already have someplace to stay. When he said I wouldn't be a burden, I gladly accepted. Not long after her dad and I returned to his cabin, Tsula found me and drug me back out into the woods. I wasn't going to refuse her.

Quickly and quietly she passed ahead of me, and though I tried to make as little noise as possible, it seemed each branch I stepped on and each muddy patch I failed to avoid echoed through the woods. I felt like a clumsy oaf trudging after her. We were going a slightly different way than her father had taken; the path was steeper, and I felt the climb in my calves. Along the way Tsula remained silent. I knew she struggled with her grief and the stress of the last few days, and I wanted to give her space, yet as we continued, I thought I needed to say something. I'd come all that way to see her, and now we were alone.

As soon as I mentioned her mother, I regretted it. If this was Tsula's retreat, I had just thrown the burden back on her shoulders. Although Tsula didn't immediately respond, she did stop and let me catch up to her. She looked at me, the evening sun peeking through the trees, exposing the weariness around her eyes.

She tried to smile. "We'll be there soon."

"Where are we going?"

"I want to show you where I ran to when I was younger and needed time to myself."

She turned and resumed her climb, jumping over a fallen

pine tree. As I followed her, I noted the spot where the pine had broken, the splintered chaos of exposed core.

Weaving around the trees and pushing through the underbrush, I tried to keep up with her, until I saw sudden movement to my left. Several yards away a light brown blur leaped behind a tree. By the time I identified it as a deer, it was gone.

I looked back to where Tsula was and couldn't see her, so I jumped ahead, hoping to catch her, and in moments I stumbled out into a clearing, the ground a rippled gray rock. After the hike in the shadows of the trees, my eyes struggled in the brightness of the orange tones of the evening sunlight. My ears picked out the rushing, gurgling sound of nearby water, and I realized we were yards away from a small waterfall, a gentle pool stretching between it and the rock where we stood.

Tsula was leaning against a tree to my right, a large grin on her face. Though I was glad to see it, it was also a bit unnerving.

"Took you long enough," she teased.

"I saw a deer."

"You saw its tail, you mean."

"It *was* running away."

"You need to learn to step softly." She paused, glancing at the waterfall and then back at me. "So what do you think?"

"It's breathtaking."

"If it were another time of the year, I'd take you swimming, but it's a little too cold today. I wouldn't want to be held responsible for getting you sick."

Remembering the blue feet I pulled out of the stream after her father's story, I counted myself lucky she wasn't going to test me in that way, but my mind then latched onto the image of going down into the pool with Tsula, when it was warmed by summer heat. We laughed and swam, and she dared me to follow her into the dark hollow behind the falls....

But winter's edge was here, and we had serious things to

discuss. I followed Tsula to a spot near the pool as she motioned for us to sit down. I was expecting to sit side-by-side facing the falls, but when I was seated, she was perpendicular to me, the falls to her right. She asked me to turn to my right and mirror her position, the falls to my left. After I moved, we finally sat across from each other, legs crisscross, our knees not quite touching, the rock cold beneath us. There was nowhere to hide.

"Why did you come, Don?" A cold wind blew a lock of her dark hair across her face, but she ignored it.

I swallowed before answering. "I was concerned about you."

"It hasn't been easy."

"I can't imagine…"

"It doesn't make any sense. Why did this have to happen? Why did he have to run into her?" She looked down, her face tightening, tears forming at the edge of her eyes.

I reached out and touched her knee. She wiped her eyes with the back of her hand, looked up at the sky, and finally again at me.

"Mama was beautiful. I regret you didn't get to meet her. Papa has pictures from when she was younger, when she was closer to my age. Times when he was busy, I would pull them out and look at them. Sometimes I'd get mad she and Papa didn't get along, that Inola and I couldn't spend time with both of them together. Sometimes I'd get out a mirror and wonder how much I looked like her. There were old ladies around town who said I looked just like her. I noticed Papa got real quiet when they said that."

Tsula's voice quickened. "I remember a time when Mama and I went dress shopping. I was going to go to a dance at school. It was ninth grade, and I needed a dress. Papa didn't think I needed one, but I convinced Mama I did. She wanted to make it special, so we drove into Asheville for the day. We went to the mall and a fancy department store. We stopped at the perfume counter and tried the different fragrances. She got the lady at the counter to help me pick out some makeup. We finally found the spot with the dresses. I went to a green one, all sparkly, and pulled it off the rack. When she said I could try it on, I rushed to the dressing room. I was so excited when I came out, and Mama said I was her princess as she hugged me tight.

"While she was holding me from behind, I saw in the mirror that she carefully pulled out the price tag. When I saw her frown, I told her it was okay, I'd look for another dress. She started to say something, paused, then hugged me closer, telling me she loved me. Mama made the best of what she had."

"What'd she do?" I asked.

"She was a hostess and head waitress at a little country-cookin' place when Inola and I were little, when Papa had his job dressing up for the tourist shop. When he quit, though, Mama said she had to look for a better job and went to work as a hostess at the casino."

"Casino?"

"Mostly bingo," Tsula explained. "Mama said she was forced into it, but I think there was part of her that liked it."

"Why do you say that?"

"There was this time when Papa had to drop us off with her, and she hadn't finished her shift, so he took us there, though he tried to avoid it as much as possible. He believed gambling was a cancer holding our people back, and he didn't want Inola and me seeing what went on there. When Papa walked us in, we saw a man rolled up, sleeping at the edge of the parking lot—I don't know if you noticed him at the funeral today. He was there. He tried to clean up; his hair was slicked back, but he still had smudges on his face, neck, and hands. His clothes didn't fit. He's so thin.

"Anyway, Uncle Jim was the man lying on the ground outside the casino."

"Uncle? Were you related?" I asked, trying to put the pieces together.

"No, everyone in town just called him that. I'm not quite sure. Uncle Jim Stone."

"Gem Stone? G-E-M?"

"No, J-I-M, but that was the joke they'd tell, that he was the gem that lost its luster and was just a plain ol' stone now. Mama told me later he'd once had some money, but had fallen on hard times." Tsula was frowning. "Papa told us just to walk past him, that we shouldn't worry about him. I think he was trying to protect us, but I felt there was something wrong. Inside, he pushed us quickly past the people. I remember the bright lights and the smell of smoke. When we finally found Mama, she and Papa exchanged cold greetings, and I watched as he left, the tinted doors closing behind him.

"I asked Mama about the man, and she explained to me he was having trouble, that we shouldn't say anything bad about him even if we heard other people doing so."

I smiled, and Tsula continued, "Mama pulled out a game of checkers, so Inola and I had something to play while we were waiting on her. But Inola and I didn't have our minds on the game; we kept looking around at the people who were there, wondering why Papa didn't like this place. Several minutes later I recognized Uncle Jim; he was clutching a crumpled green piece of paper. He had gotten some money from somewhere. I asked Papa later about it, and he said he'd given a little something to him. I didn't have the heart to tell Papa what I saw Jim do with the money, though. He went to the window and purchased his bingo cards. He must have used all the money, 'cause he didn't get any change."

"When Mama finally got off work and we were riding back home with her, I asked her why she worked at a place that would take Uncle Jim's money. I could tell from her voice she didn't like the question, but she told me the moments when Jim held his bingo card and expected to win a lot of money were what he paid for. A little bit of excitement that made him feel

204 • CHANDLER BRETT

better. Mama told me not to judge her for working there or Jim for spending his money."

"Sounds like a tough situation," I offered, unsure of what else to say.

"I know Mama didn't like to hear others say bad things about Uncle Jim. I think she tried to help him some, but she didn't have extra money to give him. One time when we were older, she took us to the trailer he was staying in. She was there to clean it for him. Once the door opened, the smell turned me away. Mama saw the look on my face and told me I could watch Inola, that she'd only be inside for a little while. When she was finished, she came out, pulled off bright yellow gloves that went up to her elbows, and put a large black trash bag into our trunk."

"Wow. She's sounds like a special lady."

Tsula went quiet and looked out at the waterfall. We sat there for several minutes, and I watched the water crash onto the rocks below.

Tsula spoke again. "I don't know if I can go back to school, Don."

"Is there anything I can do to help plead your case to your teachers?" I offered.

"It's not that."

After a moment she explained, "I'm upset with one of my roommates. When my sister called to tell me Mama was in an accident, Barbara was close enough to overhear part of it, and after I got off the phone, she asked if I was okay.

"I said I was fine, but then she pressed me, asking who was responsible. She evidently has an aunt who's a member of an organization that speaks out against drunk driving. She was too interested, and I didn't want to talk about it. She then asked if it was one of my people."

"When I asked what she meant, she replied, 'Your sister said a drunk driver caused the accident.'"

I struggled to understand her roommate's logic.

Tsula continued, "I couldn't believe she'd said it. In the shock of the moment, I shot back, 'A drunk Indian didn't kill my mother! It was a damn drunk tourist!'"

I looked down, suddenly aware again of the crash of the waterfall.

"I probably shouldn't have said that, but I didn't expect it from her. She retreated to her room, and we didn't speak another word before I left."

"I'm sorry."

"It's not your fault."

"Was Danae there?" I asked.

"She didn't hear the conversation. I told her about the phone call later, when she came into my room, but I didn't mention the fight with Barb. What do you think I should do? Would you apologize?" Her amber eyes studied me.

"I don't know," I said to give myself some time to think. Then I turned to the practical, "It's not going to be much fun having a roommate that doesn't speak to you. You've got one more semester, don't you?"

She nodded.

"If she doesn't apologize first, you might have to come to grips with what you value most, standing your ground or having a relatively peaceful apartment for the next six months."

"Have you and Mick ever fought?" Tsula asked.

"We've had our times." I didn't say that most of those disagreements had been over her.

"So your great wisdom comes with the voice of experience."

"I'm not perfect. I've had my share of fights." Now that her attention was on me, I couldn't escape the temptation of shifting the conversation. "And now there is part of me that doesn't know whether I should be angry with you."

"You have every right to be angry with me," she said in a way that caught me off-guard. I did not have time to respond. "I was too hard on you. You were right. I should have trusted you to make the best decisions."

I finally caught on. "I should have told you about Tsunami, but that's not what I'm talking about."

She seemed surprised.

I jumped in. "You knew I didn't want my name associated with the video, yet you went out of your way to highlight it when that reporter interviewed you."

"So you saw that?"

"I couldn't avoid it when Justin was using it as evidence against me."

"I didn't know."

"Didn't you?"

"I thought you should get credit for your work," she defended. "There may have been a small part of me that wanted you to get into trouble, but I didn't imagine your boss would see it."

"I could see you sending it to him."

She frowned and leaned back. "So has anything changed?"

I leaned closer; I wasn't going to let her get away. "I would say quite a lot has changed. I don't work for Tsunami Games anymore."

She seemed genuinely surprised. "What happened?"

"Justin gave me an ultimatum, and I made a decision."

"Decision?"

"There was a moment when he had paused the video of the interview. Your picture was frozen on the wall behind him, and he said he didn't understand why I had been a part of this protest. He threatened to fire me unless I could give him a reason not to. He asked me to make a choice, and at that moment I chose you."

Tsula sat across from me, watching, thinking, not saying a word. Then she reached forward and took my hand in hers.

"So you quit?"

"I told Justin I couldn't give him a reason not to fire me.

That's when his voice turned cold and he told me not to cause any problem in leaving the company. He reminded me about the confidentiality agreement, that I shouldn't talk to any reporters. I found that an insult, and proof he didn't know me if he thought I would become a sellout."

Tsula smiled, still holding my hand.

"But something strange happened then. Justin got another text. I could immediately tell he didn't like it, and it took him a moment before he looked up and told me Mr. Sadayoshi wanted to see me."

"Who's Mr. Sadayoshi?"

"He's the genius behind the company. He's the one in charge, but few people ever get to talk with him, much less see him."

"That's strange. How'd it go?" Tsula leaned forward, giving me her full attention.

"I'd never been to his office, and I'd only seen him a couple times, so I was a little nervous, and quite curious, about heading up that way. As I rode the elevator up to the top floor, I found comfort in knowing Justin didn't like that Mr. Sadayoshi had requested to see me."

"What'd you find?"

"When the elevator opened, there was a security guard who looked me over and had me empty my pockets and leave behind my Reality glasses to pass through some sort of detector. On the other side, he said Mr. Sadayoshi was expecting me. I then followed him down a hallway that had floor-to-ceiling mirrors on either side, the image of the guard and me reflecting endlessly into the distance. It was disorienting, and I had to focus on the floor in front of me."

"A hall of mirrors...." Tsula said thoughtfully.

"We finally came to a door, and the guard opened it for me, saying Mr. Sadayoshi would be with me shortly. On the other side of the doorway, I saw mountains."

"Mountains? What do you mean?"

"It was the most realistic display I've ever seen. All along the wall, again floor to ceiling, was a view of a mountain, presumably a Japanese one. It was even more disorienting than the mirrors. When I looked that way, it honestly felt like I was only feet from walking out onto the side of a real mountain. The guard told me I was to sit and wait, and then closed the door behind me. I noticed then there was a simple, yet amazingly beautiful table in the middle of the room, only a few inches from the floor, which was an ornate hardwood. I walked to the side closest to me and then focused on the one other door in the room, on the far side. I gazed out at the mountain, trying to come to grips with how real it looked. A few moments later I heard a voice, soft, yet powerful, call my name.

"I turned, and there he stood, dressed in dark navy. Though he wasn't dressed in a suit, I still felt out of place in my jeans and T-shirt. When he motioned me to sit, I noticed he sat on his knees with his calves folded under him. I didn't know how he could hold that pose on that hard floor. And he sat there in silence as if he were waiting for me to speak first. But then he finally said he knew all that Justin knew. He said he was disappointed because he had been impressed with my potential, my attack on virtual reality."

I waited for Tsula to react; she just nodded quietly.

"He valued loyalty, though, and could not ignore the situation; thus, he understood my decision to leave the company and would not stand in my way—a price had to be paid. But he said he would watch my career closely, and if I realized my vision, then he would offer me a way back in if I ever were to need it."

A skeptical twist at the edge of her mouth showed me Tsula did not value those words in the same way I did. I continued, "We stood, he shook my hand, and then he disappeared behind the door at the far end of the room. His guard immediately opened the door, escorted me back to the elevator and down toward the main door. He wouldn't let me go back to my station, but Trevor intercepted us. He'd gathered my personal things into a box, which he handed to me, after the guard inspected them. I think that was the hardest part, facing Trevor—he looked hurt. But then the guard escorted me out of the building, and that was that."

"I'm sorry," Tsula said again.

"I thought I'd be happy at Tsunami for years. I still can't believe I walked out on my dream job. But I feel like I did it for you."

"I don't want you to have done it for me."

"Why?"

"I want you to have done it for yourself."

"Can it be for both?" I said with a grin.

"Don't look back. Think about where you can go from here." She held both my hands now, and it was my turn to study her eyes. What did she want of me?

"I've already been working on some ideas. I've even pulled Mick in as a consultant."

"What's your plan?"

"Now what kind of entrepreneur would I be if I were to spill my great ideas before they'd come to their fruition? Who's to say you're not a corporate spy out to weaken my defenses so that you can run off with the fruits of my creative labor, leaving me high and dry?"

"Would I do that?" She opened her face to an exaggerated look of innocence, then switched her expression, narrowing her eyes and purring, "How secure are your defenses?"

She slid onto her knees to lean toward me, her breath warming my neck, her voice caressing my ear. I could now hear her clearly over the sound of the waterfall. "Shall we find out?"

❧

I celebrated having Tsula near again. There were moments when I wondered if I was taking advantage of a time when she was grieving and needed company, but Tsula's reactions were too genuine, her emotions more like a river steady in its bed rather than rivulets of rain on a muddy hillside. After our reconnecting before the waterfall, we returned to her father's cabin, and I tried not to get in the way of her family's grief. I had the chance to meet Inola for the first time, and it seemed from some of her comments she was much more impulsive than her elder sister.

Families from the community had brought all sorts of food, from fried chicken to corn casserole to pumpkin pie and apple cobbler. We sat around a simple pine table, and Tsula and her sister shared memories of their mother. Mr. Watie was more reserved, his face drawn in exhaustion. He decided to turn in early, and as he passed by me, he placed his hand on my shoulder—I felt the weight of it—and then he quietly disappeared down the hallway, which darkened when he closed the door to his bedroom.

Sensing Tsula needed some time with her sister, I retreated too and found my spot on the couch. In the darkness I wondered what I was doing. The scents, the textures, the interactions were not mine. I was a city boy; Atlanta was my home. Tsula had asked me what my plans were, and I had dodged the question. I still was not quite certain what she expected of me.

I had talked with my parents, though, about the ramifications of leaving Tsunami. My mother seemed more concerned, asking what I would do after graduation. My father—I could see it in his eyes—was more relieved than anything. On the way to playing tennis the day after I told them, he said sometimes it was good just to step back from the serious decisions and do something fun. At first I was a little surprised to hear that from him, but then I knew how much he valued exercise and good health—that had been another issue with us, my not spending enough time outside being active.

After the game was over, I had to admit my father was right.

I did enjoy myself. He seemed encouraged by my smiles and decided to take advantage of the moment.

"I didn't always know I'd be a doctor. Sometimes I forget that, but you reminded me of a time during college when I almost jumped ship and went into politics."

He stopped. Loquacious my father was not. He had baited me, though, and I tried to pull the story out of him. "Really? What was that about?"

"I knew I wanted to make a mark on the world. You know I've always kept up with the news, and that year was an election year—it was before I met your mother. I began to wonder if I could influence more people as a representative or a senator, rather than as a surgeon. Laws affect many more people than individual surgeries."

"What changed your mind?" I asked and then took a swig out of my water bottle.

"I spent a semester trying to work it out. I enjoyed the political theory classes, but they didn't grab me like the pre-med classes did. I needed to see a direct result in front of me. I remembered my dad's quoting of Schweitzer. The ending of suffering was the highest calling. I needed to feel that in my hands."

I found myself admiring my dad despite the tension we struggled through during my teenage years. It was not easy being his son. I never knew how to argue with him.

"Don't worry, Don. You'll know what you need to do when it comes along."

"Thanks."

The game helped straighten out my relationship with my dad. The visit had been a good one, including some of my mother's brownies—she was branching out from cookies—and I came away more hopeful. As I was walking out the door to drive back to school, my dad grabbed my arm.

"Son, I don't think you should abandon your research."

I was speechless.

"Have you thought about what your work might mean to someone who is a quadriplegic?"

"A little." I had gone down this path once to try to justify my research to Dad, but that conversation had not gotten far. I think he knew my interest had been a smokescreen at the time.

"I think you could invent something that could ease the suffering of a host of bed-ridden people." There was my dad again.

I smiled, a little half-heartedly, and said, "I'll think about it."

Back at school I spent hours thinking about it, usually when I failed to think of another way to pull my research out of the gaming industry. The clock was ticking on my doctorate; I did not want to delay my graduation. I had indeed talked with Mick about some ideas, and we had even toyed with a joint venture into something that looked more like educational software, helping people understand animals better. I still felt immersion was the key. I had a feeling Tsula would approve, but I did not want to jinx it by revealing things too early.

Suddenly feeling a soft pressure on my cheek, I jumped.

"Sorry. I didn't think you were asleep."

"No. It's okay."

She slid in close to me on the couch and pulled my free arm across her. "Don, I apologize for interrupting you."

"What?"

"You asked me a very important question, and all I could do was interrupt you."

"I don't understand."

"That stormy night on the beach. You picked a great spot." She laughed softly.

I searched for something to say.

"You asked me a question, and I never gave you an answer."

"Tsula, we've got time."

She lightly jabbed me with an elbow. "Don't interrupt me, please." She paused, settled back down, and then continued. "I want you to know my answer is yes. Yes, I will."

13

ON THE RUN

KAN WAS TORN. THE PACK NEEDED TO MOVE IMMEDIATELY to find a new home; the tigers were too great a threat for them. Doda and Etsi, the alpha pair who had raised and shaped this pack, had already fallen, and in an impulsive rescue attempt, the pack had also lost Taline. Lana's story had only stoked Kan's growing concern. He imagined her crouching low under the evergreen branches while the second tiger breathed in wolf scent. If it had not been for Koga, would he have lost Lana too? There was no question the pack had to find a new hunting ground far removed from this dangerous territory.

Yet even after a few hours rest, he still did not feel his best. His leg was burning again, the exchange with Danuwa having reopened the wound. He counted himself fortunate, though, when he looked at Oni and Sasa. The light of day exposed the swelling around Oni's eye; it was difficult to tell whether he would lose sight in that eye. Oni's other eye watered under the strain of being the only one left. The omega wolf tried to keep largely to himself, slinking lowly around the others, but Kan checked on him several times. He would not let Oni's sacrifice go unrewarded.

The biggest hindrance to quick movement, however, was Sasa. Kan and Lana struggled to find a way to help her.

She did nothing to deserve this, Lana whispered to him away from the others.

She again suffers the greatest pain for her brother's ambition. I'm glad she has Noya.

Kan watched Noya licking Sasa's wound. The bleeding had stopped. After hours of lying still, Sasa was now occasionally turning and moaning, her eyes still closed and her breathing labored.

I think she has a fever, he observed aloud.

We can't lose her too.

I can't leave her. Danuwa and Sikwa would have succeeded in taking me out if she hadn't been here.

She straightened her shoulders. *No, I don't want to leave her either.*

But this is not the safest place.

How did we end up here? Why did Danuwa attack you here?

Kan looked away into the woods back toward the tigers. *This is where I gave up yesterday when Yona was leading me back to the new hunting grounds. I didn't want to leave you behind. I knew there was no real chance you'd made it back to the hollow ahead of us, but I didn't know which way to go, so I decided to wait for you here.*

We are too exposed. We need to try to get her back to the hollow as soon as she is able. We need to get her water, and we need to find some fresh kill. If she is to recover, she needs food. As she spoke to him, he heard the gurgle of her stomach.

How long has it been since you've eaten? Kan asked.

Over half a moon cycle maybe since we've had good meat. We've spotted prey several times recently, stalked them, but the hunts in the end were unsuccessful. The pack needs to feed well before we push for a new home.

Hunting then is our priority, he said decisively.

We need to have a couple scouts patrol the border with the tigers, just in case.

Agreed.

She and Lana worked quickly to recruit for these posts. Since Noya refused to leave her sister's side, they left her to tend to Sasa and Oni. Koga seemed willing to patrol the area. Kan was irritated to leave such an important task to her. If he had had more time, he would have asked Lana more questions about her. The pack needed to move quickly, though, and their numbers were down.

The remaining group of Yona, Wesa, Unalii, and Askai joined him and Lana. His first hunt as alpha, and he had never hunted with a group so small. Kan knew the odds were not in their favor. Even a skilled pack ran many more unsuccessful hunts, all those times when the prey escaped. Now their numbers were down, cornering and taking down prey would be even more difficult. Kan hated to admit it, but Danuwa and Sikwa would be missed here—the two rivals had not made an appearance since they had run off in the night.

Yona's size, Wesa's speed, Unalii's stamina, Askai's dexterity, and Lana's determination would have to be enough. Since his leg was still a liability, Kan knew he was little more than a figurehead at this point. As if she were reading his mind, Lana brushed up against him. *We'll be all right.*

I'll follow your lead, he said, trying to keep his voice light.

And off they ran. Kan fell behind quickly, but he pushed ahead despite the burning. He wondered if his leg would ever feel normal again.

In the next breeze, it came, the slightest smell. Kan saw Lana sniffing the air; she'd picked up the scent too. They had to act quickly. Running with the pack, Kan picked up on their excitement; he could feel the expectation of the hunt. They moved through the woods swiftly and quietly, fanning out in a wide formation in preparation for rushing down on their prey. Wesa and Askai would join Lana in selecting and running the prey while Yona and Unalii would join Kan in intercepting and cutting off its escape.

Sounds up ahead—munching, breathing, stepping—made them more cautious. Kan crouched, slowing slightly. Through the branches, he saw a light brown form, white spots decorating the fur along its back. There were other sika deer nearby, feeding. One of these would do nicely.

Suddenly an antlered head sprang up; the deer had sensed the wolves. Lana dashed forward, the others at her side. They needed to move quickly before their prey outdistanced them. The male sika, though, had warned his companions, who were all retreating rapidly across the dew-covered field, the early sun obscuring their escape.

So it's going to be a long hunt then, Kan thought. There were rare moments, after the pack surprised a baby boar or an older deer, when they could take down prey earlier and get to their meal. More often than not, they would have to settle in for a pursuit that could last hours. The pack would have to run down and exhaust its prey.

It was a herd of about twelve deer, rumps flared in retreat. As they ran ahead, Kan watched as his pack measured which would most likely fall, and he spotted one female, rounder in the middle, who always stayed in view, never gaining ground to get ahead of any of its herd. When Lana also picked the doe, she and Wesa drove forward, cutting her away from the rest of the herd, who ran on, leaving her behind. Askai nipped her on a rear haunch, and the sika panicked, kicking wildly back, just barely hitting Askai in the shoulder. He went down.

Unalii and Yona ran past Kan on the other side. The two-prong attack caught the deer in between, causing her to stumble, allowing time for Unalii to gain enough ground to attack from the front. Kan saw the panic in the doe's eyes and jumped back as it kicked again. Since the kick was to the rear, Unalii took the chance to leap at her neck, but he missed, and the doe threw up her front legs to fend him off. Taking advantage of the moment, Lana latched onto the sika's spotted haunch, teeth sinking in. The doe screamed. Kan, who had now circled to Lana's side, sprang up and startled the deer at the moment she pulled in from Lana's bite. When the doe turned sharply, Yona jumped forward and knocked the deer off balance. Once the doe slipped, Yona grabbed her snout and pulled her to the ground, and Unalii reached her throat, clamping out her breath, the deer thrashing weakly, then giving in. One last twist, and the doe became still and silent.

The wolves celebrated the successful hunt. Lana tore into the flesh below the rib cage, blood matting the fur of her muzzle. She looked at him expectantly, and Kan joined her, taking his first bites as alpha. Never having fed first, he felt self-conscious with the others watching, but once the meat was in his mouth, his hunger took over, and he tasted warm blood.

After those first bites, he decided he needed to check on the rest of his pack. He looked first for Unalii, but the beta wolf was missing. Turning his head, Kan found Unalii over with Yona; they were standing over Askai, who, attempting to stand, stumbled and landed hard on the ground.

Something's wrong, Kan thought, as he left his place of honor. As he drew closer, he studied the wound in Askai's shoulder. It did not look life-threatening, but it was going to hurt for some time. Kan whined in empathy. Since Askai had defended him in Danuwa's last vicious attack, Kan needed to do something now to honor that commitment. He jogged back to the deer, tore a section of muscle off the haunch, then returned to lay it before Askai, who slowly started to gnaw on it. Once Askai was showing some signs of settling down, the others went and took their portion of the kill, each in turn according to pack rank.

After feeding, Lana came over to Kan. *We need to notify the others. I'll share mine with Sasa. She's too weak to come here, but Oni should be able to make it along with Koga.*

I'll double-back with you.

Bellies full, Kan and Lana set a leisurely pace.

Do you expect Danuwa and Sikwa to come back? she asked when they were several paces down the trail.

I don't know. You know I'm glad they're gone.

The others might not take their absence well. What will Oni do without his brother?

Oni's help saved me last night, Kan quickly defended, but Lana's question began to sink in. Oni had stepped in to prevent Danuwa from killing him. Kan had been thinking Oni was now on their side, but Lana's question made him doubt.

She continued. *They are close, and if Sikwa does desert the tribe, there's no telling what Oni will do.*

Kan remained silent. He did not understand why Oni would trade the support of the tribe for his brother's bullying, but he knew Lana understood the pack better than he did. These thoughts then led to another. *Do you think Danuwa will return?*

Leaving a pack isn't easy, and he's had a good life here, intimidating the others. She paused, thinking through something. *I know how frustrated he was when I knocked him off of you, but I didn't see him last night. What do you think?*

Has anyone stood up to him before?

It is difficult to say. I think he has mostly picked his fights in the shadows, where there are no witnesses. That is where I had to push him back when he moved to be my companion.

He came after you?

I didn't let him.

Imagination got the better of Kan. He envisioned Danuwa making advances. He spat, *If he dares to come back, I'll drive him off.*

We will handle him together.

Kan felt her head brush against his left ear. Her presence calmed him, the tightness in his face and shoulders easing. He returned a loving nudge, thinking, she almost won him over, but he could not let this go. He thought again of the moment he released Danuwa's throat, and he vowed not to make that mistake again.

❧

Noya did not want to leave her sister's side at first. Approaching carefully, Lana brought some of her chewed meat back up, placing it right before Sasa's snout. There was no change until Lana licked up some of the meat and placed it in Sasa's mouth. Finally Sasa responded, her muzzle tightened, and she swallowed. Slowly she took down the rest of what Lana fed her. Evidently feeling her sister was safe and acknowledging her own hunger, Noya finally ran off with Oni and Koga to join the others at the kill.

Kan and Lana watched over Sasa as she fell back into unconsciousness. While the sun progressed across the blue, crisp, late-winter sky, the other wolves made their rounds, circling back to where Sasa lay. Unalii, Wesa, Koga, and Noya were first to return and stayed closest during the pack's vigil. Kan saw how the fresh meat lifted the pack's spirits, for though the others still kept a respectful, gentle step and attitude around Sasa, the wolves displayed a new nervousness, the desire to move on. Even Oni, who largely kept to himself, had more of a spring in his pace even when he stumbled because of his limited vision, the wounded eye still swollen shut. On the other side, however, with a fresher, deeper wound, Askai spent the day resting.

Several in the pack began to display more openly their unease with their current location. Yona and Koga seemed the most restless. Weaving back and forth through the trees on the side closest to the tigers, the brown male and the black female ran their patrols, eyes vigilant, ears and nose alert for any signs. Kan noticed, though, they worked independently of each other; Koga had not blended entirely with the pack. On her side Wesa also kept a steady patrol as she crept quietly and steadily around them in a circular pattern, keeping Kan, Lana, and Sasa in the direct center. Her demeanor was steady and cool; nothing would get past her.

Toward evening Sasa finally opened her eyes and pushed her way to a standing position, where she wobbled and stumbled. Noya quickly moved to steady her sister, and Sasa, who seemed to register the restlessness of the pack, was able to walk. Feeling Lana's gaze on him, Kan turned and noted her relief and surprise.

During the ensuing march back to the spot they hoped would not be home for much longer, Sasa displayed a deeper strength than Kan had seen. He, Lana, and Unalii kept a tight formation around her and Noya while Wesa continued to circle them and Koga and Yona kept up the rear. When the pack reached its temporary destination, no one begrudged Sasa's dropping to the ground or her renewed sleep. Although he knew the journey was just beginning, Kan found comfort in leaving those woods behind—he wished he could abandon as easily the memories and effects of those two close calls with Danuwa.

﹗

In the middle of the darkness of the night, Kan awoke to Wesa's whining. As his head was clearing and he focused on the shadows in front of him, he felt Lana stirring next to him. Something was wrong; he could feel the tension in the air.

Then another wolf came thumping up to them; it was Koga, barely visible under the moonless sky. When she echoed and intensified Wesa's warning, the turn of her growl particularly prescient, Kan jumped to his feet.

Have the tigers found us? Lana yipped beside him.

It must be. I don't know of anything else that would agitate them so.

Koga barked, and Kan knew they had little time to make a decision.

Lana felt the same. *We've got to get the others and go.*

What about Sasa? he asked.

We don't have much choice. If those tigers find us, then we'll definitely lose her.

Kan nodded, and as Koga and Lana went off to wake Sasa and Noya, he went in the other direction to gather Unalii and the remaining male wolves. He discovered Oni, Yona, and Unalii were already awake and alert, knowing instinctively something was threatening the pack. Askai walked stiffly and awkwardly, occasionally whining, obviously in some pain, but even he seemed ready for action.

Kan met Lana at the river's edge.

We'll follow the river's course. Hopefully the noise and the scents here will help obscure our trail, Lana barked.

Agreed. He looked back and saw Sasa on her feet, Noya close beside. Koga was running back and forth between their position and the spot where she had emerged from the wood. In that moment Kan felt as if the gnarled, leafless branches of the trees and underbrush were reaching out to grab them.

Lana was already several paces away when he jumped to join her, the water's edge cold on his paws. The image of the monstrous tiger invaded his imagination, her arms outstretched, lunging and enveloping poor Taline. They could not afford to lose any more of their pack. It just did not make sense. Wolves were supposed to be the top of the chain; they did not know how to behave if they were the prey. The nightmare was descending on them—they had to run.

We're all here, except for Danuwa and Sikwa, Lana whispered to him.

We're fortunate no one was out exploring.

I think the pack knows we need to stick together now.

Do we have a plan? Kan asked. *Is there a way to cover our tracks so the tigers won't be able to follow us?*

It's difficult to cover the scents of an entire pack.

Could we create a false trail?

We could split up again. You could lead the wounded through the river and come out on the other side, and I could take Wesa, Noya, and Koga in the other direction.

Do we have to split up again? he asked. Kan did not welcome the prospect; she was the reason he was there, and now it seemed they were doomed to be separated again.

Do you have another idea? she asked, her voice insistent.

He tried to measure out the situation. If they were going to split the pack as she suggested, both groups would need guidance. If he went with her, could they trust another? And again, since his leg was still recovering, he could not include himself among the faster wolves in the pack. He would only slow them down, and this time the success of the false trail would depend upon the speed of the wolves. They would have to run out far enough to make the diversion believable, yet they would also have to double-back along their path to the river before the tigers caught up with them. It was a risky mission particularly since they did not know how far away the tigers were. Koga's agitation had been real, so the threat had to be close.

What else could they do? They did not dare stand their ground against these two beasts. The pack could not afford to lose anyone else, and in their weakened state, Oni, Askai, and Sasa all would become easy targets. Playing out a series of strategies, Kan conjured one mental image, his primary goal: he and Lana would escape through the river and come out on the other side—and then they would run and run until they were safe. He cared most about making her safe and happy.

But she would never abandon the others, that was what this was all about, wasn't it? The bonds of the pack. Then he wondered whether he could leave the others either. What of the sacrifices of Oni and Sasa? What of the friendship of Unalii and Yona? What of the devotion of Noya and Wesa? Kan knew then he had to stay.

No. I'll do what must be done, but I don't want to lose you either. Kan hesitated. He was tempted to tell her his suspicions about the tigers—who they were and what kind of threat they represented. But would that knowledge change anything? Wouldn't it only add to her worries?

She quickly responded. *We'll be on our guard; we know what to expect now. I promise to be careful.*

Kan resigned himself to the plan. *Shouldn't we have the entire pack leave the river first, and then split up out in the woods? I'd lead my group back first and then you'd take yours out to forge the false trail.*

Yes. She yipped quietly, thoughtfully.

And don't we need a place to meet back up?

We shouldn't have any trouble tracking you, she barked playfully.

They decided to get some distance before implementing the plan. As the pack loped along the river's edge, Kan felt the rhythm of their steps; it felt to him like a heartbeat, the steady pumping of life. They were running for their survival. Even poor Sasa understood this beat as she struggled to keep pace with the others. Kan pushed against his anxieties. He did not want to leave Lana again.

As soon as they came to a point where the river forked into two separate directions, Kan knew this was the spot; it allowed for more variety, more confusion for those who pursued them. Just as they planned, he and Lana led the entire pack out into the woods, following along the river's right branch and then abruptly out into the woods beyond. They were pushing the limits of the territory they had patrolled. Night was thick upon them, and they navigated primarily by smell, and though the scents here were similar to those in the part of the forest they had called home, the familiar mixed with the unfamiliar in new and unpredictable ways, leaving all the wolves cautious.

Here's where we need to break up, Lana voiced while turning her head back toward him.

He could just see her white fur in the dim light. He stepped forward and buried his face in the fur of her neck. When he finally pulled back, they licked each other's faces.

Be careful, he repeated. Then without a word, she circled, gathering Wesa, Noya, and Koga. Kan was glad she would be running with the fastest hunters in the pack, yet as she blended into the darkness of the woods, he again found himself doubting Koga's presence.

Kan finally gathered his group with Unalii's and Yona's help. They would be guiding Oni, Askai, and drooping Sasa. They needed to step carefully to pass without leaving a trace of their backward movement. He led the group to the river, where they entered the chilling water and swam upstream back to the fork. Swimming against the flow of the river was a challenge, particularly for Sasa, but she held on. It was a great relief when they reached the fork and were able to move with the current along the branch on the other side. Though he wanted to get out of the water as soon as possible, Kan pushed as far as he thought his wounded were able along the other branch of the river, before finally exiting on the far side.

Once they were out of the water, Sasa dropped to the icy mud, and Askai followed her example. Oni struggled, his eye still giving him trouble even though the swelling looked like it was beginning to retreat. Kan, Yona, and Unalii shook off the water. Because the trip through the stream had wet their underfur, they could now feel the icy touch of winter. Kan knew they had to keep Sasa warm, or she would catch a chill. They could not rest yet; they had to make sure they did not leave obvious markers on this side either. Lana and the others would be able to track them from subtle clues, but the pack did not want to leave signs the tigers could follow. With all the effort, and with the risk of losing Lana, Kan wanted to make certain this trick was going to work.

He trotted over to Sasa and nudged her with his nose, pushing up on her neck, whining insistently. Her eyes fluttered open, then shut again. When Kan barked and pushed again, her eyes opened a second time, and she struggled to stand. As she took steps up the bank toward the trees, Yona and Unalii dashed ahead of her, clearing a path for her to follow. Kan then checked on Askai, who had already regained his feet and was shaking off the river's water. When all his group were finally up in the woods, Kan returned to the river's edge and kicked water back onto the spots where Sasa and Askai had lain in the mud, hoping to dilute the scents of their presence. Not wanting to fall too far behind and feeling a twinge in his leg, Kan finally moved to join the others.

As soon as he caught up to Sasa, Kan watched her closely as they took several more paces into the woods. Her gait was slow, her shoulders slumped, her paws slipping in the mixture of snow and leaves. Would she survive this journey? She needed to rest. Kan barked ahead to Yona and Unalii, who doubled back, the other wolves pausing in their tracks. Kan started to dig out a hole in the drier dirt, and Yona and Unalii joined in the task. When they had hollowed out a couple spots, Kan guided Sasa to one, and he saw Askai headed to the other. The wolves huddled, snuggling closely in these shallow shelters. Kan licked Sasa's wet fur, and feeling the chill on his tongue, he pushed in closer to her, trying to keep her warm. As his group rested, Kan wondered how Lana and her group were doing and whether the tigers were drawing near.

❧

When the morning sun rose over the horizon, pale in the misty sky, Kan and his group were marching again. The rest had helped everyone; even Sasa had been able to recover some, though she had looked limp and unresponsive when Kan had first tried to wake her. Kan felt guilty pushing her now and even doubted his decision to keep moving forward, but he still felt the tigers were too close. The wolves needed to get way out of range, and in the light of the sun, Kan had set his sights on the mountain in front of him. It was a mountain that they had seen from a distance from their former home; they knew its presence, but they had never drawn this near, and the prospect of passing over its majestic height had never been a possibility—until now. Kan had not talked with Lana about a destination beyond the fork in the river, but his imagination now locked onto that massive rock. Surely they would be safe if they traveled over it and into the land beyond. Kan did not know what lay beyond, but he felt a pull; they would make their new home there, and the mountain would be the great barrier between them and the tigers.

Turning back to check on Askai and Oni, Kan found they were holding on. From there he circled to check on the others and soon realized he had lost track of Unalii. The beta wolf's scent broke off from the others. Where had he gone? Was there a reason? Was he just scouting? Whatever Unalii's motive, his path broke from Kan's direct line toward the mountain. Trying to control his irritation, Kan signaled to Yona that the others should stop and rest again. Then he followed after Unalii's scent.

It took Kan longer to catch Unalii than he had expected, but as he moved through this section of the woods, he began to notice a faint scent in the air and to understand the reason for

Unalii's sudden and unexpected turn. When Kan finally caught sight of Unalii, he found his friend sniffing the base of a pine. Unalii lifted his head and made the motion to bark, but kept his voice soft. Kan found it a strange expression, but immediately took the meaning. His hackles went up, and he slipped quietly to join Unalii, crouching to examine what Unalii had found. The scents were strong and undeniable; it was a marker for another pack.

Kan cringed at the thought. They did not need this confrontation; they were too weak, and the morale of their little group was at an extreme low. Kan wondered whether they were running by the edge of the pack's territory or headed into it. As he tried to estimate how large a pack—and it was a big one—this was, he caught a scent he remembered and opened his mouth to breathe it in. The pain returned to his leg. How could this be? The scent was Danuwa's, and then Kan seemed to discern Sikwa's. What were they doing out here?

He looked at Unalii, who pawed nervously at the ground. He knows, Kan thought. I'm glad you found this. We do not need a confrontation with another pack or with Danuwa and Sikwa—and certainly not both in one. A sense of urgency filled Kan again. His group had to move through this area before the other pack noticed them. Unalii joined him as he raced back to the others.

While they returned, a howl broke through the silence of the snowy wood, and then another and another. The sound startled Kan, and Unalii tensed too, head raised, ears twisting one way, then another, trying to pinpoint the sound. One of the howls stood out from the others; Kan immediately recognized the timbre of Danuwa's voice. The howls suggested camaraderie, not aggression. Had Danuwa and Sikwa found a new pack already? That didn't make sense. Kan could not see Danuwa bowing to the leadership of another, and yet how could he have gained the loyalty of strangers already? Kan did not know how to interpret what he was hearing, but he did know his rival and these other wolves were not far enough away. They were dangerously close, and Kan wondered if this new pack had picked up some sign of the presence of his pack. Danuwa and Sikwa knew them well enough to track them easily, and if the two were part of a new pack, how many wolves would they bring down with them? The scent marker had been ominously strong.

Kan motioned to Unalii, and they picked up their pace. Before they could reach the others, they heard another howl; it came from in front of them, from their group. Kan recognized Oni's voice. What was he doing? Oni's voice suddenly crumpled into a whine and then silence. Someone had stifled the howl— probably Yona—but it was too late, Kan thought. If Danuwa and company weren't aware of Kan's wolves before, they certainly knew of them now. Kan cursed Oni's stupidity. Though it was probably an innocent howl of excitement over hearing his brother unexpectedly, Oni's impulse could instantly bring an end to all Kan's planning.

As if in confirmation, Sikwa's howl sounded with intensity. Kan knew he had to act quickly. He ran in spite of his leg. When he and Unalii finally joined the others, he saw Askai pacing about. Yona stood over Oni, his mouth clamped over the omega's, growling. Upon seeing Kan, Yona finally let go of Oni, who then quietly cowered nearby.

Kan spotted Sasa and saw she was still huddled in the spot where she had collapsed. When he reached her, he licked from her closed eyes up to her ears. She finally lifted her head, but when he saw the weakness in her eyes, he knew she could not handle this pace. Running from the tigers, swimming in the river, trying to stay warm, it had all caught up with her. Kan wondered what he was supposed to do. He could not leave her. She had saved him from her brother. He could not abandon her to Danuwa now—her brother would only finish off the job he had started, and poor Sasa in her weakened state would not be able to offer up any defense.

What about the other wolves? Kan had a bad feeling a large pack was headed their way, one that would not take kindly to the presence of outsiders on their land. Kan knew Unalii and Yona would be able to stand against Danuwa and Sikwa, but if there were four, six, or eight other wolves, how would they fair? Askai, like Kan, could only offer so much help because of his wound. That left Oni whimpering at the edge. Kan could not forecast what Oni would do when he saw Sikwa—not that Oni would turn on Kan, but he might not join the fight either.

Kan made his decision. He circled around the others, herding them back onto the path toward the mountain. He barked at Unalii, who took up the lead. Then when Askai and even Oni were in formation, with Yona taking up the rear, Kan doubled back to Sasa's side.

Kan leaned down, licked her again, and then tried to prepare himself for what was coming. What was he going to do? He listened closely, but there were no other howls. What did that mean? Was the other pack coming to investigate or not? Surely they would, but that meant they were approaching silently, cautiously. What did that say about how this new pack worked?

Then in this silence another howl sounded, one totally unexpected. It was Lana's, and her voice sounded urgent. She needed help. But what was he supposed to do with Sasa? He didn't want to leave her. He licked her face vigorously, trying to get her to move. The cream-colored wolf responded, managing even to stand, but after several steps, she stumbled and fell again.

It's been too much for her, Kan thought. How can I ask her to go any farther?

Lana needed him, yet how could he leave Sasa, who was wounded because of him, when the other wolves were coming?

Is this what it meant to be an alpha? Kan wanted no part in it. He looked down at Sasa, whose eyes were closed, her head shaking slightly with her breathing. He lowered his head to touch hers. I'll come back for you, he promised. Then he took the first step in the direction of Lana's call. He took another step and hated himself for it. Pushing against the urge to look back, Kan took off running into the woods.

What had caused Lana's howl? Was she in trouble? Had Danuwa or the stranger wolves reached her? Had the tigers followed? Kan tried to run faster, but he was in a land he did not know.

Then he saw her. She was backing up slowly, watching something, her hackles raised, her ears back. What was it? Kan pushed harder and caught sight of a larger wolf, one he had never seen before. The large male rivaled Yona for size. His teeth were not bared, and there was no growl, but with each deliberate, graceful step, he showed his sights were set on Lana. As Kan neared, he resisted the urge to bark; he did not want to draw any more attention from the pack that converged on them. He instead threw himself between Lana and the giant golden wolf.

Run! He barked at Lana while turning to face the stranger.

I won't leave you. He heard Lana behind him, coming up close.

The large male paused, and Kan noticed the other was studying them. It was only a flicker, but the brown eyes seemed surprised and then showed some sort of recognition. Kan did not know how to respond. He stopped growling, but still stood his ground.

Before he could discern what was happening, Wesa and Koga appeared, running up barking and gnashing their teeth. The stranger turned his head at their approach.

Now! Lana yipped as she dashed behind Wesa and Koga.

Not having time to think, Kan followed. Wesa and Koga

232 • CHANDLER BRETT

soon were running behind them. They ran as swiftly as they could, and to his surprise Lana led them back to Unalii and the others. The pack was reunited. Glancing over his shoulder, Kan saw no sight of the large male. Why was he not following?

What's going on? Kan asked.

We've spotted several wolves roaming here, and they all are as large as the one you just saw. We found Unalii and his group, but when you weren't there, I went to look for you. That was when that male cornered me. I'm sorry I panicked for a moment.

He rubbed up against her. *We've been through a lot recently. I'm glad you got away from the tigers.*

She licked his ear. *But we have to go. We don't have any time. They know we're here.*

Kan looked over to Noya, who stood looking out toward where they had come. *But I left Sasa.* The realization of it weighed on him. He saw the concern in Lana's eyes as she recognized the no-win situation.

I don't want to leave her, but we can't go back. We're no match for those wolves.

I was going to stay with her.

As if anticipating his thoughts, Lana consoled, *Sasa fought to save you before. If she were able, she would do the same again. The others are depending on us. If there is a chance later, we'll come back for her.*

If there is... he whispered coldly.

Where's Oni? Lana asked.

Kan looked around. *I don't know.*

He wasn't with you and Sasa?

No.

He wasn't here either.

He must have run off to find his brother.

We heard Sikwa's howl too. Lana looked around. *Our numbers are getting smaller, but we've got to go. We don't have time to look for him.*

Kan simply nodded. He wondered how much the pack could endure, but if the small group they had left was going to survive, they had to press forward. He closed his eyes and saw the last image of Sasa, suffering from pain and exhaustion. With a sigh he opened his eyes and resumed the path toward the mountain. Within heartbeats his and Lana's pack was on the run again.

※

As the sun set that evening, they paused to rest.

I don't see any signs they're following us, Lana said, cozying up to him.

Maybe they won't. Kan guessed Sasa and Oni were providing enough of a distraction, but he didn't say anything. Somehow voicing it would make things worse. Instead, he looked up at the mountain; they had reached its base. Its height seemed even more imposing up close.

And if the false trail doesn't distract the tigers, then maybe those wolves will.

Did you see the tigers again when you were laying out the false trail?

No, but we smelled them. They were close.

They sat in silence for a long time. Kan looked around at the others. Their pack now only numbered eight, and they had been pushed to their limits in the last days.

He finally broke the silence. *So what do you think lies on the other side of the mountain?*

Lana looked up at the mountain, then back at him. *Our new home.*

He smiled. There could be new dangers there, but they had run from tigers and giant wolves. He liked her optimism. *The pack needs order again, something to pick up their spirits.*

They were silent for a moment.

I have a plan for that, Lana said with a smile.

You do?

Puppies.

Puppies? he repeated, wondering if he had heard her correctly. How could she be talking about puppies at a time like this?

Yes, puppies always raise spirits.

And where.... He finally understood. If they were the alphas, it was their responsibility to conceive the new generation for the pack. She had surprised him, but he bounced back quickly. *Let me know when you're ready,* he joked.

I will. She wasn't joking.

In her look and her voice, he heard something telling him there was no point in arguing; he had been with her long enough to know once a vision came she would see it through to its end despite any opposition around her. Her determination would see the pack to a new home; it could be their salvation if the land beyond delivered what she dreamed. But if it didn't—he didn't want to think of that.

Kan pushed away the thoughts of the tigers who were out to get them along with the images of Danuwa and Sikwa and what they might be doing to Sasa and Oni—and how he might fulfill his promise of returning for Sasa. And he even pushed away thoughts of the strange wolf who had shown some sort of recognition of him. In this moment those concerns had to wait.

They were together again, and for the first time in a long time, she had driven the darkness away; she made him smile about the future. He looked up at the mountain in front of them, considering again the new home that lay on the other side, as the last sun of the day shone brilliantly on the snow ahead.

14

ZOV TIGRA

"**D**O YOU THINK MICK MEANT TO STRAND US OUT here in the woods?" I asked, stepping back from the broken-down ATV, looking up at the towering evergreens surrounding us. We were lost in the middle of a Russian forest, somewhere miles north of Vladivostok.

"What? He said he was coming back for us." The tone in her voice caused me to turn back to her, and the late-afternoon autumn sunlight clearly revealed her frown.

"It was just a thought. You know he's been a little odd recently."

"How could you say such a thing? He's your friend, and he's been a great host."

"What if this is an elaborate practical joke?"

"Isn't this a little more serious than that? And wasn't this your idea anyway?"

"I'm not so sure now," I said, turning back to the ATV.

"So there's no way to get it running again?" She leaned in next to me, studying the engine.

"Something blew in here. I think a mechanic would have a challenge getting this hunk of metal going again anytime soon." I paused, then added, "That's why I'm a little suspicious."

Ignoring my theory about our situation, Tsula pressed on to more practical matters, examining the compartment at the back of the ATV. There was a tattered old tarp and a rusty flashlight that showed no signs of working. "Looks like we've got a superb survival kit here," I joked.

"Not helping." She looked around; the trees stood in thick patches on both sides of the road. "If we're going to be waiting for Mick, we might as well get some research done while we're here." She was actually smiling.

"Are you serious? Do you realize how soon our daylight is going to run out?" She raised an eyebrow, but I continued, "Sorry, but these aren't your woods, and this is tiger country. We need some good shelter." I pulled the old tarp out; it smelled like stale turpentine, and there were dark stains on it, like old blood. I let it fall to the ground behind the ATV. Pointing into the woods, I suggested, "We could go a few yards that way, climb a tree, and keep tabs on this spot in case Mick does come back."

"When Mick comes back," she corrected. "So we need to use our time wisely."

We stepped off the path and into the nearby brush. I breathed in the earthen smell of the woods and realized I was chilled here at the end of September. Too many new things had been thrown our way—earlier in the day it was exhilarating, now it was overwhelming. The beautiful had moved to the verge of the deadly. I suddenly felt vulnerable in that unknown forest.

"We shouldn't go far from the road," I cautioned.

"We'll be fine. I'll hear Mick. Get your camera out and take some scans of the area," she suggested as she walked up to a nearby Korean pine, inspecting the lower branches. She crouched down and inspected the ground nearby, smiling.

"What is it?" I asked.

"Looks like we're in wolf territory."

"Really?" I said while taking a three-dimensional scan of the woods around us. Her words and my scans sparked a memory of the forest-and-feather dream I had experienced not long after meeting her. Imagining again what it was to be prey, to be running from a creature with insatiable hunger, I found my free hand was rubbing the scar on my arm, the scar the mastiff had given me. I suddenly regretted having chosen Vladivostok as our honeymoon destination.

"Are you sure we should be out here?" I was embarrassed to hear hesitation in my voice.

"Cold feet?" Her question was also a challenge. A moment later, though, she decided on a different tack. "This is a great opportunity, Don. Look at this beautiful wilderness around us. There are dangers here, no doubt, but we can see it also as a place of retreat, even a place of shelter."

"Shelter? That's what we need right now, but all we have is that smelly tarp if it gets cold tonight."

"We can keep each other warm," she smiled.

"Mick's guaranteed to come back then."

She huffed, then gracefully shot up the tree, perching in a branch above me. I attempted to follow, slipping several times before finally pulling myself up on a nearby bough. "How long do we wait?" I asked.

"Waiting makes more sense right now than walking down the path, not sure where we're going. I expect Mick to be back soon."

We sat there quietly, each of us wrestling with our own thoughts, trying to find some solution to our situation. I wondered whether Mick and his adoptive father Pavel were okay. If anything happened to them, or if Mick was playing a terrible joke on us, we were in for a significant trial once the sun went down. How had we gotten ourselves into such a predicament?

§⁂

"Vladivostok certainly is a different place for a honeymoon. I would have expected at least the Caribbean," my dad commented as he helped me with the bow tie of my tuxedo.

I smiled. Dad had not offered much advice since Tsula and I had told him our plans back at Christmas, some nine months before. He and my mom had been noticeably happy to learn we would be waiting until after Tsula's graduation—and at the time we were hoping my graduation as well—for the wedding. My dad seemed genuinely excited for us, but I also had the feeling he thought my relationship with Tsula was finally going to get me to "grow up" and abandon my obsession with video games.

"I looked into all the typical destinations, but they didn't seem to fit us. You know Tsula loves the outdoors, and I was hoping to find a place where we could have both a resort and then a place to go hiking—preferably where we could see some wolves. I looked at Yellowstone and Yosemite and some other national parks here, but I finally went with a place where I've got inside connections."

"So Mick convinced you."

"I like to think I made my own decision, but he is always going on about how great his home is. It seemed to have all the components—a seaside resort, the Zov Tigra national park, and they'll all be celebrating Tiger Day this coming week. Besides, Mick's promised to give us the grand tour, and if we're going to be in another country, it makes sense to have a guide we can trust."

"Did you run the plan by Tsula?" he asked, his eyebrows rising slightly.

"The ceremony was her responsibility, and the honeymoon plans were mine," I defended. "She asked me to surprise her, that she just wanted to see something new."

"From my experience women who ask to be surprised often don't mean it. At least, your mother has rarely been happy when I didn't involve her in making such important decisions. I'd hear about it many times later."

"I haven't told Tsula directly, but I think she's guessed. She knows we're flying and we're headed out of the country, obviously. She seems excited."

At that moment I heard the doorknob turn, and Uncle Jack entered the room. "I think it's about time for us." Of the three of us, he looked the most out of place in a tuxedo. I looked down at his feet, almost expecting to find sandals, but found he had worn the matching black shoes. I knew it was a sacrifice for him.

I took one last look in the mirror. The bow tie, the cummerbund, the cufflinks, all seemed in place. Although I was tempted to put my sunglasses back on, I instead slipped them into my jacket pocket and followed my uncle out the door with my father close behind. It was the 25th of September, and I was getting married.

Although we had used rooms inside the church to get ready, we walked outside for the service. I was glad when Tsula decided on having the wedding outside. Even though she had been inside the church several times since December, I had not seen it since the funeral, and something about that did not sit well with me.

As we had rehearsed the evening before, my father, uncle, and I assumed our places at the front of the crowd, just to the right of Reverend Watie, who would be presiding over the ceremony.

I cannot adequately put into words what I—standing in that afternoon sun, the tops of mountains all around, trees just hinting at the golden transformation of autumn—felt when Tsula came into view around the standing crowd. There is a private language between couples, and though a small crowd gathered to witness our union, only Tsula and I understood when our eyes met. Others could observe the beauty of her profound simplicity. The dress had no train; there were no puffy sleeves, no satin, no trendy cuts. It was the whitest of dresses I have ever seen, and it fit her, nothing out of place, nothing too large or too tight, nothing calling undue attention to itself. Yet all these were only symbols of something greater, something more important, I witnessed in her face. She walked down that path toward me, and no other.

Although Tsula had tried to prepare me, the ceremony overwhelmed me. In the years ahead, she would make jokes about how her uncle's hand had to steady me to keep me from fainting, and I would half-heartedly defend myself, wondering if I had an intimation of what those vows meant. How could I have known? In my hopeful moments I look back and see a plan and a purpose, but in my melancholic moods I doubt. Was it a mistake, not so much for me, but for Tsula?

The ceremony was not all joy; we all keenly felt the absence of Tsula's mother. Just before Tsula reached me, she paused and her sister Inola came forward to light a special candle. Then her grandmother—her dad's mother—walked to her side, draping a blue blanket over her shoulders. Cherokee society is matriarchal, and husbands marry into their wife's clan, but Tsula's mother had been an outsider and had been adopted into her mother-in-law's wolf clan.

At the same moment, her uncle placed a similar one over my shoulders. When Tsula finally joined me, I saw the wet sheen in her eyes, and I had to fight the sentiment within me as we joined her uncle before a large ceremonial bonfire. When Tsula first told me about the fire, I had immediately thought about the night of the wolf makeup, her protest video, and our first kiss. But in the moment, while I smelled the burning wood, felt the warming heat, witnessed the smoke rising to the clouds, my thoughts were on Tsula.

"Our Creator has blessed us with the union of man and

woman," Reverend Watie started. "Marriage is something holy, and the vows Tsula and Don exchange here today will mark the beginning of their journey as husband and wife. May our Creator bless them when they travel to the north, the east, the south, and the west. May their union be like this fire, glowing warm and strong. May their union be like the river, flowing, cleansing them of all selfish thoughts. May they rely on each other, and pray for each other. May the Holy Spirit be upon them that their family be a blessing to them, to wolf clan, to our Cherokee tribe, to our nation, to our world, to our God."

Her uncle sang prayers for us and read from the Bible verses about the endurance of love—how those motivated by it keep no record of wrongs and hope for the best. He spoke about the blessings of family, the challenges we faced in the blending of our cultures, and then his confidence in Tsula and me, that we had the creativity and perseverance to make it work. Then after asking for the rings, he led us through our vows.

I reached for her hand. "Tsula, I promise to be a loving husband for you through the challenges of life, in good times and bad, in health and in sickness. I promise to devote my best efforts to providing for you and our family should we be blessed with children. Know that I love you deeply." I managed not to drop the ring, but quickly slipped it onto her finger.

"Before our Creator and these witnesses, I promise to be a loving wife for you, Don, down the path of life, through storms and sunny days, through health and sickness. I promise to care for you and our children, to nurture harmony with the world around us. Know that I love you deeply." Her hands, though smaller than my own, were firm as she slid the ring onto my finger.

Before I knew it, her uncle had removed the blue blankets from our shoulders. Then as I looked to him, he wrapped a much larger white blanket over both of us, and I welcomed its warmth and the intimacy of sharing it with Tsula. As we turned, her uncle declared us wife and husband and extended our invitation to those who had gathered to stay for a time of celebration. Then to kick off that celebration, following what we had rehearsed, my father handed me a basket, which I presented to Tsula—inside was a venison ham. After receiving it, she turned to her father who handed her a basket filled with corn, which she then presented to me. While we held up our respective baskets, her uncle explained they were symbols of our responsibilities in marriage, how we were to build our household together. He finished by offering a brief retelling of the Cherokee myth of the first man, Kanati the hunter, and the first woman, his wife Selu.

During the celebration that followed, late into the night, there were moments for friends and family to speak and for the presentation of gifts. Tsula's father gave us one of his masks. I had seen some of his wood carvings before in his shop, but this one was something special. I knew he had put hours into it. Though the mask was hard wood in my hand, the wolf face in it seemed fluid and alive, beautiful and mysterious.

"This mask is an expression of our culture and our clan," he said formally, and I knew he expected me to take care of his daughter. I felt the weight of the responsibility as he hugged her and when he patted me on the back. At the last, though, he winked at me, and I breathed again.

My father told us how happy he and my mother were for us, and then he said they wanted to help us with the cost of the trip. He slipped a piece of paper into my hand, and when I lifted it, I discovered it was a check. The amount surprised me.

"Thank you, Dad, but you don't have to."

"We want to. It can be a challenge just starting out as a couple."

I looked over at my mom, who was smiling broadly. When we first told my parents about the wedding, my mom had been quiet and reserved. I think the news shocked her, and she didn't know how to take it. I wondered if she were a little jealous, but as the months progressed, she warmed up to the idea, and now I was glad to see she was indeed a part of the celebration. She had had her input in the honeymoon plan, insisting I arrange some spa time for Tsula at the resort.

Considerably late that night, after saying goodbye to the friends and family who had driven up to our wedding, Tsula and I drove down to Atlanta to hop on the first plane of our journey to Vladivostok. Although Tsula had guessed our destination, it was not fully confirmed until I handed her the ticket at the airport. She grinned and asked if Mick was going to get a kickback for the tourist dollars we were bringing to his home country. I laughed as we carried our luggage into the terminal.

&.

Mick was not able to attend our wedding. Months back I had felt awkward about asking him to return to the States for the wedding. His plan upon finishing the semester in May was to go home to Russia for several months to conduct some final research on Siberian tigers for his doctorate. So it did not make sense to put that pressure on him when we would see him a few days after it anyway. Tsula kept pushing me, saying it was the polite thing to ask him and let him make the decision. Rather than putting him on the spot in person, I decided just to mail an invitation. One evening several days later, when he came to the door of my room, I could see his hesitation, so I quickly gave him an out, saying he did not need to feel obligated to come; we could show him pictures when we caught up with him in Vladivostok. He quickly accepted the plan, enthusiastically declaring he would make our visit to Russia memorable.

We were not supposed to see him until the fourth day, but life rarely goes according to plan. Sometimes we are given glimpses into things we do not understand. On the third day, I caught sight of him across the massive crowd that had flocked to the streets to celebrate Tiger Day. Mick had warned me of the thousands who would be out, but I didn't believe it until I saw it. People of all ages were dressed in orange, red, and black, with tiger tails hanging and faces painted in elaborate tiger patterns.

When I saw the first painted face, I turned to Tsula and smiled, "I think you could find a place here."

I saw in her eyes she was impressed too.

An elaborate parade progressed down the street and circled the downtown square. The brightly colored orange costumes and blue balloons starkly contrasted with the neutral gray and sand-colored historic buildings looming in the background. Below a dark charcoal-colored statue of three soldiers, one little girl posed for a picture. She must have been about six, and something about her costume and the smile on her face mesmerized me for a moment. I was going to point her out to Tsula, but I saw she was watching a group of dancers dressed in royal blue costumes. Since I thought the little girl's costume was more authentic, I turned to watch her, and as I did, I spotted a familiar head bobbing above the crowd several yards away.

It was Mick. For a moment I had the urge to call out, but then I realized there was no chance he could hear me above the celebrations of the day. He was headed away from us, and it looked like he had not seen us. So out of curiosity, I watched him and discovered he was not alone. Beside him walked a woman, dressed in a tight blouse, shredded jeans, and sneakers. From what we knew of Mick, she seemed a strange companion, but I noticed he was different too, dressed in a black T-shirt and camouflage pants, no longer the classy-dressed graduate student we knew. Since they were walking quickly through the crowd on the other side of the street, I almost missed them, but I could not mistake my friend.

By the time Tsula responded to me in the noise of the crowd, too many other people had obscured them. My wife could not corroborate my sighting. I am not quite sure why, but the difference in Mick confused me. Here we were in his homeland, and he was different. I began to wonder how different.

The next day, when we finally did meet Mick at a little cafe, he was back in a polo shirt and designer jeans. He swung his arms out in a big gesture, and I prepared for the biggest of bear hugs. He greeted us in Russian, and I tried to play along, but my Russian was terrible.

So he quickly turned to English to make us feel at home. "Welcome to Russia, my friends! You are finally here, and now you will never want to go back."

He smiled mischievously. I was surprised how good it felt to see that smile and to hear his voice after being immersed the last days in a culture and language we did not know.

"You were right, Mick. I'm impressed," I said after he released me from the quick hug.

"Your hometown is beautiful," Tsula said with genuine excitement.

"So what have you seen?"

We told him about our hotel's view of the Bay, the historic monuments, and the ornate Orthodox churches. We mentioned our adventures with Russian food and the general warm greeting we had received from the people we had met. Then last of all, we spoke about the grand spectacle of Tiger Day. I decided not to mention spotting him with the woman in tattered jeans—I would interrogate him later about his lady friend—and Tsula honored my desire to keep it quiet.

"So what's the plan?" I asked.

"Are you ready to find some tigers?"

"Lead the way," Tsula chimed in. "We trust you."

As we walked to his car, Tsula and I shared the sparsest of details about the wedding festivities. We would have given him the web address of pictures if he had asked anything about the ceremony, but he never did. Instead, conversation quickly moved from us to Zov Tigra and to the outing he had lined up for us in the woods.

"How's your research?" I asked.

"It's good."

"Only you could earn graduate credit by staying home," I teased.

"How can I help if you chose the wrong degree?"

We eventually reached his car, and I let Tsula take the passenger side while I took my place in the backseat, sitting in the middle so I could see them both. On the trip out of the city, headed north, Mick explained we were going to meet up with one of the rangers who patrolled the borders of the national park, a man named Pavel. Although there were only about eight Amur tigers in the entire park, Pavel would be one of the few who would have an informed perspective on the roaming patterns of these animals. Going out into the forest with him would increase the chances of a tiger sighting, and even if we did not see one, he could offer stories of the times when he had seen them.

The countryside around us quickly changed from the developed coastal city to a forested area, transitioning soon into a mountainous terrain. We were not quite sure where Mick was taking us. At the moment, I missed my cell phone and the map app that would show us where we were. I had looked into bringing my American phone, but the Russians used a different network, requiring a more expensive phone and plan, which did not make sense to me if we were only going to be in Russia for a week. Leaving my cell phone and Reality glasses at home, I had opted for a phone card, which Tsula and I had already used to reach out to family from the hotel. It was only during this car ride I realized I had forgotten to ask Mick if he would help me buy a throwaway cell phone in Russia. I wondered how much he knew we were in his hands.

We eventually pulled down a long dirt road, Mick saying we were near the national park, but from the surroundings

I could tell we were not at the tourist entrance. There was no main gate, no signs pointing the way.

As if he read my thoughts, Mick explained, "We're going behind the main tourist section. There's too much noise over there to count on a tiger sighting."

We came up on a truck with a trailer, and a man was working on unloading a motorcycle, to add to the other bike and the ATV parked nearby. As he parked, Mick said, "That's Pavel."

When we stepped out of the car, Mick led us over, and the other man greeted us, his English hidden by a thicker accent than Mick's. He was older than I had expected, a round face with wrinkles, cracks at the outside corners of his eyes—signs of frequent squinting in the sun. Although he wasn't thin and he had a slight stoop, he proved to be stronger and more sprightly than he looked as he pulled the last bike into place. He was dressed in camouflage from head to toe.

"Pavel knows these woods better than anyone," Mick said with pride. It seemed he was almost asking us to applaud his choice.

"We appreciate your working this out for us," Tsula responded.

I took the opportunity to shake Pavel's calloused hand. "Thank you for taking time out for us."

Pavel grinned, and I noticed he was missing one of his upper teeth. It distracted me as he spoke. "Any time I help Mikhail's friends learn about tigers."

"The Sikhote-Alin mountains were set up as a preserve all the way back in the 1930s, though the Zov Tigra was only established in 2008, to call attention to the need to save the Amur tigers and their prey. We've slowed the logging—it was bad back in the 1980s—so the forests are recovering, but we need to make certain there is enough food for the tigers, but you two probably already knew that," Mick was rattling on, obviously excited to be sharing this finally with us.

"When did you first come out here?" I asked.

"You remember I told you one of my father's friends helped raise me after my father died. That was Pavel. He took me out here first when I was about ten."

The older man chimed in, "Yes. He was natural."

Tsula whistled at the surprise.

Mick was holding back; I wanted to learn more. "So how's it been working for the government?" I asked Pavel.

He frowned in confusion. He must not have understood me.

Mick jumped in, "As a ranger for the tiger park."

Pavel seemed to catch on, but only offered, "Tough."

Mick then said, "Many of those who got into poaching in the past did it because they needed the money. Many people are very poor. Though we want to save the tigers, it hasn't been fun enforcing the laws either."

Something unsaid passed between Mick and Pavel, but if this old man was essentially Mick's dad, we would probably see a lot of that.

Mick next explained that Tsula and I could ride together on the ATV, for he and Pavel would take the motorcycles. Although I was interested in taking the keys, I acquiesced when Tsula told me she wanted to drive. We followed them out into the forest. It was a bumpy ride, and I developed a headache a few miles in. When I saw Tsula was enjoying herself, though, I started to feel a little better. So this would be a memorable honeymoon.

We did not see much wildlife thanks to the motors, but at one point we shut them all down and followed Pavel several paces off the path. He showed us a tree with long gouges in it; they began way above my head and followed down close to the ground. I marveled at the animal and the claws that could leave behind such deep marks. A pungent smell made me take a step back, my hand to my nose. Mick laughed, explaining the spot was a scent post.

Returning to our rides, we travelled several more miles in. About that time we were rounding a sharp bend in the path, Pavel's walkie-talkie clicked and hissed, and then a frantic voice started yelling things in Russian. Pavel grabbed the transceiver, stopped his bike, and shouted something back into it. Mick and Tsula pulled up beside him, and we listened as a conversation ensued, Pavel looking serious. I turned to Mick for some explanation and saw he was watching Pavel closely, a frown clouding his face.

"What's going on?" I heard Tsula ask.

"Please wait," Mick responded in a clipped fashion.

Finally putting the walkie down, Pavel spoke to Mick. Their conversation was in Russian, but Mick finally said, "The rangers have spotted poachers in the woods not too far from where we are. They've asked Pavel if he can run in that direction, perhaps to cut them off."

"I am sorry. I have to go." Pavel finally addressed us in English again.

"If he can make it, we'll meet up with him later down the path," Mick explained further.

Pavel nodded, turned, and revved the engine of his motorcycle. Within seconds he passed out of sight down the path in front of us.

"Looks like it's just me now," Mick said. "If you hold on, I have this spot not too far from here where we might be able to find some signs of a wolf pack. Just a few kilometers to go."

Tsula followed Mick, and since the motorcycle and the ATV made a good bit of noise, we did not have much of an opportunity to ask any questions of him. As part of the research I'd done in preparation for this trip, I had read about tiger poaching and the problem it presented to the region. I wanted to know if there was any risk of coming across poachers in the forest. I did not want to put Tsula at risk. Hadn't I just recently promised to care for her? And I didn't relish running into strangers myself in that context, particularly when I couldn't speak their language.

Only a few minutes later, there was another click and hiss, and I realized Mick had his own walkie-talkie. As we stopped in the path again for Mick to carry on another conversation in Russian, I looked down to see if we had a receiver in the ATV and was disturbed to find we did not. When his conversation was over, he turned to us, a look of confusion on his face. "I am not certain what to do. Pavel told me they need help. They do not have enough volunteers."

"We could help," Tsula immediately offered.

"Poachers have guns," Mick responded. "I would not ask that of you," he said, then paused. "Especially on your honeymoon."

Tsula was quiet for a moment, and I jumped in. "Should you go?"

"They need my help, and I have faith you two can manage here without me for a little time."

"What do you do if they have guns?"

"Stay out of their way," he said with his trademark grin.

"Then why go?"

"Most poachers run; they do not know whether I have a gun or not. They just do not want to get caught." He looked at Tsula. "Do not worry. I will return soon. When I am gone, just keep down this road. We are not far from the spot I mentioned. You will not miss it; the road bulges off to the side. I promise to meet you there after we scare off these poachers."

"Be careful," I said simply.

"You know me." He glanced in my direction, then kicked his motorcycle in gear.

He zipped along down the road and soon disappeared. Tsula and I now were to explore the area on our own. Although I had done some reading about Zov Tigra, I was not ready to navigate the area without a guide. Tsula did not step into the role either, so we naturally fell into following Mick's suggestion.

About fifteen minutes later, though, a loud pop in the engine surprised us, and as the ATV rolled to a stop, smoke rising from the engine, I groaned. When I gave up on it, Tsula tried to get it started again, but the engine was dead. We were stranded in the middle of the Amur forest.

ॐ

Sitting in my perch up in the Korean pine, looking back at the road and the broken ATV, I ran my hand over the needles in front of me, momentarily fascinated by the prickly stickiness. I eventually turned my attention back to Tsula.

"What are we going to do now?" I asked.

We had been sitting up in the tree for close to an hour.

She did not answer, so I tried another tactic. "We could get frisky."

"You'd fall out of the tree."

"So what's next?" I asked again.

At that moment we heard a squeal yards away, back into the woods.

"Sounds like a boar," Tsula commented, and as she spoke, a dark round shape tore through the underbrush—and close on its heels were two gray forms, taller and thinner than the first.

Two wolves closed in on a wild boar as Tsula and I watched from our perch on the other side of the forest. A third wolf suddenly appeared from another direction, trying to close off the boar's escape. One of the first two wolves got a tooth-hold on the boar's haunch, allowing the other two wolves to catch up, and together they pulled their prey to the ground. The squealing gave way to growling, tearing, and crunching as the wolves began to feed.

I checked with Tsula, who had raised her finger to her mouth, signaling for me to be silent. Looking back, I watched a fourth wolf join in the feast while a fifth paced at a distance, head lowered. I pulled my camera out and quietly filmed the feeding, the wrestling for turns to eat, the systematic dismantling of their prey.

We knew we were in the midst of a rare event, the chance to witness a wolf hunt. Although I filmed the feasting, I wished I had had the prescience to have captured the chase and the bringing down of the boar. Zooming in with the camera, I could see the sharp teeth ripping flesh, the wildness in the eyes, and the grimacing as each sought to protect its place at the meal. I lowered the camera reflexively as if to remind myself I was a safe distance away, but then I started to wonder what a safe distance was from a pack of ravenous wolves. Would the boar have sated their hunger, or would it have been merely an appetizer to a main course? In the vast majority of cases, wolves just ran from people. There were stories of occasional confrontations, though, and a fresh kill nearby seemed to me to be one of those bad situations—the wolves would want to defend their meat. If there were any chance the wolves would come after us, I was not going to leave the perch in that Korean pine anytime soon.

As the afternoon faded into early evening, my back and legs turned numb from sitting in the tree that long. The wolves had made short order of the boar, and once the initial feast was over, and even the last pacing wolf was allowed to eat, they seemed to be in a good mood, for one of them found that a piece of bone was a great toy to challenge the others to a game of keep-away. This wolf, one of the larger ones, tossed the bone up into the air, another grabbed it, and the first would chase the one who caught it. I was delighted to be able to capture these moments on my camera; I knew I would be studying them closely later.

Tsula seemed as excited as I was. We knew not to whisper and hoped our scent would not be carried down to the pack. We seemed to have lost touch with the fact that Mick and Pavel had abandoned us in a forest we did not know. At one point I thought we probably could retrace the path we had taken into the woods, but there was no telling how many hours it would take on foot to make it back to Mick's car. It was only a cursory thought, for the wolves were a magnificent distraction. We had planned for this part of our trip to involve some research, and here we had stumbled into the middle of it.

Suddenly a loud crack reverberated in the distance. I saw the recognition in Tsula's eyes. The sound was a gunshot. Was it the poachers shooting at Mick, Pavel, and the others? Several of the wolves immediately lifted their heads, tensed, ears rotating, listening. Perhaps they had known we were there all along, but did not see us as a potential threat. I froze. To my surprise one of the wolves, the one I was guessing was the alpha, sounded a howl. The beautiful and eerie roo-a-roo sound touched something inside, and I felt the shiver one feels in the presence of something powerful.

Then the pack in unison trotted off, disappearing in the green brush beyond.

I heard Tsula's voice, "Gunshot?"

"Don't think it was a car backfiring."

Unamused, Tsula continued, "Do you think Mick's okay?"

"I think he can take care of himself. I just hate we lost our wolves."

"That encounter made our trip."

"And nothing else."

She grinned, then dismissed the tangent. "Did you get some good footage?"

Turning the camera over in my hands, I said, "I think so. Hopefully the stabilizer compensated for my shaking hand. It was a long time to hold the camera steady."

There was a moment of quiet as we readjusted to our predicament.

I asked, "Any thoughts on what to do? I'm getting kind of hungry."

"I wouldn't recommend eating anything out here. Most

of it would probably make you wish you hadn't. The two first priorities are warmth and water. Let's check the ATV again to see if we missed anything."

She slid off the branch and dropped to the ground.

My legs were stiff, and my exit looked more like a fall than hers did. I immediately looked around, a little spooked after the encounter with the wolves.

Back at the ATV, we relocated the tarp and the flashlight.

"I'd have to be really cold to wrap up in that thing," I said, catching its stench again.

"Let's hope we don't have to." She looked down the road again. "I pray Mick's alright."

"I doubt we could help."

"Despite the tracks from the bikes, we'd probably get lost, and we don't know where that path would take us."

"So do we stay put or go back?"

"That's a hard choice. We assume we could find the same path back, but it will be dark soon, and once we're in the dark, there is a greater chance we'd end up off path."

"So we're staying?" I asked, a little nervous by the prospect of a night in these woods.

"We're not going to get much sleep out here. I still don't understand what's keeping Mick. Something doesn't seem right."

There was another pause; then I looked back in the ATV, saying, "Too bad there wasn't a tent in here."

But at that moment, I heard the revving sound of a motorcycle coming toward us from the path Mick and Pavel had taken, and within seconds a single cyclist came into view just as twilight was settling in, the headlamp obscuring the rider from my vision. I had the urge to run, but there was no time. I took a few steps back until I realized it was Mick.

"Mick!" I heard Tsula yell.

He pulled close.

"What was that all about?" I bombarded him.

Not looking me in the eye at first, Mick said, "Sorry. I didn't count on that happening. We found the poachers, and Pavel and I tried to catch up to them. They gave us a long chase. One of their bullets hit Pavel in his arm, and I couldn't leave him. I eventually had to radio someone in to help him. I didn't have a way of letting you know."

"Is he going to be okay?" I asked.

"I think so," he answered, finally looking up. "To tell you the truth, I didn't know if you'd still be here."

"The engine in the ATV blew. I couldn't get it to crank again."

"I don't think we can get three people on this motorcycle, and I can't get my car back in here," he thought aloud.

I immediately started doing the math in my head—we were living one of those tortuous word problems from middle school, but now there seemed no viable solution. The bike carried two people, and the trip was a little under two hours one way. We were in for a long wait before we could finally leave the park.

Tsula volunteered, "You two go ahead; I can wait it out."

"No," I answered. "I won't leave you behind."

Mick stepped off the cycle, "You two go, and I'll stay. I know these woods better than you do. Don, you can then double-back for me."

"What if we meet a ranger or someone else? You know how bad my Russian is," I interjected.

"Don, I don't like this," Tsula looked to me.

"Do you have a better plan?" I asked. I really wished she could have surprised me again.

"Isn't there a chance we could get lost in the dark?"

Her question stood, and we were back at square one. Mick knew the path best; it made most sense for him to drive.

I finally said, "Mick, you've got to drive. I'll stay behind."

There was something in his eyes I could not read as he again mounted the motorcycle.

"I don't like this either," Tsula said, grabbing my arm.

"Go, Tsula. The sooner we start the sooner we'll be able to get back to our hotel room. I think I can manage. I'll climb a tree and hold out like you taught me."

She kissed me and got on the bike behind Mick.

I leaned in and whispered in Mick's ear, "You better take care of her."

"No need to worry, Tovarishch." He narrowed his eyes.

They drove off, Tsula looking back, frowning. When they disappeared in the dark, the weight of my decision suddenly hit me. I was now alone in the wilderness, only yards from the spot where the wolves had dismembered the boar. As I imagined the pack surrounding me, creeping forward, teeth bared, I darkly speculated how loud my squeals would be.

15
THE WILDERNESS

"I F I'M GOING TO BE YOUR WIFE, DON'T YOU THINK YOU should tell me what you're going to be when you're grown up?" Seated on the other side of the small table, just outside a coffee shop near campus, she began her assault, the book she was holding lowered just enough so I could see her eyes, but not her mouth.

I smiled. We were supposed to be studying, but here was the question again. Tsula started asking it just a few weeks after she had accepted my proposal, and it seemed to crop up at least once a week.

"What do you mean 'if'? Are you having second thoughts?"

"That depends. Are you having second thoughts?" Her eyes were full of mischief, the rest of her face still hidden behind the green-cloth library book.

"Do I need to propose again to convince you?"

She finally put the book down. "It wouldn't hurt."

I looked around and saw everything was quiet on the street, only one other student was outside with us and she was facing another way, so in mock chivalry I got down on one knee next to the table and held up an imaginary ring. "Tsula Watie, will you do me the honor of—?" I paused.

She leaned forward.

"Paying for my coffee."

She immediately grabbed her book and threw it at me.

As I recovered, picking up Tsula's book, I saw a young lady at the window inside the coffee shop watching me. She was shaking her head. When I regained my seat, I heard Tsula say, "You're pleased with yourself, aren't you?" Tsula now was frowning too. "I had something else in mind."

"What?"

"Do you trust me?"

I recognized the loaded question. "Yes."

"That's too easy."

"Ok." I paused and then said, "I want to." A second later I decided to return fire. "Do you trust me?"

"I want to."

The tone in her voice kept me silent. It was tender, yet guarded. I studied her amber eyes and saw her intently gazing back. I felt her sincerity, but found her elusive. A cool spring breeze chilled me.

I had not forgotten what had started the conversation. "I'm waiting for the right moment." And I was. Her persistent return to the subject had turned our exchanges about my career plans into quite the game, and as I faced each new assault, every temptation, my initial reserve had morphed into a desire not to disappoint. Now there was simply too much buildup for me to let her down.

"I'm waiting too," she whispered.

§

I made her wait several months. Although I am certain she

uncovered many clues on her own, I resolved not to help her. I decided I was not going to reveal my plans until I could show her.

When I left Tsunami Games, my research suffered well into the fall semester, yet as I talked to Dr. Stanley, as I kept thinking about my dad's suggestion about redirecting my research, I threw around a new idea. Mick proved to be a good sounding board.

"So what do you think about the idea of a virtual zoo?" I asked him on one of those days we hung out at our apartment, probably in October, before I reconnected with Tsula.

He kicked back in his sofa chair, and I watched him chew on the idea for a moment. "What do you mean by 'virtual zoo'? Just a simulation of a zoo? How could that compete with a real one?"

I defended, "People wouldn't have to travel to visit it. They could experience all sorts of animals they wouldn't see otherwise. And they would be guaranteed to see them. Come on, Mick, you know you've visited a zoo, come to an exhibit, and seen only a bunch of plants and a sign telling you there should be an animal running around in front of you."

He frowned.

I continued, "And there would be no animals to suffer the abuse of people who shouldn't be anywhere near the animals—like that couple that caused us so much grief with the tiger cubs."

Mick nodded in recognition, but then said, "Is this not tame in comparison to what you were doing for Tsunami? Are you sure you should not go and beg for your old job back?"

"Thanks for the support. No, I'm thinking about something more immersive than a petting zoo. I'm thinking about a simulation that would allow you to experience the world as an animal. Imagine what it would be like to see and hear and smell like a tiger. Imagine what it would be like to hunt an elk. Imagine what it would be like to run from a hunter's gun."

"And how do you plan to do that?" I heard the skepticism in his voice, but also a note of curiosity. I knew I had him if I could convince him on the next point.

"I'm working on the hardware and software that will take brain scans of different animals and then superimpose them over human brain scans to show us which areas to stimulate."

"What do you do when an animal like a tiger has a much more advanced sense of smell?"

"The human brain has more potential than the human nose. That's what I've been trying to argue with the VR technology. It's all outside us, limited by our own senses. If we tap into the brain, then we have a game changer."

"And you are the mad scientist to do it?" Mick grinned.

"I could use some help," I admitted. "Care to join me on an impossible quest?"

"Are you sure you want me along?"

"You've got the expertise in biology the project will need."

"You finally acknowledge my superior intellect."

Knowing he was trying to bait me again, I ignored him and blazed ahead with the idea. "And my dad, the brain surgeon, can help with the medical side of things, particularly in developing something that is safe. To pull it off, we'll have to assemble a team with some others we can trust."

"Sounds like a big project. Who is going to pay for it?"

"I'm still working on that side," I admitted. These were the beginning stages; practical concerns would come later. I knew, though, Mick's question was an important one. "I'll try to look into some research grants. Maybe we'll get lucky and win the lottery or something."

"Now I know why you need me. I'm the lucky one."

"So you're in?"

"Sure, *Tovarishch*. Maybe along the way I can convince you to turn it into a video game so that we can become billionaires."

"Maybe," I said softly.

Leaving Tsunami Games, in my mind, had also been a stepping away from a potentially lucrative career. After that conversation with my dad about redirecting my research, and previous ones with Tsula about making a difference, "helping others" started to seem to me as important as "making money." Mick's offer seemed the voice of temptation, pulling me back into old patterns of thought. At the time I was uncertain which way to go.

Yet as spring semester rolled around, and Tsula and I became engaged, I began to envision the project more as an opportunity for education, to influence people, rather than a chance to make money. My conversations with Tsula only solidified this plan, particularly the day I showed her the simulation.

"It's only a prototype," I said as I held up what looked like a pair of sunglasses and a baseball cap.

"I like the wolf," she said looking at the embroidery on the cap.

"Just for you. It took me a little while to find it," I answered, then moved on to more technical issues. "Inside the band of the cap is the secret tech, the product of my doctoral research, the part that makes this more what I hope will become Immersive Reality, rather than Virtual Reality. It's the part that communicates directly with your brain," I explained as I placed the cap on her head. "For now there are also earbuds that fold down for your ears and glasses similar to Reality glasses. I hope one day I might be able to streamline the gear even more."

"Is it safe?" she asked.

"Do you trust me?" I helped lean her back in the sofa chair. For privacy I had locked us in the lounge off the computer lab, one of the privileges of being a graduate student.

She smiled. "It's your turn to paint my face?"

I laughed at the memory. "You could look at it that way." Stepping back, I sat down across from her and put my own cap, buds, and glasses into place. "This is just a start. I hope to develop it more. You'll begin with a blank screen which will then fade into the simulation."

"I'm ready," she said.

"Then press the button on the side of your glasses."

I watched her slender hand follow my instruction. Then I leaned back and touched the button on the side of my glasses. My vision immediately went dark, and all became quiet.

Since Tsula and I were sharing the same sim, I could just hear her breathing. In seconds light started to grow around us, and my vision came into focus. We stood on a sandy patch, a swamp stretching out before us, the thin trees sticking up out of the water. The one closest to us was a blackgum, a patch of neon green moss growing up its mottled gray trunk.

When I looked to Tsula, I saw her staring at a series of Venus flytraps—one had just closed in on something.

"The transition can be disorienting at first," I offered.

She finally turned to look at me, and I saw a note of confusion in her eyes. "Is that you, Don?"

"Yes, look down at yourself." I watched her closely as she did.

She lifted a paw and studied it a moment. "We're red wolves?"

"I wanted to surprise you. You might check out your reflection in the water."

She looked up and around her. "So this is the Alligator River Refuge?"

"Now you know what I was doing with all those 3D scans. It hasn't been easy putting all this together."

She took a few steps toward the edge of the water, where she tried to find an open spot among the plants growing there.

"Do you see it?" I asked.

"I look like the wolf we lost that summer."

"I wanted to commemorate her in some way. I knew she was

special to you."

"Thank you, Don. She's beautiful. I do miss that summer." Her voice was quiet and reflective as she stared into the water.

"Do you want to explore a little? There's not much beyond this sandy patch, and we can't go swimming—I'm still working on the mechanics of that—but there are a couple more things to see."

"I wish we could have caught the one who shot her."

The emotion in her reaction surprised me. A small part of me had wondered if the simulation would push her back into that unsolved case, but I was hoping the wonder of the simulation would dominate. I did not expect this turn.

She was quiet, and when she spoke again, she surprised me. "How do we sign out?"

"Are you sure I can't convince you to look around some more."

"I can tell you've put a lot of work into this, but I'm ready to stop."

"Alright then," I said, trying to keep any irritation out of my voice. "Close your eyes, and keep them closed as you count to thirty. Then say clearly, 'Exit.'"

I watched her follow my instructions, and when her sim disappeared, I exited as well. All went blank again before I became conscious of the glasses in front of me and pushed them up to see Tsula awkwardly pushing hers up.

"Hold on," I said, jumping to my feet. I wanted to protect my investment.

When I got to her, I lifted the cap and glasses away. Since her dark hair was hiding her face, I crouched down next to her, and she looked at me, a solemn expression on her face.

"So what do you think about it?" I asked, hungry for affirmation.

"I don't know what to say. The images were so sharp." Her tone continued to be reserved.

"You didn't like it?" I fished.

"It is unlike anything I have ever experienced. I appreciate your work to preserve the memory of the wolf we lost—that is a true gift."

"But it's more than a memory. It's a chance to experience what it's like to be a red wolf."

"I'm sorry, Don, but can we do that?" she asked. "Do we know what it is like to be a wolf?"

"It's a start," I defended. "I plan to do more research into wolf DNA and wolf sensory perception to try to bridge the gap with human senses."

"Why?"

I paused a moment. I knew the importance of this answer. "Maybe we can get more people to support the cause of the red wolves if they could experience just a little bit of what the red wolves do. I think these sims could do more to raise awareness of endangered animals than any lecture ever could."

"I can see that. Maybe I need to think about it some more."

I had not expected this response from her, so I remained silent as I put my gear in a safe place and picked up her backpack.

Recovering, she finally said, "Thank you, Don, for showing me. I hope it does raise awareness for the red wolves. They can use all the help they can get."

"Well, let's go grab some lunch." I changed the subject to hide any disappointment.

As we left the lab, I wondered if she was holding something back; I had the nagging feeling I had not yet convinced her of the power of the simulation. Would I ever?

❦

The night Mick and Tsula drove off and left me somewhere in the middle of Zov Tigra, I found myself thinking back to that moment, wondering how I could capture the essence of the wilderness around me. What was it about the wild woods that drew her, and why could I not copy it in my simulation?

Out there in the forest, inundated with the strange, the wild, the beautiful, the intimidating, I felt so small. As I listened to the clicks, thumps, and rattles, unable to identify what was moving in the dark around me, I was not sure what to do. The first strange sound or two, I pulled out my pocket flashlight, but the light was not strong enough to see anything beyond a couple feet. All I was doing was calling attention to myself.

I did not stay on the ground long, but quickly scrambled up the tree where Tsula and I had perched earlier. A breeze blew by, making me realize I was getting cold. I closed my eyes and tried to calm myself, slowly breathing in and out. It helped until a sharp sting on my arm startled me and I jerked reflexively, slipping on the branch and then falling. Grasping out, I landed on my chest, my arms scraping and holding onto the branch, my feet dangling below. Not knowing what it was in the dark—I had visions of a spider or some poisonous insect—I decided not to climb back up, but to drop the rest of the way to the ground. Using the flashlight to inspect my arm, all I found was a small red mark, but it throbbed, along with the scrape on my chest, and I really began to feel I wanted to go home. This honeymoon was proving too memorable.

After the sting and the fall, I decided not to climb another tree, but to crouch on top of the ATV. Even though the perch was lower, I was hoping the smell of the machine would be a deterrent for any creatures that might sneak up on me in the dark. When my legs tired of the crouching, I had to give in and sit, my legs tingling. I checked my watch and saw it had been a little over an hour. I did not know if I could hold out. These minutes seemed unbelievably long.

To occupy myself, I thought back over the day and the strange behavior I had seen in Mick. My imagination ran away, and I wondered if Mick had been lying to us. Was this afternoon all an elaborate practical joke? I saw in all Mick's awkward moments a hidden affection toward Tsula. I knew from the beginning he liked her, and he had been her TA too, the semester Tsula and I were estranged. Tsula told me she had enjoyed the class with him; he had always been a gentleman around her. At the lowest point, when the woods around me felt massive and threatening, I began to think this moment was the perfect opportunity for Mick to get rid of me if he truly resented my marrying Tsula.

In the midst of that thought, I felt a presence nearby—even though it was very subtle, perhaps a breath or a soft pad on the ground. I froze and fought the urge to bring out the flashlight, but instead reached for the camera. Although I couldn't see anything, I knew the camera had the capacity to pull in more light than I thought was there. As I lifted it, I saw two shining orbs; they had to be eyes. I almost dropped the camera when I came to the realization they were aimed at me. Then I remembered the camera was still at full zoom—the animal was farther away—and relaxed a fraction. The animal was large, not a raccoon or even a boar. It did not look like a deer either.

Then a low grumble sounded, almost like a boat motor. It had to be a large cat, but which kind I could not tell in the dark. How could this be? Then I thought of the carcass of the boar. Even though the wolves had pretty much devoured it, the smell was probably still in the air, drawing other predators. Had this beast—tiger or leopard—come only to be disappointed at how little was left? Was its appetite only whet for something else? Was I to be its next meal?

I was filming now. How much did I want to risk to get some good footage? I did not think Tsula would believe me without it, and I knew it would also help with my project. The eyes seemed to move closer; it was a slink, and I was betting it was a leopard. It was a little too curious, so I called out, my voice a higher pitch than expected—not so intimidating—but the form paused and lowered. When it did not move, I decided to risk using the flash, and as the bright light blinded me, I heard a thrashing in the leaves. Blinking several times, my eyes finally readjusted; the cat appeared to have run, for I could not find the reflective orbs anywhere. Finally, feeling I could check the picture, I discovered a lithe form, covered in rosettes, mouth open, eyes wide in surprise. One of the rarest creatures in the world—it had to be an Amur leopard.

My emotions ran high. Not only was I wondering whether the animal would come back, strategically creeping around to another side, I was also celebrating the sheer luck of capturing an image of this critically endangered animal. As I sat in the dark, wishing I had a blanket, I panned my camera for another potential sighting, but the leopard had run back into the sheltering wilderness.

When I heard the rumble of the motorcycle, my shoulders relaxed. I no longer had to doubt Mick's return. The headlamp blinded me, and I threw up my hand to try to see around it.

"Don!"

It wasn't Mick.

Tsula pulled the bike up next to me. "Are you okay?"

"You'll never believe what I saw," I answered.

"What?"

"A leopard."

"In the dark?"

"I'll show you the picture when we get back. I had to fight it off with my camera."

"Only you," she said with a laugh, then switched subjects. "I had quite an argument with Mick about who was coming back for you."

"I was expecting him since he knows the roads better."

"I've been down the path twice, that's all I needed."

I smiled in the dark at her confidence. "How'd you finally convince him?"

"I told him you'd rather hug me for two hours. He couldn't

argue with my logic."

I laughed and slid onto the motorcycle behind her, indeed hugging her close, her back warm against my chest. It felt so good I didn't mind the bumps on the way back.

୫୭

Mick surprised me with one other gift the next evening. In preparing for the honeymoon trip, I had asked him if there were going to be any interesting concerts in the area while Tsula and I were there. He explained there would be some big concerts, actually connected with Tiger Day. The pop rock star Bastion was singing in the Central Square, and there would be tens of thousands of people there. Although I knew some of Bastion's songs, I had never seen him in concert, and it surprised me a little when Mick explained to me, the day after the night adventure in Zov Tigra, that Bastion was an activist and was giving the proceeds of that evening's concert to the tiger effort. Tsula was immediately interested.

What surprised me even more was Mick's reveal that he had backstage passes for us. He explained he had a friend who, working as one of the ushers, was able to secure these highly limited passes. I had never been behind a concert and had no clue what to expect, but it sounded exciting. The only problem was I was still a little hungover from the previous evening's adventure—the only thing helping me was Tsula and I had slept late that morning.

Mick also dropped a hint; he was thinking he and I could pitch our idea of the wilderness simulation to Bastion. Mick seemed to think the activist side of this superstar would jump at the chance to fund our cutting-edge technology to raise awareness about endangered animals if we centered our presentation around the plight of the Amur or Siberian tiger. Easily caught up in his excitement, I considered the possibility, thinking it was so far-fetched, but then if anyone had told me I was going to see, by the end of my honeymoon, a pack of wolves take down a boar and defend myself from an approaching leopard with the flash of my camera, I would have laughed them off. Even though I was reluctant to share my carefully guarded idea with a complete stranger, I felt I should trust Mick on this one—he was invested too.

And if Bastion could punch a wild lottery ticket for us, then we would be on our way to settling a problem we had been tossing around for the last several months. Over the course of the past academic year, both Mick and I had been making plans for our fifth and final year, aware graduation was only two semesters away. We even started to brainstorm what we might do after securing our degrees. Mick became increasingly interested in and committed to my virtual-zoo idea.

His tiger research served a double purpose, completing his degree and informing the simulation I was developing. The first and most developed part of it involved red wolves, as I showed Tsula, and I was able to draw on my summer's research and design a full habitat. But Mick and I had another sim, less-developed, centering on a tiger. Since I knew little about tigers and their habitats, all I was able to work out were some basic tiger designs. I reached the limits of my own computer and supplemented with university resources. When we began to realize after graduation we would not have the resources to keep our project going, Mick and I began talking about putting the tiger sim on hiatus until we could get the funding. If we were to start up a company of our own, we could look for investors, but I did not know how to play that game. We needed to be creative.

When we finally met up with Mick the evening of the concert, outside the Central Square, not far from where I had seen him on Tiger Day, he still seemed apologetic.

"Hopefully this will make up for last night," he said as I noticed he had one of our Immersive Reality sets with him.

I had not told him yet I thought the stress of last night was worth it for the footage of the wolves and the picture of the leopard. Tsula told me she had mentioned the wolves to him, and he had been incredulous at first. I had only told Tsula, though, about the leopard, and I teased that she was just as incredulous until I showed her the proof.

"There's nothing to make up," Tsula consoled.

Mick then led us back into one of the older buildings along the square, and I marveled at the architecture. Mick showed his badge and our passes to the security guard at the door, who let us enter. Inside, there was a slight musty smell, though all seemed tidy. Coming down the hall to greet us, a seductive smile on her face, was the woman I had seen with Mick on Tiger Day. She was in a red dress now, her golden chestnut hair bouncing on her shoulders.

"This is my friend Yuliana; she's the one who helped secure the passes," Mick said.

She greeted him with quick kisses to the cheeks. Tsula had a wry grin on her face. I felt she was thinking the same thing—Mick had a secret flame. Yuliana nodded quietly when Mick introduced her, only briefly looking at Tsula and me. An exotic beauty in her features fascinated me, but she kept her distance, like a model resenting her charismatic power over others.

She and Mick guided us down the hall, and I noticed she slipped her arm inside his, resting her hand on his forearm. We came on some more guards in front of a large wooden door, and Yuliana spoke to them in Russian while holding up the passes. On our side the squint-eyed guard with a bulldog face nodded and then let us pass. I smiled at Tsula; we were enjoying privileged access.

We found a small crowd inside a large room, ornate couches sporadically placed around—I guessed most of those present were musicians in the band with family and close friends there to help pass the time. We were a few hours still from the concert.

Sitting on one couch, leaning with his forearms resting on his thighs, his feet arched, rocking slightly, was the man I guessed was Bastion. I had seen pictures of him, of course, but what confirmed my suspicion immediately was that magical quality, charisma, which drew several others around him. Though several nearby had shaggy, long hair, and stereotypical rock dress with shredded jeans and black leather bands with studs, he had a black silk shirt, hanging open slightly at his chest, and shiny slacks of a material I could not identify—exclusive and expensive.

Yuliana led us close, and rather than interrupting, we fell into a conversation that was already underway. Since it was in Russian, I could not decipher what was being said. After a few minutes, the man in silk addressed Yuliana, and in the next moment, she confirmed that he was indeed the pop star Bastion.

"Yuliana already introduced me to Mick, so you must be the American with the great idea," Bastion addressed me.

I was surprised how much time elapsed before I was able to respond. I did not think I would have trouble speaking to a celebrity, but I did. "Yes, Mick and I have been working on a computer program that hopefully will increase awareness about endangered animals."

Mick jumped in. "I've got the gear here if you'd like to see it." Mick knew to strike quickly—we could not predict how much time we would have.

"Give me an idea how it works first."

"Just put on the baseball cap. It helps if you keep your eyes closed at first. When you open them, you'll have a different perspective; you'll see the world as a tiger. It may be a little disorienting at first," I explained.

"How is this different than VR games?" he asked.

Helping Bastion with the earbuds, Mick jumped in, "We will let you answer that question after you see our work."

Tsula was watching, arms crossed.

The sim Mick and I had prepared with the tiger was fairly simple. You could control the movement through the woods.

Then after a few minutes, a hunter would come out and start shooting at the tiger. If you could not move quickly enough, the sim would end. Short and to the point, but we felt it was as realistic as we could get it with our current resources. I still wanted something more.

We watched Bastion turning his head, raising his arms. Mick advised him not to stand, and his friends tried to ask him a few questions, but he was wrapped up in the experience. Although I still was protective of my project, I must admit there was a rush at having this pop star, this person that millions of people idolized, going through the simulation I had coded.

Suddenly Bastion jumped. Mick and I grinned at each other; the hunter must have gotten him. Then Bastion was still; Yuliana asked if he was okay. He reached up, and Mick helped him remove the cap and glasses. His face was blank at first— was that shock? Had we gotten him? The expression melted as he looked up at us, a wide grin spreading.

"Ha! Bastion loves it!" he said with Russian gusto. His excitement spread among those around him. I could tell others wanted to try it, but Mick and I were not at that stage. We just wanted the big fish.

"Is that it?" he asked next.

"That's just the start. I'm hoping to develop a full open-ended simulation that actually gives you even more sensory experience of the animal, so that you can feel, smell, taste what it's like being these different animals."

"Which animals?"

"Just red wolves and Siberian tigers right now," I answered. "We're hoping to expand to Amur leopards, snow leopards, and gray wolves soon. Maybe even polar bears. But I'm not just focusing on the endangered animals. We're trying to develop sims of endangered habitats, so that requires a broad knowledge of flora as well as fauna."

Mick saw something and interjected, "But the Amur tigers

are the priority."

"That is what Tiger Day is all about," Bastion championed.

Yuliana attentively watched Mick, who struck again. "We are looking to develop this into something we can market, but the two of us are just starting out and do not have the resources."

Bastion took the hint. "So you need a partner with resources."

"Yes, sir," I said.

Looking first around the room at his friends, Bastion threw his arms up in a grand gesture, "Bastion will be that partner. We will talk details later, but I pledge to set up a fund for your venture—it just has to have tigers in it!" He paused and then asked, "But what are you going to call it?"

Mick and Yuliana looked to me, and I said, after glancing at Tsula, "The Wilderness."

༄

I had set up one final surprise for Tsula the last morning we were in Vladivostok. After packing up our things for a quick after-lunch escape to our afternoon flight, we found and rode the funicular up to the highest point in the city, over an extinct volcano, to the Eagle's Nest Mount and the Alphabet Monument honoring the missionaries who were responsible for the Cyrillic alphabet which grounds Russian and the other Slavic languages. I celebrated when I noticed Tsula pause before the breathtaking view of the city—the golden domes of the Orthodox churches, the bridge, and the bay—only partially obscured by the remnants of an early-morning fog. We could see several places we had explored over the last few days, and as I located each, the world was a grand and beautiful place.

When Tsula finally looked back at me, I walked her past the statues of Cyril and Methodius to the railing behind, and as we approached, Tsula noticed the series of strange shapes all along the railing.

"What are all these locks?" she asked as she reached down

and pulled several forward for inspection.

"The people of Vladivostok have a tradition that couples who place locks here will have a long and happy life together."

"That's sweet," she said. "Each one of these has a story then."

I put one hand on her shoulder while I reached into my jacket pocket with the other and pulled out a golden padlock. It was a heavy thing to smuggle, and I was glad finally to unleash the surprise.

Tsula took it from my hand and studied it a moment. "Our names are on it?"

"I had a jeweler engrave them. I also have a second one we can keep at home on the mantle."

"So you knew about this?"

"I've been planning it. You just need to pick a spot."

Tsula promptly adopted the rules of the game, taking a few steps, scanning the view of the city. Several places were heavily populated, but she finally found a spot that made her happy. After bending down, taking her hands, and guiding them to the rail, I pushed them gently closed, and she snapped the lock in place.

She kissed me. "Thank you, Don, for all of this."

"I thought the trip needed a finale. Now whenever you think of our honeymoon, you can think of this lock—it will still be in place, and so will my love for you."

We stood back up. "So you have a mushy side after all."

"I'll never admit it." I said, putting my arm over her shoulder and pulling her in. "It looks like it's time for us to get back to the real world. It's been fun."

As we took one last look out over the city, Tsula asked, "So what've you learned?"

"Learned?"

"Yes, what have you learned over the last couple days?"

"That you're clearly much more comfortable without clothes than I am."

She laughed. "Anything else?"

"Since we didn't get to talk much last night.... I finally feel good about the wilderness simulation."

Tsula remained quiet, but I kept running with the idea, hoping I could pull her in. "You know I've been worried how we could support the venture after leaving the university. We just didn't have the funds."

"Looks like you might now."

"It's a beginning. I'm still hoping to pull together some grants. If I emphasize this as an educational opportunity and highlight endangered animals, then I think we've got a good shot. When we move to D. C. and you settle into your job, maybe we'll discover some other leads."

"You might also find a job teaching at one of the universities nearby."

"It's a possibility." Tsula saw me more as a teacher than I did. "So if we manage to pull this off and develop a wide-scale simulation, will I be able to get you to be a part of it? I could use your expertise."

"Don, you know that I just don't have the love for virtual reality you do."

"Immersive reality," I corrected with a smile.

"You know what I mean."

"You wouldn't be interested even if I could develop a full blown wolf simulation?"

"Maybe." Her voice betrayed her distraction.

I wasn't going to let her off so easily. "So what kind of wolf would you like to be?"

"I don't know."

"You love wolves and that's the best you can do."

"I guess I'd be a gray wolf."

"Not a red wolf?"

"That's too close to home."

"So gray wolves it is. If that's the case, then I think I'd like to be a black wolf."

She smiled. "That suits you."

"And since I'm in charge of the simulation, I know what you'll be." The alarm on my watch went off, interrupting my thought, sending me in a new direction. "Looks like we've got to go if we're going to catch lunch before our flight."

"I am getting hungry."

"But let's get a picture of our lock before we go."

After taking some close-ups of the lock, I set up my mini-tripod, framed a shot of us with the old city in the background, selected the timer shutter-release, and then ran over to crouch beside Tsula. As I held her close and watched the flashing light on the camera, I smiled, anticipating the importance of the picture, hoping for a bright future together. Yet what did lie ahead of us? What would we think years from now when we looked back at this moment? Now that our paths were joined, where would they lead? An uncharted, and uncertain, world stretched before us, one ripe for exploration.

After the camera finally flashed, I gathered our gear, and we rushed on with our schedule to lunch at a restaurant Mick recommended and finally to the airport, where we boarded our first plane back to the United States, but the golden padlock and our engraved names remained behind to weather sunlight and storms, a testament to our week in Vladivostok, a promise of our commitment to each other, a silent record of the final words I whispered to Tsula there, "You'll always be my white wolf."

WOLF CODE

BOOK 2: WILDERNESS WAR

In an effort to make the land over the mountain their new home and to lift the spirits of their pack, Kan and Lana give birth to a litter of puppies. The young ones offer the promise of new life, but Kan still remembers his promise to Sasa. When will he be able to go back to find her, and what will he discover? How will he face the pack of golden wolves? Meanwhile, when tigers cross into wolf territory again, what daring plan can Lana pull off to save her pack, and her new pups, once and for all?

In the human world, Don and Tsula have challenges of their own as they move to Washington, D. C. An unexpected turn and the following diagnosis disrupt their plans. Under this stress Don feels his simulation may provide some relief; however, he retreats from his design team, who has different plans for their work. Fighting his own pressures, Mick resists in unexpected ways. The struggle between Don and Mick has lasting repercussions for their friendship, for Don and Tsula's marriage, and for the fate of Kan and Lana's pack.

ABOUT THE AUTHOR

Wolf Code is Chandler Brett's debut series. Chandler grew up appreciating stories of many stripes, but had a special love for "Rikki-Tikki-Tavi," *The Call of the Wild*, *Watership Down*, and *The Last Unicorn*. He also grew up visiting Cherokee, North Carolina, admiring the history, culture, and artistry of the people there. This novel represents a blending of these two interests, and Chandler hopes those reading this story will come to their own appreciation of the Cherokee people and of the wildlife that share this world with us.

You may discover more about his books, including future release dates, online:

www.chandlerbrett.com.

Proof

Made in the USA
Charleston, SC
10 December 2015